THREE BROKEN BODIES

An absolutely gripping crime thriller with a massive twist

MICHELLE KIDD

DI Jack MacIntosh Mysteries Book 5

Joffe Books, London
www.joffebooks.com

First published in Great Britain in 2024

Cover art by Nick Castle

ISBN: 978-1-83526-331-0

CHAPTER ONE

Time: 8.30 a.m.
Date: Wednesday 27 August 2014
Location: St Benedict's Street, London

It wasn't the best place to hide a body, he knew that much.

When the effects of the initial sedative had worn off, the woman had become quite feisty — but she was curiously docile right now. From the first-floor window, Jimmy Neale kept his eyes trained to the street outside. The road was quiet, which unnerved him. The busier the surroundings, the easier it was to blend into the background, go about your business without catching anyone's attention.

It was quiet places that could be dangerous.

In quiet places you could be seen.

Jimmy bit his lip and sipped the bitter black coffee he'd been nursing for the past half an hour. He hadn't wanted this job — but when the boss told you to do something you either did as you were asked or . . . He swilled the now-cooled liquid inside his mouth, pushing the alternative from his mind. Jimmy had yet to refuse a job when it was offered to him. He was rather attached to his kneecaps.

More muffled moaning and kicking came from the packing crate.

He had half a mind to wrench the lid open and finish her off, get it over with — but apparently that wasn't the plan.

The Plan.

To Jimmy it sounded like a half-baked, hastily put together idea that would only get them all a one-way ticket to the inside of the nearest prison cell.

But what did he know?

He was just the hired muscle.

Finishing the last of the foul-tasting coffee, he tossed the empty cup into the corner of the room and reached for the plastic bottle he'd been forced to use during the night. The boss had left strict instructions that he wasn't to leave the room under any circumstances. He'd slipped out during the night, under cover of darkness, nipping to the all-night café three streets away. What the boss didn't know wouldn't hurt him — and it wasn't as if the woman was going anywhere. But now it was daylight outside — and that had left him with one of only two options. Piss on the floor, or use the bottle.

The woman inside the crate had even more limited options than he did. The thought made his nose twitch and a cruel smile crossed his dry lips.

Leaning forward, he positioned the bottle underneath one of the crudely punched breathing holes set into the side of the crate. Taking a plastic straw from the takeaway he'd had for his dinner, he jammed it into the bottle and poked the other end through the hole.

He grinned. "There you go, missy. Somethin' to perk you up. You must be thirsty."

* * *

Time: 8.30 a.m.
Date: Wednesday 27 August 2014
Location: The South Bank

It was the second body in as many days — and that was enough to make Detective Inspector Jack MacIntosh nervous.

"What can you tell me, Elliott?"

Elliott Walker, crime scene manager, wore a perturbed look on his face — something else to add to Jack's growing disquiet. "Not a lot at this stage, as you can imagine." He held the blue and white crime scene tape up, allowing Jack to duck beneath and enter the inner cordon.

The back street was quiet at this time of the morning. Jack followed Elliott along the metal stepping plates towards the white forensic tent that was already in place at the end of the alleyway. As they walked, Jack noted the lack of through traffic and absence of buildings directly overlooking their route.

The perfect dump site.

As they neared the tent, Jack recognised the balding head of the force's chief pathologist — Dr Philip Matthews. The tall, wiry man straightened up, catching Jack's eye as he turned.

"Morning, Jack."

Jack nodded his greeting. "Another?"

The pathologist let the question hang in the air for a moment before responding. "I'll leave that connection for you to make, Jack. But all the hallmarks are there." He held one of the tent flaps open, gesturing for Jack to step inside.

She lay on her back, hands bound together at the wrists, feet bound together by the ankles. Empty eyes stared up towards the ceiling of the forensic tent, the coarse fabric now acting as her temporary shroud. Even from this distance, Jack could see the bruising — some purple, some black — covering swathes of her partially clothed torso and limbs.

Sensing movement behind him, Jack turned to see Detective Sergeant Chris Cooper hovering at the entrance to the tent, his ginger hair tucked beneath the hood of his white protective suit.

"Another?" DS Cooper repeated Jack's own thoughts from only moments before.

It wasn't really a question that needed answering.

Not when they saw what had happened to the poor girl's mouth.

* * *

Katarina forced the bile back down into her throat. Vomiting inside the crate wasn't going to be pleasant. So far she'd managed to keep control of her bladder and bowels, but that wasn't going to be for much longer. A faint cramping in her lower abdomen told her that much.

How long had she been in here?

The panic that had initially coursed through her when she'd first regained consciousness was now evolving into a cold, unadulterated fear. She had calmed her breathing down, willed her heart rate to slow, and eventually the fog of confusion disappeared to reveal, in startling clarity, her new predicament.

She was inside a coffin-like box, the lid closed and tightly secured. She had found that out the hard way after expending a good deal of energy kicking and thumping, trying to force her way out.

The crate was made of wood, rough with razor-sharp splinters on the inside. Her knuckles were bleeding from her futile attempts to escape. Random holes had been punched through the sides — breathing holes she'd assumed. Maybe the crate had been used to transport animals at some point. The thought made her nose wrinkle.

When she'd spied the plastic straw poking through one of the holes near her head, she'd realised just how thirsty she was. She couldn't remember the last time she'd had something to drink.

Shivering, she swallowed — trying to rid herself of the nauseating taste of concentrated urine. She wouldn't fall for that one again any time soon.

Her mouth wasn't gagged, which was a blessing — but her shouts and cries went unheard, merely absorbed by the heavy blackness surrounding her. So she'd soon stopped screaming, her throat dry and hoarse.

She knew there was someone close by, someone guarding this makeshift tomb she now found herself in. She could hear his movements — a scrape of a chair, an occasional cough, heavy footfall on the wooden floorboards surrounding her as he moved around. He even spoke to her sometimes — a gruff sounding voice, no accent that she could detect.

A solitary tear escaped her eye. She felt it trickle down the side of her cheek and drip. Her lips began to quiver as a fresh wave of fear engulfed her.

Why was she in here?

And, more importantly, how was she going to get out?

CHAPTER TWO

Time: 10.30 a.m.
Date: Wednesday 27 August 2014
Location: Metropolitan Police HQ, London

Hard copies of the crime scene photographs from both locations were tacked next to each other on the first whiteboard, beneath the words '*Operation Scarecrow*'.

"I don't think we can be under any illusion that these two cases are not connected." Jack tapped one of the first images with a marker pen. "Victim one. Found two days ago by the river close to Southwark Bridge. So far, no ID has been forthcoming. As with the victim found this morning, bruising of a variety of ages is visible to the torso and limbs. Hands and feet bound with the same type of twine. Both victims are female. No identification found with either body."

Jack eyed his team — it was small, but perfectly formed. DS Chris Cooper was his most experienced officer — a bundle of ginger-haired energy with a deep-seated love of anything remotely bacon flavoured. DS Amanda Cassidy, not long promoted to sergeant, was an exceptionally astute officer. Always on a health kick of some sort, she had yet to convince Jack to swap his sugar-laden coffee to green tea but she was working on it. And then there was Trevor. DC Trevor Daniels had joined the investigation team back in September last year and instantly won a place in Jack's heart as a loyal and hardworking police officer. Originally labelled as the station 'nerd', with a brilliantly quick mind and a love of anything historical or supernatural, he'd rapidly turned out to be a very valuable part of Jack's close-knit team — and Jack couldn't envisage working with anyone else.

"Cooper. Tell us what we know about our first victim."

"Like you said, boss — found two days ago at low tide close to Southwark Bridge. No ID found with the body. Missing Persons don't have any matches. No matches with fingerprints, either. DNA obtained but not on the system. And there was little or no CCTV in the vicinity." Cooper woke up his computer screen. "Nothing more yet from the lab — I'll give Jenny a ring later and see if she can find out where we are with that."

Jack nodded. Cooper's girlfriend was Jenny Davies — head of Central London Laboratories — and the pair had just moved into a new flat together. "Thanks for cancelling your leave, Cooper. It's appreciated. I know this investigation has come at a bad time for you, what with the move and everything."

Cooper gave a grin, wrestling open a fresh packet of bacon-flavoured crisps. "No worries there, boss. I think Jenny's more than happy to see the back of me — reckons I'd only end up getting under her feet."

"Anything much come out of the post-mortem for our first body?" Jack turned back to the image of the first victim on the whiteboard.

"Nothing that isn't already in the report." Cooper pulled out the post- mortem report from the pile of papers next to his keyboard. "Extensive bruising to the torso and limbs of varying ages. Although widespread, a beating wasn't felt to be the cause of death. That was attributed to asphyxiation. Time of death any time within the preceding three or so days, depending where the body had been kept. Usual samples

7

taken — skin and fingernail scrapings. Swabs. Bloods. Results pending."

Jack's gaze rested on the headshots of both victims. The feeling of unease he'd experienced at the scene earlier that morning continued to grow. Forty-eight hours on from the discovery of the first body, and they were no further forward in finding out who she was or what had happened to her.

And now they had another.

He switched his gaze back towards his team. Disquiet continued to multiply.

They'd all dealt with many a dark and twisted case before — murders were never pleasant, whichever way you looked at it. But this was already fast becoming an investigation like no other they'd seen before.

"Let's get cracking and see if we can't find out who these people are."

* * *

Time: 10.30 a.m.
Date: Wednesday 27 August 2014
Location: McSweeney Malthouses, Juniper Lane, London

Natalia shivered and hugged her knees close to her chest for warmth. She no longer felt the chafing from the metal cuffs around her ankles, her skin so used to the discomfort by now. With just the one window high up near the rafters, itself encrusted with decades of city grime, virtually no light from the outside world filtered in. For most of the time they sat in near total darkness — and silence if they knew what was good for them. An occasional paraffin lamp was all they had to lift the gloom.

Leaning back against the damp brickwork of the wall behind, she looked over towards Stefan.

He'd been the first person to speak to her when she'd arrived — how long ago that was now, Natalia could only guess. Each day seemed to just roll into the next — before you knew it weeks had passed, then maybe months. The only clue as to the passing of time came with the lengthening of her hair. But Stefan had been kind and looked after her in the early days; the pair of them drawn together because of their shared Romanian heritage.

Natalia soon realised that today wasn't a work day for her when the others were dragged from their straw mattresses, but she was left behind in the dark. Sometimes that felt worse; left all alone with just your own thoughts for company.

And Stefan's dead body lying opposite.

She tried not to look — but it was impossible not to. Which was exactly what they wanted.

That was how they kept you quiet.

Stefan had lain there in the far corner of the abandoned brewery long after his heart had stopped beating. Natalia couldn't think how long ago that was now — a week? Two? Maybe even more. A dozen or so flies were buzzing around his lifeless body, enjoying the feast presented to them. Maggots crawled in and out of every available opening.

Natalia wasn't sure how Stefan had got hold of the phone. But when it was discovered, their captors had taken great delight in smashing it to smithereens in front of them all — and everyone was left in no doubt that next time it might be their skulls.

* * *

She was oblivious to the stench now. To begin with, it had made her eyes water and her stomach heave — but now she barely even noticed.

The body was hideously bloated — Stefan's torso ballooning as the decomposition process took hold, and the noxious gases bubbled up within.

Putrefaction.

It was a term Natalia understood well. Long before this nightmare began, she'd dreamed of being a doctor — of one day going to college, then maybe to university somewhere in Europe. But coming from one of the poorest towns in north-east Romania, she knew it was just that. A dream. People like her didn't go to college. Or university. And they certainly didn't become doctors. But then she had been offered a way out — a way to realise her dreams and fund her education, and also provide for her family back home. Looking back, she'd been dumb to fall for it. But fall for it she had. And she wasn't the only one.

Many others had come and gone in the time she'd been here — some just stayed for a night, huddled together in the corner in the dark, disappearing before dawn. The last had been a group of Vietnamese — men and women just like her. People prepared to leave their families in search of a better life.

Natalia pushed thoughts of home out of her head.

It wasn't the strong smell of decay, or even the swollen torso that horrified her the most when she looked across at Stefan. As disgusting as that was, the true horror came when she looked at his face.

The stitches were crude, pulling the top and bottom lips tightly together. — but they did their job. Natalia remembered hearing Stefan's blood-curdling screams as he was pinned to the floor, but the shouts had been short-lived, soon muffled and swallowed by the inevitable darkness that followed.

And Stefan wasn't the only one to die. He may have been the first that she'd witnessed, but he certainly won't have been the last; Natalia was sure of that. Both Danika and Elina were absent from their straw mattresses and had been for several days now. Natalia knew better than to ask where they were.

Her eyes flickered back to the bloated body of her decaying friend. She was convinced they kept him there as a constant reminder of what would happen if you didn't do as you were told; if you weren't *obedient*. Stefan had overstepped the mark and paid for it with his life in the most brutal way imaginable.

Again, Natalia shivered.

Was her fate to end up like Stefan?

Before she had a chance to even entertain such a horrific end, the door to the building crashed open.

"Move!" Two hands roughly manhandled her to her feet, another wrenched the chains from her ankles. "Now!"

* * *

Time: 11.00 a.m.
Date: Wednesday 27 August 2014
Location: Metropolitan Police HQ, London

DS Cassidy wrinkled her nose as she studied the headshots of both victims. "Why on earth would someone sew their mouths shut?"

Jack rose from his seat. The images were sickening, no mistake about it — and not something he'd seen before in all his years of police service. And by the expressions he saw on the other faces in the room, the rest of the team felt the same. These weren't just your ordinary run-of-the-mill murders — there was another element to them. Something darker; something evil; something more sinister than just cutting short another person's life.

"Looks like a punishment of some sort to me." Cooper scrunched up his empty crisp packet. "Someone making a point? Sending a message?"

Jack nodded — he had to agree it looked likely. And punishment crimes usually meant one thing, and one thing only — *gangs*. It wasn't a particularly pleasant thought.

He turned his gaze away from the headshots. "Daniels — I want you to head over to the mortuary for the post-mortem of this morning's victim. I'm not sure when it'll be — the mortuary will no doubt ring when they're ready. While you're waiting, both you and Amanda make a start on requesting any CCTV in the area. Fixed cameras, too." Jack grabbed his jacket and started heading towards the door. "And, for what it's worth, trawl missing persons again. I doubt we'll have any luck but it's got to be done. Cooper — let's go and revisit the first scene and see if there's some connection between them that we're missing."

"Don't forget the Chief Superintendent wants to see you." DS Cassidy flicked her jet-black fringe from her eyes, giving Jack a knowing look. "He's called down twice now — sounds urgent."

Jack glanced at his watch. The first message from upstairs had come through not long after he and Cooper had returned from the crime scene that morning.

'When you've got a minute, Jack. Pop up.'

He knew it wasn't a request he could ignore for long, but he silently put it to the back of his mind. Dougie King was a man he respected, and Jack believed the feeling was mutual. The Chief Superintendent was one of his staunchest supporters, pulling more than a few white rabbits out of hats when Jack inevitably landed himself in hot water. But as far as he knew, there weren't any outstanding complaints that had landed on his senior officer's desk — which was just as well, because right now the case in front of him needed his fullest attention.

Plucking his car keys from his pocket, he headed for the door. "I'll catch up with him when I can. Come on Cooper, we've places to be."

CHAPTER THREE

Time: 12.10 p.m.
Date: Wednesday 27 August 2014
Location: Canterbury Lane Industrial Estate, London

Although the warehouse wasn't exactly soundproof — with just one sheet of battered corrugated iron acting as a door, and none of the grimy windows having an intact pane of glass between them — Lance Carson was unconcerned.

The industrial estate was deserted, abandoned several years ago in favour of a new retail park some thirteen miles away. One by one the businesses had shut up shop and shipped out, leaving nothing but boarded- up units behind.

Which suited Lance Carson.

Because this way no one would hear the screams.

He kicked the corrugated iron sheet closed, sending vibrations and echoes around the empty warehouse, and strode towards a solitary wooden chair sitting in the centre. "Let's try this again." Carson fixed his cold stare on to the terrified face of a small-time pimp and weasel known as Dion Fuller. "I don't think you quite heard me the first time."

Dion's whole body shuddered.

Bindings around each ankle fastened him to the chair's legs — a further strap winding its way around his thighs to secure him to the seat. For now, his arms were free from restraints.

Carson stepped closer. "Coming all the way out here to deal with you makes me unhappy, Dion. I'm a busy man with far better things to be doing with my time than listening to excuses from a runt like you." He bent down so his eyes were level with Dion's. "And when I get unhappy, I get angry."

Carson's mouth twitched as he flicked his gaze up towards the hulk of a man standing behind the chair. Their eyes met for the briefest of seconds, but that was all that was needed. They both knew what was coming next.

Carson turned his attention back to the terrified man seated on the chair. "So, what's it to be, Dion?" He kept both his voice and gaze steady. "At the last count, you owe us fifteen grand, plus some small change — and each week you come up with some sorry excuse for why you can't pay. I'm not running a charity here. You borrow money, you're expected to pay it back."

Carson saw the man's chin start to tremble, his chest rising and falling with increased frequency beneath the fake Nike T-shirt he was wearing. Carson didn't have much time for people like Dion Fuller.

"I . . . I had a bad week." The man's voice was high-pitched, each word grating on Carson's already irritated nerves. "Some of my punters got busted. Some of my girls are off sick. I can't . . ."

"This isn't what I want to hear, Dion." Carson straightened up, his expression as stony as the grey of his eyes. He glanced back towards the man behind the chair and nodded. "Let's do it."

Wayne Carson grabbed hold of one of Dion's wrists, holding it in an iron-clad grasp. The larger of the two Carson brothers, the six-foot former cage fighter wasn't to be messed with. One hundred and twenty kilos of pure muscle rippled beneath his expensively tailored suit.

Lance Carson whipped a pair of pliers from his pocket and stepped swiftly to stand by his brother's side. Dion moaned and tried to wriggle free, but such efforts were futile. Wayne Carson's grip merely tightened.

The first fingernail came away with surprising ease — ripped from its bed with one quick pull. Dion screamed, the sound reverberating emptily around the abandoned warehouse. A smile flickered at the corner of Lance Carson's mouth. Pain. Sometimes it was such a sweet sound.

The second and third fingernails were a little more troublesome — Dion had bitten them to the quick and the pliers struggled to find their purchase. Lance Carson merely took a chunk of fingertip with them; he didn't have time to waste on niceties.

Blood began to trickle down Dion's left hand and forearm, staining his skin a deep crimson.

The fourth and fifth fingernails soon followed suit, ripped away cleanly with the now-bloodied pliers.

Dion Fuller was all screamed out. Tortured moans were the only sounds left to gurgle in his throat. His body crumpled in on itself, every limb shaking.

Lance Carson handed the pliers to his brother and brushed himself down. Kneeling down beside the chair, he grabbed hold of Dion's quivering chin, pulling it towards him so they were staring face to face, eye to eye. "You've got three days, Dion. Or next time, we'll take your fingers too."

* * *

Time: 12.15 p.m.
Date: Wednesday 27 August 2014
Location: Southwark Bridge

Jack felt the goosebumps prickle the moment he stepped from the car. Although a little upstream from London Bridge, Jack knew the impressive structure was just a short distance away to his right. As he made his way down to the water's edge, he felt a flood of memories swamp his thoughts for what had occurred little more than three months earlier.

It would be a long time before he could forget the suitcase with little Maisie Lancaster's body inside — if he ever did.

Turning away, he purposefully looked in the opposite direction. He could do without such distractions today.

"From the crime scene photos, it was just about here, boss." DS Cooper gestured towards a section of the shingle bank a few yards to their left. With the tide mostly out, the waters had receded enough to allow them access to the riverbed itself.

The aroma of the receding tide met their nostrils.

Despite the grim find being only two days before, there was little evidence now of the meticulous crime scene investigation that had followed. After the removal of the body, the investigators had done their best — but there seemed to be little useful evidence left behind, judging by the meagre findings so far from the forensic lab.

Cooper pulled up copies of the crime scene photos on his phone and passed the handset to Jack. The first image showed the deceased lying by the water's edge, face up. Hands bound by the wrists, feet bound by the ankles. Extensive blue-black bruising to the torso was evident even from the photograph.

The next image was a close-up of the deceased's face.

And the hand-sewn mouth, shut fast.

Jack handed the phone back to Cooper and looked around. Numerous small streets fed down to the river all along this stretch. Plenty of buildings in the vicinity, yet seemingly no one had seen or heard anything out of the ordinary. Or, at least, weren't prepared to come forward. And very little by way of cameras in the immediate area.

"What are you thinking, Cooper?"

Cooper slipped the phone back in his pocket. "Well, this victim was found in an almost identical position to the one we saw this morning. Face up. Hands and feet bound. Mouth sewn shut. And . . ." Cooper broke off, using a hand to shield the sun's glare from his eyes as he looked behind him. "It's not all that far away — from this morning's scene, I mean."

"Exactly what I was thinking." Jack began to head back towards the Mondeo. "Let's see how long it takes us to get to the second crime scene from here."

The answer was less than three minutes. And that included a stop at a red light.

Here, the crime scene investigation was still very much underway. Jack raised a hand in greeting through the windscreen at the crime scene manager, Elliott Walker, who was still in attendance.

Little seemed to have changed in the intervening four hours. The white forensic tent was still in situ — the victim still inside. She wouldn't be moved until Elliott's team had extracted all the evidence they could from the surrounding area. It seemed a heartless decision to the uninitiated — leaving the poor girl there half-dressed and exposed. But the body was a valuable crime scene on its own — and extreme care needed to be taken to get the best possible evidence from around her.

The location itself was similar to the one on the riverbank. Secluded, with numerous side streets that would swallow you whole, especially at night.

"You think they were both killed somewhere around here?" Cooper looked out of the side window of the Mondeo as a black private ambulance backed up to the scene.

"Well, I doubt they were taken far. It would take a pretty confident killer to cross London with a dead body in the back of their vehicle. Twice." Jack gestured towards the brick walls lining the alleyway at their side. "Someone could easily bring a car along here and no one would ever know. No street lights."

"Another scene with no cameras," added Cooper.

Jack switched his gaze to the Mondeo's rear-view mirror, and the main road that he knew would be some way behind them. Southwark Bridge was close, too.

"When we get back to the station, find out what bus routes pass along the main road back there." Jack paused.

"And across the bridge. The streets down here might not have cameras, but most buses sure as hell do nowadays. Let's see if they caught something interesting."

* * *

Time: 12.30 p.m.
Date: Wednesday 27 August 2014
Location: Canterbury Lane Industrial Estate, London

Lance Carson sat behind the wheel of his sleek BMW and sighed. Although inflicting pain on others often gave him a sense of satisfaction, and even pleasure, it was usually short-lived. Already the delight in seeing Dion Fuller's agony, hearing his blood-curdling screams as pain consumed his body, was beginning to fade.

Wayne Carson sat in the passenger seat, staring stonily out of the windscreen ahead. Dion had been released from the chair and sent on his way, minus his fingertips; the offending appendages now sitting in a bloodied tissue inside the younger Carson's jacket pocket.

Lance examined his hands on the steering wheel and noted a smear of blood still present. Tutting, he reached for the box of wipes he kept in the glove compartment and carefully removed the evidence. As he did so, his mobile began to chirp. Pulling it from his pocket he noted the number and immediately hit 'accept'.

"Is it done?" he barked, not giving the caller a moment to speak. He listened to the reply. "Good. At least something's going right today. Update me later."

Swiftly ending the call, Lance Carson fired up the BMW and pulled out of the abandoned warehouse car park. They had plenty more visits to make that day — more payments to chase. The Carson Brothers didn't have a reputation of being particularly patient when it came to honouring their repayment plans. Sighing, he wondered whether he might need to pick up a clean pair of pliers.

CHAPTER FOUR

Time: 12.50 p.m.
Date: Wednesday 27 August 2014
Location: HMP Belmarsh, Thamesmead, South-East London

New books always brought a smile to Jason Alcock's face. From the outside — with his closely shaven head, scarred scalp, and strong tattooed arms that revealed a multitude of healed track marks — ex-drug addict and life prisoner Jason Alcock didn't look like your archetypal library user.

But then again, Jason Alcock wasn't your archetypal inmate. Entering the criminal justice system at fifteen years of age, it had taken almost three decades for him to be reformed. *Better late than never*, he always joked when people had the gall to ask. Sentenced six years ago for the brutal murder of a London taxi driver — high on a cocktail of drugs, he'd almost beheaded the poor man with an axe, and all for less than thirty quid in the cash box — Jason had managed to surprise everyone by turning his life around. But although he'd put his drug-fuelled, violent past behind him, his reputation as a hard man still persisted and most of those inside Belmarsh tended to leave him alone.

Which suited Jason just fine.

He made his way over to a stack of books piled high in the middle of a large, oval table. Each book had already been examined and checked for its suitability to be stocked in the prison library — and once they'd passed that initial interrogation, they landed in the library for Jason to deal with, logging them on to the computer system and finding a spare place on the shelves.

Although a hardened career criminal on the outside, Jason was a surprisingly well-educated and intelligent man on the inside. With statistics suggesting some fifty per cent of prisoners in England and Wales had a reading age of eleven or less, Jason somewhat bucked the trend. But it was something he was content to keep hidden while incarcerated within the thick walls of Belmarsh. Some might see it as a weakness, a way to attack or intimidate — and it didn't take much, not in here. Generally speaking, the less people knew about you, the better. A hardened shell is what kept you alive in here. That and the ability to keep a secret.

"All right there, Alcock?"

Jason spun round. He hadn't noticed anyone slipping into the library and a faint shiver rippled beneath his prison sweatshirt. It wasn't like him to let someone creep up like that — you needed eyes in the back of your head in here; something you learned very quickly once the prison door slammed shut behind you. He silently chastised himself for his lapse of concentration and gave a curt nod.

Lindsay Jenkins made his way towards one of the shelving units close to the door. Jason watched from a distance as the man started to browse the shelves, his head cocked to the side.

Seconds ticked by.

"You looking for anything in particular?" Jason eventually broke the silence and nodded towards the shelving. "I didn't have you down as a big reader." Although Lindsay Jenkins was renowned for various things within Belmarsh, a love of literature wasn't one of them. In fact, Jason couldn't remember ever seeing the six-foot-five ex-wrestler with a book in his hand, or any other reading material for that matter, save for the occasional copy of the *Daily Mirror*. A fan of the Brontë sisters he was not.

Jason watched Jenkins' fat, stumpy fingers trail along the spines of the books in the classical literature section.

"Just browsing," he eventually replied, still managing to inject a subtle element of threat into those two simple words. "Just browsing."

Jason glanced at the wall clock. The end of the morning session was in ten minutes and by then everyone would be returning to the wing for lunch and those who had spent the morning locked in their cells would be released. "Don't you need to be heading back? It's lunchtime in a minute or two."

Jenkins' hand hovered over a copy of *Jane Eyre*, the muscles in his thick neck tensing. He turned, slowly, to give Jason a cold stare.

"I'm well aware of the time. I'll make it back in good time for a bit of scran."

More seconds ticked slowly by.

It wasn't the first time Jason had noticed Jenkins showing up unexpectedly in recent days. Behind him in the queue for breakfast, on the way to the visitors' centre, coming back from exercising in the yard. But never in the library.

Until today.

Another faint shiver rippled beneath Jason's prison sweatshirt. Although Jenkins didn't scare him in the slightest, the man's presence immediately made the room feel that bit smaller.

"So, what can I help you with?" Jason's voice was tinged with enough sarcasm to show Jenkins he was no fool. "The children's section is at the back."

Before Jenkins could reply, another figure entered the library — one which Jason was silently grateful for.

"If you're not checking a book out, Jenkins — on your way. I don't believe this is your allotted time to use the library services." Louise Freeman flashed Jason a concerned look. "Everything all right while I've been gone?"

Jason hesitated for a split second, but gave a nod. "Nothing I couldn't handle." His eyes remained firmly fixed on the retreating ex-wrestler.

Jenkins reached the door, turning at the last moment to give Jason another hardened stare. "You take care now, Alcock — and give my regards to that policeman friend of yours next time you see him. I assume you're still best mates?"

Jason let a smile cross his lips. He knew it irritated Jenkins how he refused to be intimidated. Once top dog himself when he'd first arrived in Belmarsh, Jason had been happy enough to relinquish that honour to Jenkins when the man had arrived a year or so later. Jason might be smaller and lighter, but he was smarter than the ageing hulk standing in the doorway. And being smart gave you an edge in here.

"I'll do that," replied Jason in an even tone, watching as Jenkins retreated into the corridor. "And, in the meantime, I'll look out some picture books for you. I know how these big words can be difficult for you sometimes." He flashed Jenkins another grin before the prison librarian closed the door.

"Friend of yours these days?" she enquired, a small smile playing on her lips. "I thought you'd have more sense than that."

Jason made his way back to the table and the stack of books waiting for him. "I wouldn't call him that exactly."

"Good. You let me know if he becomes a nuisance."

Jason pulled a book from the stack towards him. He liked Louise. She was a no-nonsense kind of person, firm but fair. And the library was her domain. She wouldn't let the likes of Lindsay Jenkins take so much as an inch on her territory. She may be petite in stature but her bite was most definitely worse than her bark.

Working in the library was a prestigious job, coveted throughout the prison — something Jason was well aware of. He was able to spend his days walking on carpeted floors and sitting in comfortable seats — and it sure as hell beat working in the prison kitchens or laundry. But it wasn't necessarily the carpet nor the seating that made it attractive — working in the library gave rise to many an opportunity to abuse the system. With all manner of prisoners passing through the library at one time or another, whether to check out a book or to access educational courses, it was rife for dealing in one shape or form. Be it drugs, weapons or any other type of contraband.

But Louise ran a tight ship. And she seemed to trust Jason.

Although, on paper, he may not have been the obvious choice for such a trustworthy position — jobs like this went to those who were well respected and honest, if such qualities were ever present in a bunch of incarcerated prisoners — Louise must have seen something in the convicted murderer when she approved his application. Exactly what that was, Jason wasn't quite sure, but he was grateful all the same.

"Why don't you get going? Get yourself some lunch." Louise gestured towards the door. "I'll see you this afternoon."

Jason didn't need asking twice, his stomach already rumbling. But he made sure he kept his head down and avoided Lindsay Jenkins. The man was starting to irritate him.

* * *

Time: 1.30 p.m.
Date: Wednesday 27 August 2014
Location: Metropolitan Police HQ, London

Jack pulled the Mondeo into the rear car park, just in time to see DC Daniels heading out. Jack wound down the window and beckoned him over.

"Just heading out to the mortuary." Daniels bent down by the car's side window. "Perry, Dr Matthews' assistant, just rang. They can squeeze it in now before the start of their afternoon list."

Jack nodded. "Good. Get what information you can — although judging by the first one it's unlikely to be much."

Daniels gave a wave as he left.

Once inside the station, Jack and DS Cooper headed up to the incident room. DS Cassidy was beavering away, head down, at one of the computer terminals. Without looking up she said, "No joy with Missing Persons for the second body, either. And fingerprints are a no-show for this one so far, too."

It wasn't unexpected. Jack slipped out of his jacket and headed for the cold-water dispenser. It had been a dry, hot summer and according to the forecast the heat looked set to continue for the next couple of days at least. The parks throughout the capital were parched, the grass turning a tinder-box shade of yellow. Pavements were dusty, tempers were frayed. Most shops admitted their best-selling items were ice cream and beer. He was about to ask about CCTV when Cassidy beat him to it.

"All CCTV around this morning's scene requested. Shouldn't take long to come in."

Jack quickly gulped down a paper cup of cold water. "Cooper, get that bus CCTV we mentioned earlier requested, too. Just in case." Cooper busied himself at a spare workstation.

"Couple of messages came in while you were out." Cassidy pushed herself out of her seat, notepad in hand. "First, CPS want a chat about the Maisie Lancaster and Narelle Williams cases. Said they'd either ring back or send an email. Then DI Telford popped up — said she'd try and catch you later — something about an update to the Carrie-Ann Dixon case."

"Cheers, Amanda." Jack had half expected another summons from the Chief Superintendent to appear when he got back, and was relieved that there wasn't one waiting for him. "Remind me, were there many house-to-house statements taken for the first crime scene? It wasn't a particularly residential area, by the river, so I'm guessing not."

Cassidy returned to her seat and tapped at her keyboard, opening the relevant section on her computer screen. "Not a lot. As you said, not really a residential area. There are a couple of statements from the owners of a bar and restaurant, and also a media company that has offices facing the riverbank. Skimming through them, nobody had anything useful to say. Even the poor chap who discovered the body."

Jack poured himself another cup of water. "Remind me what he said again?"

Cassidy brought up the statement. "Eric Van de Haar was taking a walk along the river shortly before sunrise, saw something odd on the exposed river bed. He was pretty sure there wasn't anyone else around — it was a little after five o'clock and the sun wasn't up yet. Used his phone torch to see what it was."

"Do we question why he was taking a walk along the river at that time? I mean, it's not like he had a dog or anything with him. Not even jogging."

"He says he suffers from insomnia and finds walking helps clear his head." Cassidy shrugged and looked up from the screen. "You think we should follow it up some more?"

Insomnia.

Jack knew first-hand what that felt like. He shook his head. "No, I think we'll give him the benefit of the doubt if he checks out otherwise."

Cassidy resumed reading from the statement. "Works in finance in the City. Stressful job and going through a divorce. Has two grown-up children. No convictions or contact with the police — not even a parking ticket."

Jack slugged back another mouthful of water. "Let's leave him be. So, we've no eye witness to the dumping of the body. Access — as Cooper and I saw earlier — is quite easy by car. It isn't overlooked and there are no cameras in the immediate area. My guess would be our victim wasn't there for very long before she was discovered — dumped under the cover of darkness. With sunset around eight o'clock the night before, this gives around nine hours before our poor, unfortunate Eric stumbled across her. Cooper — did the doc commit himself to a time of death on this one?"

Cooper quickly rummaged in the paperwork on his desk and pulled out the draft report. "Time of death always difficult to pinpoint, boss. All he would commit to was sometime within the preceding seventy-two hours. It all depends on where the body was kept in between times — whether it was outside or not. Day and night temperatures have been high for some time though."

"Tide times for that part of the river suggest the body was probably dumped sometime after two a.m.," added Cassidy. "The tide would be receding around then."

"That narrows the window somewhat." Jack tossed his paper cup into the bin as he passed. "Only a few hours before our Eric clocks her. Did the doc say anything more about the bruising, other than what he's detailed in the report?"

"Not much — only that it was widespread and of varying ages. Although he couldn't be specific, he felt there could be a variety of causes — some manual, say kicking and punching. Others more in keeping with a blunt weapon."

"And definitely no sexual assault?" Despite the body being found partially clothed, Jack hadn't seen any red flags to tell them it was a sexual predator they were looking for.

Cooper shook his head. "No evidence of it, no."

That was something at least. Although, in some respects, a sexually motivated killer was often more careless at leaving trace evidence on their victims — which made tracking them down a whole lot easier.

"And nothing from the labs yet?" Jack knew the answer to the question, but asked it anyway.

"Nothing yet."

Just then, one of the desk phones began to trill, Cooper snatching up the handset. As he listened to the voice on the other end, he made a face at Jack and let his eyes drift towards the ceiling.

"I'll tell him, sir." Cooper placed the phone back in its cradle. "The Chief Super — he knows you're back in the building. You're wanted upstairs right away."

CHAPTER FIVE

Time: 1.50 p.m.
Date: Wednesday 27 August 2014
Location: Metropolitan Police HQ, London

"What's your take on it, Jack? Operation Scarecrow. Are we looking at gangs here?" Chief Superintendent Douglas 'Dougie' King leaned forward, eyeing Jack across his paperwork strewn desk. "Because if we are . . ."

Jack could do nothing but shrug. He really didn't know. It was a train of thought that had been suggested but nothing more than that. "I'm not sure what we're looking at yet, sir. The two cases are definitely linked, but without IDs . . ."

"Pull in whatever resources you need. And keep the media onside for a change. You'll need their help with this one, Jack. Ask for it sooner rather than later."

Jack gave a brief nod. The mere thought of having to talk to the press made him shudder. His relationship with the media was legendary throughout the station, and possibly beyond. To date, none of the press conferences he'd been involved with had ended up in a brawl, but sometimes it wasn't far off. Jack avoided Dougie King's gaze and instead eyed up the Chief's expensive-looking coffee machine sitting idly by. A dose of caffeine from a decent Colombian would go down a treat right now. His shoulder was starting to throb.

King followed his eye line. "Needs servicing I'm afraid. I can get you a glass of water if you need one — to wash those down with?" He gestured towards the packet of painkillers Jack still had clutched in his hand.

Jack slipped the tablets back into his pocket. "I'm fine, sir."

"You sure?" The Chief Superintendent's bushy eyebrows hitched, telling Jack he was no fool. "That was some injury you sustained there."

Don't I know it, thought Jack, trying to push the dull ache coming from his shoulder into the background. It had been three months since he'd suffered a particularly nasty traumatic dislocation of his shoulder, after a certain James Quinn had come at him with a gun. The bullet had missed its intended target, luckily only tearing through superficial muscle and tissues — but Jack was left with chronic pain and a residual weakness as a result. Not that he was prepared to admit it.

"I'm fine," he repeated, looking anywhere but Dougie King's penetrating gaze.

"Well, this Quinn chap won't be seeing the light of day for a good while now, Jack. That's something at least."

"Indeed it is, sir." Jack had been more than a little surprised when Quinn had pleaded guilty to the botched shooting, expecting the seasoned burglar to take it to trial just for the sheer hell of it. But, instead, he'd held his hands up at the earliest opportunity and was currently languishing in prison as a result.

King leaned back in his swivel chair, the leather creaking. "But back to your Operation Scarecrow. It makes me nervous that it might be gang related. And if I'm nervous then you can bet your life those above me are, too. And I'm even more concerned as we seem to have a power vacuum in the city right now, what with Joseph Geraghty's sudden disappearance from the streets."

Jack felt his jaw tense but he remained silent. Once the undisputed leader of London's most infamous crime gang, Geraghty had dropped off the face of the earth last year.

Rumours circulated that he'd merely retired, taken his cut of the gang's money and run off to the sun. But Jack knew better.

The Chief Superintendent didn't know Geraghty was dead — and Jack wanted to keep it that way.

Dougie King continued. "A gap like this won't last long, you know that as well as I do, Jack. Not in this city. There'll be plenty of vultures circulating as we speak, eyeing up the potential windfall that could land in their laps if they step into Geraghty's territory. But the last thing we want is a turf war on our hands. As soon as you think this case is gang related, you let me know."

"Sir."

The Chief Superintendent ran a hand over his chin, a frown forming. "What do you know of the Carson brothers? I keep hearing their names pop up. Anything I should be aware of?"

Jack frowned. Lance and Wayne Carson hadn't made it across his radar for a long time. "From what I know of them they're small fry. Loan sharks with some low-level drug dealing on the side. Cannabis factories and the like. Definitely not big-time players to my knowledge. I don't think they particularly hold much clout out there on the streets, anyway."

"But the streets are changing, Jack. Even small fry can be dangerous these days."

Jack acknowledged the information and filed it away. "I'll look into it. Dig around and see what I can find out."

"Keep it low-key, though, won't you Jack? Don't make any more enemies than is absolutely necessary, eh? I haven't had a complaint cross my desk for at least six months — let's try and keep it that way."

* * *

Time: 2.00 p.m.
Date: Wednesday 27 August 2014
Location: Acacia Avenue, Wimbledon

It had been over twenty-four hours now and there'd been nothing. Nothing except one simple text message.

'We have your wife.'

Jonathan Spearing wasn't renowned for being frightened of much, having an exterior as tough as rhino hide and emotions to match, but right now a fear like no other consumed him.

He'd made plenty of enemies in his fifteen-year journalistic career, no question about that. His often acerbic articles ruffled many a feather, and worse — but he didn't care. In this game, if you were too nice then people took advantage — all too eager to crush you in their own scramble to the top. He'd learned that sweet chestnut a long time ago. He knew he wasn't the most likeable member of the team at the *Daily Courier* — there was certainly no secret about that; but being popular didn't win you awards, and Jonathan Spearing had big ambitions.

But had he really pissed someone off enough for them to have snatched Katarina?

Spearing sat and stared once more at the solitary text.

'We have your wife.'

They'd taken her from inside the house sometime yesterday morning, of that there was no question. When he'd returned home at lunchtime, he'd noticed nothing out of place, nothing disturbed, nothing missing.

Except for Katarina.

And just a cheap mobile phone left behind on the kitchen worktop.

Spearing knew it would be unregistered, untraceable. Whoever was behind this wouldn't be that stupid. He read the second part of the message.

'If you call the police, she dies.'

Then there had been twenty-four hours of nothing. Twenty-four long hours which Spearing had spent pacing the floor, wracking his brains to try and think who could be behind something like this. He'd come up with nothing and no one.

Several times during the early hours of the morning he'd picked up the phone, ready to punch in triple nine. But each time he faltered.

'*If you call the police, she dies.*'

It wasn't a risk he was prepared to take. Katarina meant the world to him. Even he — Jonathan Spearing, man of so many bitter words and harsh retorts — had a heart. And it wasn't as black and shrivelled as some believed.

Katarina.

Katie.

They had been married ten years now and he still sometimes pinched himself, wondering what she saw in him. He was punching far above his weight; he knew that without needing to be told — although plenty delighted in telling him just that. But they'd been happy enough, just the two of them.

Until now.

Reaching for yet another cup of bitter coffee, his nerves jangling with the amount of caffeine coursing through his system, he decided to make a plan. He would give them until six o'clock. If he didn't hear anything by then, he'd ring the police.

Yes. A plan.

It felt better having a plan.

Swallowing the last of the coffee, he picked up the phone once more and willed it to reveal another message.

* * *

Time: 2.15 p.m.
Date: Wednesday 27 August 2014
Location: Westminster Mortuary, London

"Today we have a female of approximately seventeen to twenty-five years of age. One hundred and fifty-nine centimetres tall, weighing fifty-seven kilogrammes."

The pathologist angled the overhead light towards the body lying exposed on the steel examination table. "Outwardly, extensive bruising is visible on the torso — especially the left and right flanks." Stepping to the side, he allowed the mortuary technician to take a set of close-up photographs. "Due to the range of discolouration, I estimate some of the contusions are in the region of several days old, others even older. Fresher bruising is seen on the upper thighs and around both ankles. Both wrists show skin abrasions."

DC Trevor Daniels was standing on the opposite side of the examination table, his eyes trained on the body. Dressed in a protective rubber apron and matching wellington boots, an audible squeak filtered through the chilled air as he inched closer. "From the restraints around the wrists and ankles?"

"Both wrists and ankles are bound by twine." Dr Matthews took a pair of sharp scissors and snipped a small section for analysis. "Such abrasions are consistent with being restrained." Bending in closer, a deep frown creased his brow beneath his protective hat. "But there are some additional contusions around the wrists that look somewhat inconsistent with the diameter of the twine. This leads me to surmise that at least some of the injuries were caused manually."

"By hand?"

The pathologist gestured towards the underside of the victim's right wrist. "The markings here are wider — more in line with the width of a human thumb, wouldn't you say?"

Daniels stepped closer and found himself nodding.

"And the same can be said for the bruising around each ankle. The narrower contusions could be caused by the twine, the wider bruising more likely caused by physical force."

"Held down by the arms and legs," muttered Daniels, slotting the extra piece of information away inside his head. "Which could suggest more than one perpetrator."

Dr Matthews' mouth twitched. He had a soft spot for the quietly-spoken detective. The lad was smart. "That is certainly one way to interpret the findings, detective."

The pathologist continued the external examination. "More abrasions noted on the upper and lower back, and around each shoulder, otherwise the body looks relatively healthy. The muscle tone is slack with evidence of substantial wasting. Possible malnourishment. Some puncture wounds to each forearm. Routine bloods to be taken for post-mortem analysis."

Bending down more closely, Dr Matthews waved the mortuary technician over. "Perry, take some more close-ups of the bruising around the right shoulder, here. I can see an unusual pattern beneath the contusions." The technician duly took a series of photographs, the sound of the camera shutter echoing in the chill air.

With the external examination complete, the post mortem moved to the internal organs. Had DS Cassidy been in attendance, Dr Matthews knew she would already be averting her gaze and edging as far back as possible. In contrast, the ever-eager DC Daniels stepped closer.

Internally, the examination gave up little by way of surprise. All major organs looked healthy and free of disease — although a loss of adipose tissue was evident in the subcutaneous tissues, again possibly pointing towards malnutrition. Everything was weighed, logged and photographed as a matter of routine.

The pathologist kept the examination of the head until last. Hesitating, with his scalpel raised above the victim's face, he felt his eyes flicker towards the chiller room next door. A room where an almost identical face lay inside a frozen drawer.

It wasn't often that Dr Matthews felt a shiver run down his spine. He could count on the fingers of one gloved hand how many times it had happened in his thirty-year career.

But now was one of those times.

With his eyes flicking back to the face before him, he lowered the razor-sharp scalpel down to the victim's mouth and began to steadily unpick the coarse thread that clamped the girl's lips shut. Snipping a small section with a pair of sharp scissors, the pathologist deposited the sample into a test tube and handed it to the mortuary technician. "Section of thread to be sent for analysis."

Dr Matthews turned his attention back to the victim's mouth. "Thread has been pulled through the tissue of both the upper and lower lips." The pathologist paused, teasing more of the hardened thread free from the victim's mouth. "Obvious swelling apparent at the puncture sites with evidence of bleeding into the surrounding tissues. There is some evidence of additional needlestick injuries to both upper and lower gums. This could suggest the needle missed its intended target on several occasions."

Dr Matthews cleared his throat, taking a small scraping of gingival tissue for analysis before straightening back up. He hadn't seen anything quite like it before. "Petechiae and micro-haemorrhaging can be seen in both eyes, signs of cyanosis around the lips. Bloods will clarify but the likely cause of death here is asphyxiation. Despite the extensive bruising, there are no broken bones or internal injuries. Whatever beating this poor girl endured, it didn't end her life."

With the coarse thread now removed from the victim's mouth, the pathologist began teasing the lips apart. His gaze flickered up towards DC Daniels and for a split second they exchanged a knowing look.

They both knew exactly what they were about to find.

CHAPTER SIX

Time: 4.45 p.m.
Date: Wednesday 27 August 2014
Location: Metropolitan Police HQ, London

Jack took a seat in the incident room, shoulder throbbing. Dry swallowing a couple of painkillers, he turned towards his team. "Daniels? Care to fill us in on what you gleaned from the PM?"

DS Cassidy squirmed in her seat and pushed her peppermint tea to the side. Any talk about postmortems made her stomach churn.

DC Trevor Daniels nudged his spectacles a little further up on to the bridge of his nose. "The report won't be with us until tomorrow but I got a few interesting bits and pieces from it. Firstly, the body was in pretty good shape — young and healthy. Bruising to the torso and limbs, likely evidence of being restrained. Identical to the first victim." Daniels flicked to a fresh page in his notepad. "There were some markings on one of the shoulders which Dr Matthews wasn't quite sure about — he'll put it in the report with some pictures. He also mentioned that as well as the abrasions around the ankles and wrists, presumably from the restraints, he saw other contusions suggestive of manual force. Bruises that looked like thumb and fingerprints. I floated the idea that it might suggest the victims were being held down at some point in time. While I was there, he also reviewed the post-mortem bloods for the first victim which had just come in. There was some evidence of drug use, which fits with the puncture wounds seen on both of the victim's forearms. He mentioned both bodies looked somewhat malnourished — a lack of body fat both internal and external, muscle wasting and general skin condition."

"Did the doc give you any idea as to the relevance of that?"

Daniels gave a small shrug. "Not really. I mean, they were both young and fit, so . . ." He left the rest of the sentence hanging.

"Cooper? Pop that up on to the board for us. Drug use and malnourishment. It might be relevant."

DS Cooper swiped up a marker pen and headed for the first whiteboard, writing *'Drug Use'* then *'Malnutrition'* beneath the words *'Operation Scarecrow'*. Both were followed by a question mark. "Do we think they might have been addicts then? If there's evidence of drug use in their bloods?"

Jack rubbed a hand over his chin and turned his gaze back to the crime scene photographs. Neither of them screamed 'drug addict' at him. "I'm not so sure. Anything more about the cause of death, Daniels?"

"Same as for the first body — asphyxiation. Although there were multiple areas of quite severe bruising, there's no indication that any of those contributed to the girl's death."

Jack's eyes remained fixed on the unpleasant images of both victims on the whiteboard. Even if it didn't kill them, they both seemed to have been on the end of a pretty brutal assault. "Tell me about the mouths."

DC Daniels cleared his throat, unable to stop his own gaze slanting towards the headshots pinned to the board. He didn't really need to see them — what he'd witnessed in the mortuary earlier would stay with him for a long time to come.

"Today's victim had their mouth sewn up in the same way as the first body. The same coarse material was used. A sample has been sent to the lab for analysis but Dr Matthews feels it's a similar type to that used in leather work."

Jack raised an eyebrow but nodded for the young detective to continue. "Anything else?"

A heavy silence threatened to squeeze the oxygen from the room. Cassidy's face paled against her jet-black hair, her jaw tense — even Cooper's usually bright complexion beneath his freckles took on a pallid tone.

Everyone knew what was coming next.

It was just that no one had the stomach to say it out loud.

Daniels nudged at his spectacles and cleared his throat once again. "Dr Matthews unpicked the thread from the victim's mouth and, on pulling the jaws open, he found . . ." Even Daniels, who had an insatiable interest and stomach for the goings on at a post-mortem, faltered. "He found . . ."

"I think we all know what he found, Daniels — but spit it out." Jack's mouth thinned. "Sorry. No pun intended."

The joke, if it was even meant to be one, fell flat. They all knew what was coming.

Daniels lowered his gaze to his notebook. "Inside the victim's mouth was the head of a dead rat."

* * *

Time: 4.45 p.m.
Date: Wednesday 27 August 2014
Location: Canterbury Green Industrial Estate, London

Lance Carson passed his brother a quarter pounder and large fries. They were parked in front of an abandoned timber merchants' warehouse, a stone's throw from where Dion Fuller's fingernails had parted company with his body.

"You reckon we'll need to pull out the rest of that Fuller's nails?" Wayne Carson took a large bite from his burger, most of it disappearing in one mouthful.

Lance considered it for a moment. As much as he enjoyed inflicting pain on others, it was time-consuming and an unwanted distraction from the real job of making money. "Maybe. Let's see if he finds the extra next time."

"We could do with him paying up. Cash flow is a bit tight at the moment."

Grimacing, Lance sank his teeth into his cheeseburger. *Don't I know it*, he mused. With several of their deals having been busted in the last six months — two cannabis factories raided and shut down — drug distribution in the Carson enterprise had faltered. You couldn't distribute the goods when the supply chain crumbled. Even the prostitution business was getting squeezed now, too — too many do-gooders on the prowl trying to rescue his girls from the gutter. It was bad for business. So they'd had to fall back on their second line of income — loans. And people like Dion Fuller. But even that line of work was getting squeezed. People just didn't have the money anymore, and defaulters were rocketing.

"We'll be fine," he eventually replied, taking a sip of his orange juice. "I've got another line of imports coming in through Harwich next month. And a fresh ring of dealers to work the East."

"Is that wise?" The brothers both knew the dangers of stepping into someone else's territory.

"It'll be fine." Lance Carson's voice was taut. His brother was right; they really did need the cash. The vacuum left by Joseph Geraghty was too tempting to turn down, but filling that man's shoes would take a lot of capital — and it was capital that Carson didn't have right now. But he would get it, one way or another. Lance had ambitions that went far beyond small-time loans with a bit of drug dealing on the side. He was going to *be* someone.

"We could always go after that bitch, Gina?" Wayne finished his burger with a final bite, tomato sauce smeared on his chin. "She still owes us a fortune."

Lance shook his head, wrapping up the remains of his burger and tossing it out of the open window, appetite lost.

"That debt was bought by Hughes fair and square. If we go after anyone, we go after him." Lance sometimes surprised himself at his moral stance, but deals were deals. With Darren Hughes now in prison and looking at serving a long stretch, it was unlikely they would see their money anytime soon; if ever. But Gina Simmonds owed them nothing.

For now.

"This evening should be more fruitful." Lance looked at the calendar on his phone. "Four pickups — all regular payers, so I don't envisage any issues. You able to handle those alone? There's somewhere I need to be."

Wayne Carson nodded. "Sure."

Reaching into the glove compartment, Lance retrieved a fresh pair of pliers.

"Take these just in case."

* * *

Time: 5.15 p.m.
Date: Wednesday 27 August 2014
Location: Metropolitan Police HQ, London

The office was barely bigger than a cupboard, but Detective Inspector Becky Yates wasn't about to complain. This was her chance — maybe her *last* chance — and she couldn't afford to mess it up.

She had six months to turn her fortunes around, and the first hurdle was right here. It sounded like a long time — six months — but Becky knew she'd have to hit the ground running if she was going to succeed. DI Hooper was on maternity leave, so all she was really doing was filling in, keeping Hooper's seat warm in her absence. But to be honest Becky wasn't looking much further ahead than the next day — living minute to minute, hour to hour. Six months felt too much like a lifetime.

Her colleagues at her old station had been very enthusiastic and congratulatory when she'd informed them of her move — telling her that although it was only 'temporary' there was always the chance it could lead to something more permanent if she impressed the right people. Doors might open for her. She had a feeling not all the good luck messages were genuine. She'd made detective inspector at just thirty-one, which some of her colleagues had thought was too young; that she'd risen through the ranks too quickly and was too inexperienced.

Inexperienced.

Maybe they were right.

Doubt once again flooded her thoughts. What was she doing here? Did she really think she could step into the well-respected shoes of DI Hooper, even if only temporarily? Police stations could be closed shops at the best of times — suspicious of new blood — and she knew she'd have to put in some serious work to earn the respect of her new colleagues. First impressions could make or break you — and she didn't have a lot of time.

She sat back in the swivel chair that had seen better days, hearing it creak beneath her weight, and glanced around. Buried in the middle of the building's second floor, the office had no windows — and the paintwork on the walls was a dark shade of murky brown, making the space feel small and claustrophobic. Two battered filing cabinets were pushed up against one wall, and a worn wooden desk with uneven legs sat in the centre. Becky gave a rueful smile. She had a distinct feeling this wasn't DI Hooper's office. Everything looked as though it had been salvaged from some dusty storage room somewhere — saved from the scrapheap. A bit like herself. The irony wasn't lost on her.

Reaching into her bag, she pulled out the few possessions she'd brought with her from home — just a framed photograph of her mother which she placed beside the computer monitor, and a leather-bound notepad and pen.

An uneasy nervousness began to flutter in her stomach. She'd spent the day filling out endless forms, getting her ID authorised, and being given a slew of passwords to access the station's computer systems — and in all that time she'd not managed a single bite to eat. With only a black coffee for breakfast that morning, her stomach growled.

With the time past five, she knew she could leave for home — her real 'first day' wasn't until tomorrow — but she needed to make a good impression; needed to make this move count for something.

The reality of her predicament threatened to engulf her and more fluttering filled her stomach. Could she really do this? Could she really pull it off? Now she was here, she was starting to have her doubts.

She pulled a compact mirror from her pocket and checked her reflection, tucking several wayward strands of her shoulder length dirty-blonde hair behind her ear. She wasn't one for wearing much make-up — just a bit of light foundation to cover up her otherwise pale features. She noticed a few lines were creeping in around her eyes. She felt more like eighty-five than thirty-five right now — and she had a feeling she probably looked it, too. She'd gone for an understated pair of light grey trousers with matching jacket, with an ivory shirt underneath. It wasn't exactly power-dressing at its best but it would have to do. She tried a smile — unsure if it really worked as it looked more like a grimace.

Snapping the compact shut, she pushed herself up out of the chair and took in a deep breath. Unable to put it off any longer, she went in search of her new team.

* * *

Time: 6.35 p.m.
Date: Wednesday 27 August 2014
Location: Acacia Avenue, Wimbledon

Six o'clock came and went.

Jonathan Spearing sat clutching the cheap burner phone in his hand, staring out of the living room window. Nothing outside stirred. With his stomach tied up in a series of gut-wrenching knots, he looked down at the phone screen once again.

Nothing.

Still nothing about Katarina.

He couldn't bear thinking about what might be happening to her, but his new-found confidence at giving the kidnappers a deadline was diminishing fast. He just couldn't bring himself to do it. He couldn't call the police, no matter how much he wanted to.

What if they killed her on the basis of that one decision? That one phone call?

He would never be able live with himself if that happened.

Hand quivering, he placed the handset down and cried.

* * *

Time: 6.45 p.m.
Date: Wednesday 27 August 2014
Location: Metropolitan Police HQ, London

"See what you can find out about rats, Daniels. And the sewing up of mouths, for what it's worth." Jack ran a hand through his hair. His stomach was rumbling but the thought of food was unappetising. Instead, he reached for more painkillers. "And Cooper — make sure we've asked for that bus CCTV."

Cooper pulled his keyboard towards him.

"But don't make it a late one, any of you. It's been a long day already — and we need to be back bright and early in the morning. Get yourselves off home at a decent hour." Jack grabbed a copy of the first victim's post- mortem report, intending to go through it again at home later. "I'll be in my office for a bit longer if anyone needs me."

Once back in his office, Jack sighed when he saw the mound of paperwork that had appeared in his in-tray since that morning. He knew there were urgent files buried somewhere that needed his attention, but right now his head was throbbing in tandem with his shoulder. He downed the painkillers and thought back to his conversation with Dougie King earlier. He didn't like not being entirely straight with the man — but when they got on to the subject of Joseph Geraghty, Jack knew he needed to steer the conversation into safer waters. He wasn't sure that now would be a good time for the Chief Superintendent to hear about his involvement in Geraghty's disappearance. And even less sure his senior officer needed to know how he and Geraghty had tried to set up James Quinn to take the fall. That golden nugget Jack would keep firmly to himself.

Whenever Joseph Geraghty was mentioned, Jack's thoughts inevitably turned to James Quinn — the man who'd tried to shoot him, and the man Jack suspected of murdering his mother Stella MacIntosh forty-odd years ago. The fact that he knew Quinn was safely locked up behind bars offered little by way of comfort. The man had yet to truly pay for what he'd done.

Jack willed the painkillers to start working. He didn't have time for James Quinn or Joseph Geraghty right now. Operation Scarecrow was growing by the second and didn't show any signs of stopping. Sighing, he rubbed his throbbing temples and reached for one of the files perched on the top of his in-tray. At the same time, his mobile chirped with an incoming message — and a much needed distraction.

'*Pub*?'

CHAPTER SEVEN

Time: 7.00 p.m.
Date: Wednesday 27 August 2014
Location: The Duke of Wellington Public House

"How's the case going?" DS Robert Carmichael deposited two pints of lager on to the small table by the dart board. He dropped two packets of cheese and onion crisps next to them. "Looks like it could be a big one."

Jack reached for his pint glass, immediately sinking a third. "Early days but I can see it snowballing. Only two bodies so far . . ."

"You think there'll be more?" Carmichael settled on to the opposite bar stool, ripping open one of the packets of crisps and grabbing a handful before offering it across the table.

"I hope I'm wrong but somehow my gut tells me it won't stop at two." Jack waved the crisp packet away, taking another mouthful of his beer instead. "Something tells me this is just the beginning."

"And the sewing up of the mouths?" Carmichael's eyes hitched over the rim of his pint. "That's not something I've seen before."

"Me neither. I've got Daniels doing some research, for what it's worth. Chief Super thinks it might be gang related."

Carmichael's brow hitched even further. "You think he's right?"

Jack could only shrug in response. "I don't know what I think, mate. It has all the hallmarks, I guess."

"You don't think it could be Geraghty's lot, do you?"

Another shrug. "Anything's possible. They've been quiet of late so who knows what they're up to. Although I'm pretty sure they haven't disappeared into the ether just because their trusted leader is no longer around. We're just focusing on trying to get these poor souls an ID."

Carmichael paused, washing down another handful of crisps before adding, "You look rough, mate. No offence."

Jack gave a rueful smile in response. "None taken. I feel it."

"Insomnia still a problem, I take it?"

Jack sank another mouthful of his pint. The nightmares had been with him for so long now, he couldn't really remember when they'd first started — but sleep hadn't been his friend for a while. He didn't need a shrink to tell him what had brought them on though — discovering his mother's dead body swinging from a light fitting when he was just four years old had left an indelible mark. He'd had a course of hypnotherapy, which he'd been surprised to admit had helped to some extent — but nothing could quite banish the dark thoughts from his dreams. Like them or not, he had a feeling they were here to stay.

"Have you met the new DI yet? Rebecca Yates?" Carmichael tossed another handful of crisps into his mouth. "She's covering Hooper's maternity leave."

Jack stirred from his thoughts. "Not yet. First impressions?"

"All right from what I saw. It was only a brief introduction, just before I left to come here. She seems young, nothing wrong with that. Bit nervous but hey, starting somewhere new can be intimidating — we all know that. Anyway, enough shop talk — how's the love life?" Carmichael's eyes sparked with humour as he ripped open the second bag of crisps. "Been on any more dates?"

Jack made a face. "I don't know what you're getting at. You know I don't do dates."

"Sure you do. It wasn't that long ago that Jane Telford was your plus one at your brother's wedding. And I'm sure I saw you heading over here with that psychologist on a couple of occasions recently. So spill — surely you don't have two women on the go at once?"

Jack almost spat his beer out. "I don't have *any* women on the go, as you so eloquently put it, Rob — let alone two. As you well know. Jane's a friend and Rachel and I were discussing work."

"So, back to being the eternal bachelor, eh?" Carmichael scrunched both empty crisps packets into balls, turning his attention back to his pint. "I despair of you sometimes, Jack."

"You can talk." Jack drained his glass. "You're not exactly Casanova yourself."

"True enough. My ex-wife can certainly vouch for that. She's already found someone else. I say 'already' — we've been divorced five years now so I suppose it's no great surprise." Carmichael got to his feet, spying Jack's empty glass. "Whereas I seem to be spending so much time with my bachelor mate here that it's starting to rub off on me." Carmichael grinned as he went to order Jack another pint at the bar.

With a fresh drink in front of him, Jack began to peruse the laminated bar food menu.

Carmichael pulled his bar stool closer to the table. "How's married life treating your brother?"

Jack put the menu down, nursing the fresh pint in his hands. "Good by all accounts. They're taking a bit of time off right now — gone down to stay in Isabel's family home in Surrey. Now that it's hers again."

Carmichael's pint glass hovered in front of his lips. "She's keeping it? Not selling up?"

Jack shrugged. "I guess the place has too many memories for her to give it up — good and bad."

"And the other stuff — you heard any more?"

By *other stuff* Jack knew exactly what Carmichael was referring to. Before his demise, Joseph Geraghty — long since a thorn in Jack's side and that of the whole Metropolitan Police force — had offered Jack an ultimatum. A *choice*. Dying of terminal cancer, Geraghty didn't have long to live, he had asked Jack to help him in a way that wouldn't invalidate his life insurance.

'*I cannot die from cancer, Inspector . . .*'

Jack could almost hear Geraghty's mocking tone in his head.

'*And I cannot die by suicide . . . I need you to stage a murder.*'

Geraghty had created a new identity for himself — a retired banker by the name of Roger Bancroft — and the man had been found dead from a shotgun wound in his new home in Surrey last September. No one knew it was really Joseph Geraghty — or that Jack had helped him. No one, that was, except DS Carmichael.

Rob was the only person Jack had confided in.

"Nothing so far." Jack continued to eye the menu but, suddenly, no longer felt so hungry. He'd never actually divulged to Rob whether he'd merely set the scene of Geraghty's 'murder' or whether he'd been tempted to pull the trigger himself. Jack preferred it that way. He suspected Carmichael did too.

"Good news about Quinn though." Carmichael sank the final third of his pint. "Pleading guilty like that gets him off the streets for a while, doesn't it? But I can't say it didn't surprise me — him copping to shooting at you so easily."

Jack had to agree. "You and me both, mate, but I'm not complaining. Belmarsh won't be an easy ride for him — he'll get his just desserts one way or another."

"And what about your mum's case?"

Rob was one of only two people Jack trusted enough to divulge his suspicions about Quinn's involvement in his mother's death. Just Rob and the pathologist, Dr Matthews. Apart from those two, Jack kept his suspicions a closely guarded secret. The case had been reopened after a re-examination of the post-mortem findings showed Quinn's DNA beneath Stella MacIntosh's fingernails — but the investigation had since stalled. "CPS are dragging their heels on authorising any charges. Apparently, Quinn's DNA isn't quite enough, not on its own. They want more."

"More? Such as what?"

Jack shrugged, immediately regretting it as his shoulder reminded him once more of his close encounter with Quinn's gun "Witnesses. Someone to put him at the scene, I guess."

"From 1971? What's the likelihood of them tracking down witnesses from that far back?"

The look on Jack's face told Carmichael he wasn't hopeful. "I can barely remember our neighbours myself, so . . ." He gave another shrug, despite the inevitable pain that followed.

"Well, they might surprise you and come up with something." Carmichael took hold of the bar menu. "So, are we gonna eat something or what? I'm starving."

"Thanks, mate — but I think I'll pass." Jack pushed the last third of his pint to the side. Thinking about James Quinn made his stomach churn.

* * *

Time: 7.30 p.m.
Date: Wednesday 27 August 2014
Location: Isabel's Café, Horseferry Road, London

The door to the café closed behind the final customer of the day, and Sacha Greene gave a sigh of relief. Isabel's was going from strength to strength, which meant they were rushed off their feet from dawn to dusk. They had even extended their opening hours, staying open longer in the evenings.

But Sacha couldn't help a satisfied smile crossing her face as she turned the sign in the window to 'CLOSED'. As much as her feet throbbed and her stomach grumbled, she was loving every minute of running the café, even if it was only temporarily.

Isabel and Mac — recently married — were spending some time down in Surrey at Isabel's childhood home. They hadn't taken a honeymoon after their nuptials last May — what with all that had happened, it didn't seem quite right.

The café had been Isabel Faraday's brainchild — a relaxed mix of books and coffee, with a mismatch of comfortable sofas, squashy beanbags and old armchairs with soft cushions and throws to welcome her customers. And with a resident tabby cat threading its way through customer's legs, Isabel's was a café like no other.

Sacha picked up the last stack of plates from one of the tables and headed for the kitchen. "Dom? What time's the delivery coming in the morning?"

Dominic Greene's head appeared in the doorway that led into the kitchen. He pulled a notebook from the back pocket of his jeans and flipped to the last page.

"Slot booked between seven and nine a.m. Reference number TGF00312."

Sacha smiled, handing her son the dirty plates. "Smashing. As soon as we get the new supplies in, I'll do a spot of baking." She almost felt fit to burst with pride when she saw Dom working happily in the café. With autism and notable OCD, life wasn't always easy for him. But Isabel had helped Dom turn his life around by offering him a part-time job, and he hadn't looked back since. Now attending night school, his quick brain and head for numbers was already reaping rewards; Isabel's faith in him had given Dom a huge surge in confidence. Together with Sacha's baking skills, they were a formidable team.

But they weren't running the café alone.

"Gina? Will you be OK to handle the customers in the morning, if I'm in the kitchen baking?"

Gina Simmonds looked up from wiping down the coffee machine. Her hair was plastered to her forehead, and her cheeks had a rosy glow. "Of course, no problem."

Gina had only been working at the café for the last few months, but the place had literally saved her life. She wasn't proud of how she'd ended up — ensnared into the Carson brothers' web of prostitution and drugs. No one said *no* to the Carsons, and very quickly she found herself sucked into a downward spiral. Using her ever-increasing debt against her, before she knew what was happening, they controlled every aspect of her life.

She'd been old enough to know better — well into her thirties when the Carsons had got their claws into her — but they weren't easy to shake off once they had you in their clutches. When local low-life Darren Hughes had bought her debt she'd initially felt elated — for once able to see a way out of the mess she'd managed to get herself into. But in reality all she'd done was swap one set of abusers for another, and her debt continued to spiral out of control.

Gina wasn't often blessed with luck, but when Darren Hughes was arrested three months ago — now languishing in a cell somewhere and unlikely to see the light of day for a good while to come — Gina felt her world flip flop overnight. For with Hughes' incarceration, her debt disappeared alongside him. *Finally*, she was free. And now she had the job at Isabel's — earning decent money that wouldn't just go straight back into the hands of her debtors. For her, it was nothing short of a miracle.

Giving the coffee machine a final wipe, Gina turned her attention to the counter top and began to restock the cutlery trays. "I hope Isabel and Mac are having a good break." She wiped her warm brow with the back of her hand. "They deserve it after everything that's happened."

Sacha joined her behind the counter. "If I know Isabel, she'll be dragging that poor boy from one side of the county to the other, reliving every moment from her childhood." Chuckling to herself, she leaned across the counter to refill the napkin dispenser, and as she did so she noticed a small stack of flyers sitting by the till. Pulling one from the top, she glanced at the title.

Living in a Gangster's Paradise?
Freemason's Hall, Wellingborough Street.
Friday 29 August 5 p.m.

"What's this?" Sacha waved the flyer in Gina's direction.

Gina looked up from straightening the knives and forks, a sheepish look crossing her face. "You know I said I wanted to do some voluntary work? Well, I found this outreach programme with the Argyle Foundation — it's all about gangs and gang culture." She paused, biting her lip. Her own experiences with the Carson brothers, and later Darren Hughes, still made her shudder. "I thought — well — I don't really know what I thought to be honest, but maybe I might be able to help? You know, having been through something similar?" Another pause. "It's stupid of me, isn't it? Who'd want to listen to me rabbiting on?"

Sacha placed the flyer down and went to give Gina a hug. "I think it's fantastic. Well done."

Gina made a face. "I'm not so sure now. It's all becoming a bit real — the first session is on Friday and they want me to give a talk. I'm petrified."

Sacha held Gina at arm's length and fixed her with a reassuring yet firm smile. "You'll be brilliant. I just know you will. Have some faith in yourself."

Gina shuddered. She knew this next step was fundamental in getting her life finally back on track — and more importantly getting her life back with Rosie. Now seven, her daughter was still living with Gina's parents in Worcestershire. There had been talk of a reunion — of Rosie coming back to live with her in London — but both Gina and her parents were being cautious. Some people thought her parents were cold-hearted in their approach — when Gina had hit rock bottom they'd taken Rosie in with open arms, but they hadn't done the same for their own daughter.

But it was a decision Gina supported. Maybe not so much at the time, but definitely now. She'd had to crawl her way out of the cesspit she'd landed herself in, and she'd had to do it on her own. The experience had made her stronger — more resilient and determined to never, ever go back to that kind of life again. And she had her parents to thank for giving her the motivation to do it.

Contact with Rosie had increased over the last few weeks. They spoke on the phone every weekend and sometimes during the week too. And now there was this — the voluntary work with the Argyle Foundation. It was another step towards her new life. Another step in showing her parents that she really had changed.

"If you say so — but I'll be as nervous as hell."

Just then, Sacha's mobile phone began to ring. Reaching into her back pocket, she glanced at the screen and smiled before hitting the accept button.

"Isabel — we've just been talking about you."

* * *

Time: 8.30 p.m.
Date: Wednesday 27 August 2014
Location: Kettle's Yard Mews, London

Jack eyed the pile of washing-up waiting in the sink, but instead turned to flick on the kettle. He gave the milk a quick sniff before emptying the dregs into his coffee mug. There were two bottles of Budweiser left in the fridge, but he could feel the two pints from the pub still swilling uncomfortably in his stomach. More alcohol he could probably do without tonight.

Dumping two teaspoons of sugar into the mug, he waited for the water to boil. He needed food but thinking about Quinn had killed his appetite.

Coffee made, Jack slumped down on to the sofa and stretched, feeling his back click. As he made himself comfortable, intending to go through the post-mortem report for the first victim once more before bed, he felt something lumpy behind him. Adjusting the cushions, he found one of his brother's sweatshirts, screwed up and in need of a wash. He threw it on to a neighbouring chair.

Stu.

Although almost everyone called his brother 'Mac' — a nickname he'd acquired in childhood — in Jack's eyes, Stuart would always be 'Stu'.

His brother had literally crashed back into his life two years ago — coming off his motorbike in front of him outside Isabel's Café — and after spending much of their childhood and adult lives apart, it had been nice to get to know him again. Stu hadn't had it easy. When Jack had found their mother's dead body swinging from a light fitting in their Christchurch flat, without a father on the scene or any other family they knew of, the welfare system had stepped in. Various foster families followed, resulting in their eventual separation. Stu ended up in a children's home, rapidly followed by an approved school and then juvenile detention.

It hadn't been the greatest of beginnings, but things were starting to work out for him now. And Jack couldn't help but feel a tiny bit proud of his baby brother right now — turning his life around and settling down to some form of normality with Isabel. He'd even managed to get married — something Jack had yet to even get close to.

And marrying Isabel had been good for them both; she hadn't had it easy either — losing her parents in a car crash when she was six. Jack knew more about the accident that killed them, but hadn't yet found the right time to divulge what he knew. As time passed, he wasn't sure she ever really needed to know the truth — so, for now, he kept it to himself.

Sighing, Jack took a mouthful of the boiling coffee and glanced around the flat. With Stu now happily married, he didn't stay over so much which meant Jack was often alone — again. *The eternal bachelor.* Rob hadn't been far off the mark with that one. Not that Jack really minded — preferred it in a lot of ways, if he was being honest. You knew where you stood when it was just you to look out for.

Before he could analyse his solitary existence any further, Jack's phone began to trill. Glancing at his watch, he pulled the handset from his pocket. Dr Matthews' name was flashing.

"Doc? What's up?"

"Glad I caught you, Jack. Sorry it's so late."

"No problem. What can I do for you?" Jack could count on the fingers of one hand the number of times the pathologist had called him at night.

There was a brief pause on the other end of the line, Jack hearing the rustling of papers in the background.

"Just wanted to touch base with you after the PM earlier. I'm sure young Daniels gave you the lowdown but . . ." Another pause. "I've been thinking about both cases this evening."

"And?"

"From the discolouration around the suture sites, I'm increasingly convinced your victims were alive when their mouths were sewn shut. They may have been unconscious, of course, but their hearts were still beating."

"You're sure?" Jack's cluttered mind began to race. This put an entirely different slant on things.

"As sure as I can be. I can never be a hundred per cent, you know that, but . . . I just felt you ought to know my thoughts. In case it has a bearing on things. Did Daniels mention the additional bruising around the wrists and ankles? The thumbprints?"

"He did. You think they were manually restrained in addition to being bound with the twine?"

"It certainly looks that way."

Held down while their mouths were sewn shut.

Alive.

Jack felt the coffee churn in his stomach. "Cheers, doc." Jack couldn't help thinking back to his conversation with the Chief Superintendent earlier that day. Were these really punishment attacks? Gang related like Dougie King had suggested?

"And the markings," continued the pathologist. "Did Daniels mention those to you?"

"Briefly. He mentioned there was something on one of the shoulders?"

"Indeed. I'll attach pictures to the report and send it over in the morning. I've had a good look — to me it looks a little like lettering of some sort. I don't recall seeing anything similar on the first body, but I've decided to take another look at her first thing tomorrow. There was such extensive bruising I may have missed something."

Jack ended the call.

The thought that the victims had been alive at the time their mouths were sewn shut made Jack's skin crawl. But it never truly shocked him what one human being could do to another — he'd been in the job too long for that. Abandoning the half-drunk coffee, he made his way over to the fridge and pulled out a beer.

* * *

Time: 8.30 p.m.
Date: Wednesday 27 August 2014
Location: The Glade, Church Street, Albury, Surrey

Isabel put the phone down and smiled. It had been a wrench to up sticks and leave the café — but she was pleasantly reassured that it was in very capable hands. Sacha had managed the café on her own before, introducing several themed evenings last year which had been a roaring success. Isabel had no doubt the café would thrive in her absence.

But she'd never been away for so long before — and for some reason it felt different this time. Taking her glass of wine, she pushed open the patio doors and stepped outside, breathing in the sultry evening air. Mac was taking a nap upstairs while the casserole bubbled in the oven. He'd had a tough couple of days at physio and was feeling the effects. The injuries he'd sustained in the fire early last year were healing: physically at least. But mentally, Isabel wasn't so sure those particular wounds would ever truly fade.

Stepping out on to the patio, the solar lights flickered into life as night-time beckoned. As she usually did, she found herself looking over towards the wooden summer house nestling beneath the trees at the bottom of the garden.

Taking a mouthful of wine, she felt her heart jolt. The summer house invoked so many memories for her — some good, others more painful. As did the rest of the house. Sometimes she wondered if coming back here had been such a good idea. On the one hand, it was her childhood family home — the only one she remembered — and the only place where she felt fully connected to her past. She may have only had six years with her parents, but her memories of them were special — and every one of them was locked up in this house.

But then there were other memories — ones that weren't so pleasant.

One such memory was of Uncle Clive. As much as she tried, she couldn't stop calling him that. *Uncle Clive.* He'd been there for her when her parents died — a steadying force amid all the tumultuous confusion and heartbreak — protecting and supporting her as she grew from child to teen, then teen to young adult.

Dependable Uncle Clive.

But even that had been a lie.

Isabel shivered, pulling her cardigan around her shoulders. The man she'd trusted so much had ended up betraying her in the worst way imaginable. As a loyal family friend, he'd pretended to care for her, steer her through the tough choices and choppy waters of adulthood, only to reward her loyalty by stealing her inheritance and disappearing like a thief in the night — which was exactly what he was.

A thief.

It had taken her years to get over what he'd done, only for the pain to resurface last year when the shocking truth over who he really was hit home. He wasn't Uncle Clive after all. He was Joseph Geraghty — London's infamous crime lord. Isabel couldn't get her head around it. How was that even possible? The money didn't matter to her anymore — she'd long since come to terms with that being lost forever. But what really hurt was the lying; the betrayal; the *deception*.

Isabel felt her skin prickle as she turned back towards the patio doors. Jack had told her not to worry — Geraghty wasn't coming back. And although she knew that to be true — the man was dead, after all — it didn't stop her looking over her shoulder. Because sometimes she had the unnerving feeling that she was being watched. She knew it was silly — but sometimes she just couldn't shake it.

CHAPTER EIGHT

Time: 7.15 a.m.
Date: Thursday 28 August 2014
Location: Near Covent Garden, London

Moving twice in the last nine months, what had possessed them?

Jenny Davies shoved another box to the side and wiped her brow with the back of her hand. She'd managed to slice her thumb trying to cut off one of those blasted cable ties Chris was so obsessed with, and must have stubbed her toes more times than she could count hauling boxes from room to room. Good job they didn't have any stairs, she mused, sucking the open wound on her thumb.

With an exhausted sigh, she pulled a tissue from her pocket and surveyed the piles of stacked boxes around her. Somewhere in this room there was a box of toiletries — and somewhere inside that was a box of plasters.

She knew it would all be worth it in the end, once they managed to get everything unpacked and straight. It was just sod's law that Chris had had his annual leave cancelled at the last minute because of the latest investigation. But it couldn't be helped, such was the nature of the job. And, to be honest, she felt she could get far more done without him here.

Sitting on one of the packing crates by the window, she pressed the tissue to her bleeding thumb. The ground floor flat was perfect. When it came on to the market she'd literally dragged Chris across the city to view it, before he'd even finished reading the estate agent's particulars of sale. Needing some renovation work here and there, and a quick sale needed by the vendors, the price compelled them to sign on the dotted line before the day was out.

Despite Covent Garden being a stone's throw away, the street was deceptively quiet. You could almost forget you were living in the city some days. Just then, movement from outside the window caught Jenny's attention and she smiled when she saw the familiar figure of the old woman from next door passing by, looking to be heading in her direction. Each door along the street served both the ground floor and the flats above — but luckily for Jenny and Chris, the flats above them were currently unoccupied.

Pushing herself up from the packing crate, Jenny went out into the communal hallway to answer the buzzer. "Mrs Thompson," she greeted, warmly. "How are you today?"

Betty Thompson stood no more than five feet tall and a not-unpleasant aroma of lavender followed in her wake.

"I'm just grand, my dear. Just grand. And call me Betty. We're neighbours now."

"Betty," smiled Jenny stepping back into the hallway. "Would you like to come in? I'm afraid we're still in a bit of a mess, but I have unpacked the kettle if you fancy a cup of tea?"

"Oh no, I'll not be bothering you, my dear. It's early." Betty paused, her gaze flicking to the bloodied tissue Jenny still had clamped to her thumb. "Oh, have you hurt yourself?"

Jenny gave a rueful smile. "It's just a scratch. Looks worse than it is. Are you sure you can't join me for a cuppa?" She saw a slight hesitation flickering across the old woman's face. "I was going to stop for a brew anyway."

"Well . . ." Betty cautiously stepped over the threshold. "I suppose it wouldn't hurt just for a few minutes. But I don't want to get in your way. I was just bringing you some of my baking."

It was then that Jenny spied the Tupperware box the old woman had tucked under her arm. "Oh, that's lovely, thank you!"

"It's just some of my homemade shortbread and flapjacks."

Jenny closed the front door behind the old woman and gestured towards the door on the right that led through to the ground floor flat. "You really shouldn't have gone to so much trouble — but I'm sure they'll be delicious. What a lovely thought."

"It was no bother." Betty followed Jenny through to another private hallway and then into the living room. "It's not like I've much else to fill my time with — not since my dear Harold passed on."

Jenny pulled over the only chair they possessed. "You sit yourself down here and I'll go and pop the kettle on."

* * *

Time: 7.30 a.m.
Date: Thursday 28 August 2014
Location: Kettle's Yard Mews, London

Eyeing the washing-up still waiting in the sink, Jack pulled on his jacket. The second bottle of beer last night probably hadn't been wise, but once he'd got off the phone to the doc, he felt like he needed a drink. He couldn't quite get the notion out of his head that the victims' mouths were sewn shut while they were still alive. And that had pretty much set the tone for the rest of the night.

After demolishing a leftover Chinese takeaway, he'd nodded off on the sofa again — and when he woke in the small hours of the morning he could almost hear Dr Riches tutting in his ear.

'*A good sleep routine is essential,*' the psychologist had remarked after reading one of the entries in his sleep diary. '*Your bedroom needs to be a place you associate with restful sleep and tranquillity.*'

Dr Riches had encouraged him to keep a sleep diary during the ten-week course of hypnotherapy Jack had signed up for eighteen months ago. He'd dutifully obliged, somewhat unsure what his entries revealed about him, other than a severely disturbed sleep pattern.

Even now, Jack wasn't so sure he'd managed the '*restful sleep and tranquillity*' part yet.

After dragging himself into bed at gone two o'clock, the rest of the night was plagued by his usual nightmares — eventually he'd sat bolt upright at a little after four, sweat clinging to his skin. The nightmares had never really gone away, despite Dr Riches' best efforts. But she'd never promised him that they would, and he wasn't so naive to think it was achievable. All she'd suggested was that she might be able to make them more manageable.

Might.

The visions were always the same — seeing his mother's dead body swinging from the light fitting of their Christchurch flat. And they were always crystal-clear — as if he were truly there. He could even feel the cold floor beneath his feet as he walked.

Despite their traumatic nature, however, he often found them strangely comforting — something he'd eventually admitted to Dr Riches during one of their sessions. And instead of being surprised or concerned, she'd merely nodded.

Jack thought he knew why he found them comforting, sometimes even welcoming them in an odd sort of way. During one of his last sessions, he'd unlocked a '*hidden memory*' — at least that was what he liked to call it. Dr Riches hadn't been quite so sure. But instead of seeing only his mother in his dreams as he always did, he'd also seen something else.

Someone else.

A man.

And it was a man Jack later discovered to be none other than James Quinn. Jack had seen him as clear as day — present while his mother's life slipped away.

He'd contemplated booking more sessions with Dr Riches, seeing what else he could uncover about the past — but the psychologist was understandably reluctant. And Jack couldn't really blame her. She was right; he needed to concentrate on getting his own head straight before inviting yet more drama into it.

Scooping up the keys to the Mondeo, Jack headed for the door. He had two bodies that needed his attention today, not James Quinn. Stepping out on to the landing, he spied Marmaduke — old Mrs Constantine's ginger cat from the floor below — waiting patiently outside the door. Jack had never been a great fan of cats — not until Marmaduke had sent Quinn crashing down a flight of concrete steps, breaking his leg and putting a great big dent in his skull in the process.

Jack bent down to give the tabby cat a tickle underneath its chin.

Jack was most definitely a cat fan now.

* * *

Time: 7.30 a.m.
Date: Thursday 28 August 2014
Location: Acacia Avenue, Wimbledon

Jonathan Spearing's eyes felt raw. He hadn't slept a wink all night, spending much of it pacing the floor, his stomach gripped in nauseating knots. As each hour dragged by, he'd again contemplated calling the police. Surely, he'd be better off letting them handle it?

But then he thought about Katarina.

And the threat.

If you call the police, she dies.

Spearing had no idea how genuine the threat was — but he wasn't prepared to take the risk.

In a moment of heightened emotion during the early hours, he'd pulled out all the photograph albums from the sideboard, spending time looking through each and every one. Their wedding album was the smallest — only a handful of pictures taken on the day. Spearing forced himself to stop pacing and sit back down at the dining room table, pulling the album towards him once again.

It had been a small gathering — a registry office in Lewisham. Just him and Katarina, his parents, his brother, and a friend of Katarina's from work. Noticeably absent were any members of Katarina's family. They'd all been invited, but not one of them had accepted.

At the time, it didn't matter to them; they were young and in love. But as the years rolled by, the effect of Katarina's estrangement from her family began to take its toll. They'd been a close-knit family when she was growing up in Croatia — her parents doting on their only daughter, sending her to the UK for her education when she was just seventeen.

But then she'd met the self-assured and somewhat cocky news reporter and everything had changed.

Spearing wasn't entirely sure what he'd done to cause such bad feeling within a family he barely knew. He'd been on his best behaviour the one and only time he'd been introduced to them.

Katarina had tried to brush it off, adamant that her family's views weren't her own — and that she would marry who the hell she wanted to, with or without their blessing. It was something he'd loved about her the moment they met — that fiery, independent streak. But Spearing knew, as time went by, Katarina was increasingly heartbroken by not having her family in her life.

His brother had taken on the best man duties on the big day, which was just as well. Spearing remembered looking through his address book at the time and noting he didn't really have that many friends. No one who would want an invitation to his wedding anyway — even if it did involve a free bar and cold buffet. Climbing to the top of his game in journalism had inevitably involved stomping on those around him, pulling them down the ladder as he scrambled his way up. At the time it didn't matter to him — he was so wrapped up in his career and his new life with Katarina. They didn't need anyone.

But now?

Closing the wedding album, Spearing rubbed his blood-shot eyes. Right now he wished he had someone to call; someone to help.

Someone to tell him what to do.

Suddenly the silence was disturbed by the sound of an incoming text message. Spearing raced to the window, kicking over his chair in his haste, grabbing the handset from the window ledge where it was on charge.

His hand shook as he unlocked the screen.

It was them.

* * *

Time: 8.15 a.m.
Date: Thursday 28 August 2014
Location: Near Covent Garden, London

"Another one?" Jenny got up from the packing crate and held her hand out for Betty's cup.

"Oh, I'm not sure I should, my dear — you must have much more important things to be getting on with than sitting with a silly old thing like me."

"Nonsense." Jenny took the teacup and headed towards the kitchen. "I'll be unpacking boxes for days to come yet — another half an hour won't hurt." And to tell the truth, Jenny had enjoyed the old woman's company, happily listening to her chattering on about her life with Harold, the places they'd visited, the people they'd met.

As she busied herself popping extra tea bags into the teapot and switching the kettle back on, Jenny heard the front door open and close, and then the door that led into their private hallway. Leaning around the doorframe of the kitchen she beamed. "This is a nice surprise! Time for a cuppa?"

DS Chris Cooper headed for the kitchen, pecking Jenny on the cheek as he passed. "Sadly not — have you seen my phone? I must have left it here this morning." He began moving some of the boxes on the worktops when he spied the two teacups next to the teapot. "Company?"

"Mrs Thompson from next door — Betty. Go and say hello while I finish making this tea."

Cooper entered the front room, scouring the surfaces of yet more boxes as he did so. "Morning, Mrs Thompson."

Betty beamed. "How lovely to see you," she replied. "How are you settling in?"

"Oh, you know — getting there." Cooper picked up a pile of books from one of the boxes, his frown increasing. "Have you seen a phone lying around anywhere?" As Jenny reappeared with the fresh round of tea, he turned towards her. "Can you ring it for me? It must be in here somewhere."

Jenny put the teacups down and pulled out her own phone. Tapping the screen, it wasn't long before a faint ring-tone could be heard.

"There." Jenny pointed towards an open suitcase in the corner, with piles of clothes that had yet to make their way into the bedroom spilling over the sides. "You must have put it down when you were looking for your socks this morning."

Cooper rummaged in the suitcase, eventually retrieving his iPhone. "Gotcha. Right, I'd better be heading back." He slipped the phone in his pocket and began to head for the door.

"Betty has baked some lovely shortbread and flapjacks. Why don't you take some with you for the others?" Jenny was already picking up a couple of the paper napkins Mrs Thompson had brought with her, wrapping up a few of each.

"Don't mind if I do." Cooper accepted the food bundle and grinned. "I've not had any breakfast yet. I'm starving. God knows which box we packed the toaster in."

"Don't eat them all yourself!" chastised Jenny with a smile, as Cooper waved his goodbyes and disappeared. She turned back towards Betty, handing her a fresh cup of tea. "Thank you so much again for the treats. It's so thoughtful of you."

"It's my pleasure, dear. I love baking and it's lovely to have some new neighbours at last. This place has been empty a while and, at my age, I get a bit anxious when there's nobody next door."

Jenny sat back down on the packing crate by the window. "We don't have anyone in the flats above us yet." She took another slice of shortbread. "Part of me hopes it stays that way. Do you get much noise when the flats are occupied above?"

Betty brought the teacup to her lips, a faint tremor in her hand. "Not really, my dear — I think the floorboards are quite thick. I barely hear the ones above me — just the front door going occasionally, and a few footsteps on the stairs. But then again, my hearing isn't what it used to be — especially if I forget to put my hearing aid in."

* * *

Time: 8.30 a.m.
Date: Thursday 28 August 2014
Location: HMP Belmarsh, Thamesmead, South-East London

It had been a while since he'd last been inside a prison cell — falling off a ferry in 2002 had bought him a new lease of life, free from metal bars and locked doors. And it had been good while it lasted. But all good things come to an end — eventually.

He glanced around the eight feet by six feet cell.

It didn't look like much had changed.

The beds were still as hard and unforgiving as he remembered, and the blankets still as scratchy. There was a welcome addition in a toilet and small shower — no doors, so no privacy. Not that it really mattered in here. He could pay for a TV if he wanted one, and he was allowed a radio.

James Quinn stared down at the cell floor — noticing an unusual stain still evident by his feet, resistant to scrubbing. He began to think about what might have caused it — but none of the conclusions were particularly pleasant.

He'd been given a cell to himself — something he hadn't been expecting. For his own protection he'd heard someone say, but he wasn't quite sure what that meant. And he wasn't sure it was really a blessing — solitary cells cut you off from the rest of the prison population at a time when, as a newbie, you needed to make your mark.

He'd spent much of the last three months being moved from pillar to post — initially in the hospital, then the medical wings of various prisons while he recovered from the injuries he'd sustained falling down Jack MacIntosh's staircase. His busted leg had mostly healed — a large metal plate and screws keeping him together. The laceration to his scalp had been stapled shut, leaving behind an impressive scar. But, as soon as he was mobile, the hospital had turfed him out into the care of the justice system.

And seven days ago he'd landed at Belmarsh, the inference being that this would be where he stayed for the duration of his debt to society. In the few days since his arrival, he'd quickly managed to get the lie of the land. A brick-built man called Jenkins seemed to be the top dog of the wing — it hadn't taken Quinn long to figure that one out. They hadn't officially met, but he was sure that particular treat would be coming his way soon enough.

Which was one of the disadvantages of being in a cell on your own — no cellmate to give you the low down on who to be civil to and who to avoid, or to tell you when something was about to go down. Stuck in a cell on his own, he felt blind.

He'd never been inside Belmarsh before — although one nick was much the same as another, and he'd been inside enough times to know. But something about Belmarsh was different. The induction was the same as he'd experienced before — he'd done all the necessary steps like registering with a GP, had a check-up due to the history of his injuries, and filled in enough paper forms to sink a small ship.

But now he was alone. And alone in Belmarsh wasn't somewhere you really wanted to be.

He'd been happy — well, maybe not *happy* as such — to cop to the wounding charge on MacIntosh. He didn't really have much option, according to his brief. And he'd got less jail time in his sentence by admitting his guilt early on. But there was no way he was copping to that banker's murder in Surrey, even if they did try to tell him his DNA was found at the scene. He doubted Roger Bancroft truly existed, but who the guy really was didn't interest Quinn.

What *did* interest him though was who had tried to set him up.

He suspected MacIntosh was behind it — but even a decent copper would have needed some help to pull something like that off, and Quinn was determined to find out just who that someone was. No matter how long it might take.

Nobody set up James Quinn without living to regret it.

It was almost time for breakfast — a time where Quinn would emerge from his cell and try to suss out more about that Jenkins fella. Top dog he might be at the moment — but James Quinn was here now.

And James Quinn didn't bow down to anyone.

CHAPTER NINE

Time: 8.30 a.m.
Date: Thursday 28 August 2014
Location: Metropolitan Police HQ, London

"We need the media onside early with this one." Jack failed to hide the displeasure in his tone. So far, apart from several press releases giving the barest of facts, nothing substantial had been given to the media. But that needed to change. He sighed. "I feel it's the only way forward. We need to give them photos of our victims — see if any members of the public can help identify them."

Both Cooper's and Daniels' eyes flickered towards the gruesome headshots tacked to the whiteboard. Cassidy's face paled beneath her jet-black fringe. "What pictures could we possibly give them?" she asked. "We can't give them *these*."

Jack shrugged, running a hand over his hair. He looked like crap, he knew that without needing to be told. His eyes felt like they were out on stalks from his restless night, and the crumpled shirt didn't help. "No idea, but we've got to come up with something."

"How about we use a digitally enhanced headshot?" volunteered Daniels. "You could use any of the images we have for that."

"A *digitally enhanced headshot*." Jack's withering expression told the room he had no idea what that meant.

"Good idea, Trev." Cassidy nodded her agreement. "All it needs is some photo shopping and filters. Everyone does it on their selfies these days. On their Facebook and Insta pages."

Jack gave Cassidy another one of his looks. "I won't even pretend to know what any of that means."

Cassidy hid a snigger behind her mug of chai tea. "It just something to make you look better than you do in real life."

Jack felt like he needed that himself. "So, they can take away the stitches from their mouths?"

Cassidy nodded again. "They can get rid of the stitches and make it look like a normal mouth. Lose any bruising, too. It won't be an exact likeness – more like the images you see when a missing person has been aged to try and show what they would look like now. But it might just be enough for someone to recognise them."

"Then let's do it. I want those pictures out across the media by lunchtime."

"Leave it with me." Cassidy put down her mug and grabbed her keyboard. "I'll get Simon down in the Tech Suite to look at it."

"Leaving the media aside for the moment, any further updates before we get cracking?" Jack looked expectantly around the room.

"I've been researching the sewing shut of the mouths and also the rodent aspect." Daniels pulled his notebook towards him. "It was quite fascinating in the end."

"Fascinating *and* useful?" Jack pulled his chair across the room, a hopeful look on his face. Before Daniels had a chance to reply, he added, "And the short version will do."

"There's a fair bit about the sewing up of mouths, but I'm not too sure it has much relevance to the case. Protesters have been doing it for a while, as an act of symbolism — mostly protesting about censorship and freedom of speech. Historically, however, it's more to do with keeping away evil.

I found references in Tudor times to sewing up the mouths of the recently departed to stop the devil from entering their bodies and preventing them from reaching the afterlife."

Jack sighed. "I think the devil's already got to these poor souls, Daniels. Anything else?"

"I hit a bit of a dead end regarding the rats." Daniels flicked to a fresh page in his notebook. "I found an ancient Egyptian custom that says placing the body of a dead rat or mouse on the gums would alleviate toothache — and the Elizabethans thought they were a cure for warts. Elsewhere, it's mostly the usual reference to dead rodents heralding that someone is about to die, or is already dead."

"I'm not sure any of that takes us much further forward." Jack slumped in his chair.

"Sewing up the mouths says '*keep quiet*' to me. And the dead rat's head — maybe that means '*don't rat on us*'?" Cooper unwrapped a hot bacon roll, the smell quickly wafting around the incident room. "If you don't keep your mouth shut, this is what'll happen to you."

Jack pulled himself to his feet. "I think I'm with you on that, Cooper. As much as I don't like to say it, I think we're looking at gangs here. These are punishment killings." He heard the Chief Superintendent's words echoing around his head.

'*As soon as you think this case is gang related, you let me know.*'

Then he remembered Dougie King's suspicions about Lance and Wayne Carson.

"Start looking into the Carson brothers. As much as you can find out without stirring up a hornet's nest."

"The Carsons? You think they're involved in *this*?" Cassidy blew across the top of her chai tea and reached for one of Betty Thompson's shortbread slices. "I thought they were amateurs — small fish in a very large pond."

"They are." Jack shrugged back into his jacket, reaching for the packet of painkillers in his pocket. "Just something the Chief Super said. It might come to nothing but we should at least look into it."

"If we're talking gangs, then could our victims be illegals? Trafficked?" Cassidy took a bite of the freshly baked shortbread. "With no ID on them, no fingerprints on the system, nothing on missing persons — no one missing them at all?"

"Very possible. Let's see if releasing the photographs gets us anywhere. In the meantime, I had another chat with the doc last night and he thinks both victims were alive when their mouths were sewn shut."

"Alive?" Cassidy put the shortbread down. "That's barbaric."

"Indeed. Which I feel leads us even more towards the gang angle. None of them are generally known for their niceties. Daniels, you mentioned some lettering on the victim's shoulder at yesterday's post-mortem. The doc says he'll be taking another look at our first victim sometime today, just to make sure he didn't miss anything — now he knows what to look for. He'll send through some photos later this morning and I might get you to take a look."

Daniels' eyes brightened at the prospect of another task.

Cooper pulled his keyboard towards him. "As well as the Carsons, I'll try looking for any unsolved gang related crimes with unidentified bodies — and any involving facial mutilation."

"Knock yourself out, Cooper." Jack headed for the door. "And get those photographs enhanced or whatever it was you called it. I want some images that won't put the public off their breakfast."

* * *

Time: 9.00 a.m.
Date: Thursday 28 August 2014
Location: Westminster Mortuary, London

It wasn't often Dr Matthews re-examined a body. But something was drawing him back towards the resident of drawer number four in the mortuary chiller. He'd sent Perry off to prepare the paperwork for the day's list of examinations so, for the moment at least, he had precious time alone.

The body was already lying on the steel examination table. Pulling one of the overhead lights down a fraction, he focused the glare on to the victim's upper torso. The examination on yesterday's body had revealed a small marking on the rear of the right shoulder, just above the shoulder blade. At first he'd thought it could be a naevus, a benign and very common skin condition. But on closer inspection, faint lettering could be seen in among the surrounding discoloration from the widespread contusions. At least, it looked like letters — albeit unfamiliar ones. Not your standard tattoo markings at any rate.

With a gloved hand, the pathologist turned the body to the side, focusing the light from above over the victim's right shoulder. External bruising made the inspection difficult. Bringing out a large magnifying glass, he bent in closer.

Nothing. He was sure of it. Nothing but darkened contusions.

Frowning, he walked around the table and repeated the process with the opposite shoulder. Nothing but bruising. More discolouration.

Except.

Bringing the overhead light down further, he focused it on to the base of the victim's neck. Using the magnifying glass once more, he moved in closer.

Just then, the mortuary technician pushed the double doors open, clipboard under his arm. "All ready to go with the first on the list."

Dr Matthews straightened up, pushing the overhead light out of the way. "Before we do that Perry, go get the camera."

* * *

Time: 9.15 a.m.
Date: Thursday 28 August 2014
Location: Skyline Apartments, Canary Wharf, London

Knowing he was standing in the exact same spot Joseph Geraghty once stood gave Ritchie Greenwood a curious thrill.

Joseph Geraghty.

The man had enormous shoes to fill — and Ritchie was doing his best to do them justice. He knew he'd put some of the others' noses out of joint, rising to the top of the organisation so quickly. It wasn't so long ago that he'd been the 'new boy' — Geraghty's prodigal son.

And here he was now — in control.

It made him smile.

Geraghty had known exactly what he was doing in the final few months of his life — planning things with the utmost precision. He'd wanted to bring in new blood to bolster the team — and that new blood came in the form of Ritchie Greenwood.

Sipping his morning coffee on the balcony of the penthouse suite, Ritchie closed his eyes against the morning rays. The city was already coming to life below him, the business suits scurrying like ants into their skyscraper offices. An array of aromas would be filling the air at ground level — freshly roasted coffee and pastries from the pavement cafes, more adventurous smells from the upmarket fusion restaurants touting for business. Up here, close to the clouds, Ritchie could only use his imagination.

Opening his eyes, he turned towards the marble-topped table. The plan was taking shape — Geraghty had laid the foundations, leaving clear instructions on what was to happen next. And Ritchie felt increasingly sure there was no way it could fail. The boss had thought of everything.

Two crisp white envelopes were set out, one next to the other, each bearing the same typed lettering. Draining the last of his coffee, Ritchie set the mug down and snapped on a pair of latex gloves before reaching for the first envelope.

Selecting the correct piece of white card, also containing the same typed lettering, he tucked it inside the envelope and sealed it. He repeated the process with envelope number two, but also slotted in the required number of banknotes. Used. Unmarked. Untraceable.

He slipped both envelopes into his briefcase and settled back in his chair. He had time for another coffee before he needed to leave, and maybe he'd even order in something from that new patisserie that had opened up below.

For now, life was good for Ritchie Greenwood.

CHAPTER TEN

Time: 10.15 a.m.
Date: Thursday 28 August 2014
Location: Metropolitan Police HQ, London

Becky Yates kept her eyes trained on the closed door of her box-like office as she swapped the phone to her other ear. The corridor outside was barely used, but it didn't hurt to be careful.

"Good," she said, her voice low. "I'll see you tonight."

She ended the call, eyes still fixed on the door. Her nerves were on edge, plainly evident by the gripping pains in her abdomen and the cool, sweat on her brow. She winced as she leaned back in her chair. She really wasn't sure if she could see this through to the end — but what choice did she have? She couldn't pull out now.

She'd skipped breakfast and arrived at the station early that morning, wanting to get up to speed with the pile of cases that had now landed on her desk. Her new team had given her the low down on a number of investigations that were currently under-way — a sexual assault in Green Park; a stabbing on Tottenham Court Road, and a robbery at a jewellers in Holborn. Everyone was nice enough — certainly hardworking and no question that they were good at their jobs. She just hoped she could live up to the expectations they most surely had of her.

Feeling her stomach growl once more, she contemplated heading up to the canteen for some food. She would need something to steady her nerves, or someone would start wondering what was wrong with her. And she didn't need questions right now — well-meaning or otherwise.

Reaching for her bag, her hand skimmed the framed photograph of her mother sitting by her computer monitor. It had been a while since she'd last visited. Yet another 'to do' to add to the growing mental list inside her head. But it wasn't one she could put off for much longer — her mother wasn't getting any younger. They hadn't quite mentioned 'end of life' care but Becky knew it would be on the horizon before too long. As would the next eye-watering bill for her care. With her savings dwindling by the second, another demand was the last thing she needed.

Which was why she really needed to make this work.

Just then there was a brief rap at the door, followed by DS Carmichael's head appearing around the door jamb as it opened. "You got a minute?"

Becky nodded, trying her best to give a welcoming smile. "Sure, come on in."

"It's about that witness you want me to go and see." Carmichael slipped into a vacant chair opposite, handing over two A4 sheets of paper. "This was all we got from them the last time — I know they're holding back but I'm not quite sure what I can say to get them to open up. I'm not sure they trust us enough. I suspect they're worried about reprisals if they get involved."

Becky took the papers, eyes scanning the details. The case involved the alleged sexual assault of a young woman in Green Park and witnesses were rather thin on the ground. There was some forensic evidence, but one or two witnesses as a back-up would strengthen their case no end. As she finished reading, she nodded.

"I see what you mean." She handed the papers back. "It's got to be worth another go, though. We might be able to offer some kind of anonymity if you think that might help?"

"That's what I was hoping you'd say. Something like that just might swing it." Carmichael made to get back to his feet, as he did so he spied the photo frame. "You and your mum?" He gestured towards the image of two women standing on a white, sandy beach, the turquoise blue ocean in the background. "You look very alike."

Becky gave a small chuckle, a genuine smile forming. "That's what everyone used to say about us. My dad would call us his twins."

"Used to? Sorry — I didn't realise."

Becky waved her hands in front of her face. "No, no — nothing like that. She's still with us — in body anyway." She paused, the smile slipping a little. "She has dementia — entering the end stages we think. We've had to put her in a nursing home as Dad couldn't cope on his own anymore. We can't really afford it, but . . ." She gave a shrug. "The staff are brilliant, and she seems happy enough." Becky's voice faltered as she let her gaze fall on the photograph once more. "She doesn't always recognise us these days. It hits Dad quite hard. I can see the pain in his eyes after he's been to see her — even though he tries his best to hide it."

"That must be tough."

Another shrug. "It is what it is." Becky plastered another smile on her face and got to her feet. "Anyway, you don't need to hear about my woes. See if you can get your witness to open up a little more — the case could really do with it." She grabbed her bag and headed for the door. "Before you go, I'm heading up to the canteen — care to join?"

* * *

Time: 12.00 p.m.
Date: Thursday 28 August 2014
Location: Metropolitan Police HQ, London

Jack put the phone down, a satisfied smile on his face. It wasn't often a discussion with the CPS left him in a good mood, but Carrie-Ann Dixon was going to get the justice she deserved at last. He placed the file into his out-tray, and reached for another.

He'd only just opened it when the desk phone trilled once more. Considering ignoring it just for a second, Jack tossed the file back and snatched up the receiver.

"DI MacIntosh."

"I completed the re-examination of your first body earlier this morning and thought you might appreciate my findings sooner rather than later."

Dr Matthews' low tone instantly put Jack on alert as he instinctively pulled a notepad across the desk. "Shoot."

"It was difficult to spot — I can see why I didn't see it during the initial examination. But I now believe the first victim has a similar set of lettering as body number two."

"Are we any closer to knowing what it says?"

"Not my field really, Jack. I'll send the images over. They're clearer on the second victim than the first — body number one has more extensive bruising on the upper torso which makes it hard to decipher. See what you make of it."

There was a brief pause as Jack heard a series of tapping sounds, presumably the pathologist at his keyboard. Seconds later, an email alert pinged on to Jack's monitor.

"You got it?"

"Just arrived." Jack grabbed the mouse and opened the attachment.

The doc was right. The images weren't great but . . . there was definitely some kind of lettering evident. Small, not particularly clear — but lettering all the same.

"Thanks, doc. I'll see where it takes us."

As soon as he'd ended the call, Jack punched in the number for the incident room. "Daniels? I've got another job for you."

* * *

Time: 12.35 p.m.
Date: Thursday 28 August 2014
Location: Near Covent Garden, London

Betty picked up her empty teacup and peered out of the window of her ground floor flat.

They were here again.

She'd heard the front door open and close, then the heavy footsteps climbing the stairs to the flat above. Was it one set of footsteps this time, or two? She couldn't be quite sure, but it sounded like more than one.

Making her way to the door that led out into the communal hallway, she pulled it open and popped her head around the doorframe. Whoever it was had already managed to get to the top of the stairs, slipping out of sight just in time.

She'd seen one of them a few times now — a tall man, heavily built with a beard. But he had kind eyes. And he'd been accommodating enough to help her inside with her shopping the other day, and hand over her morning post. He hadn't wanted to stop and chat, not like that lovely couple next door. Betty frowned as she tried to remember their names. What was it now? *Janice*? *Colin*?

Muttering to herself, Betty closed the door and headed for the kitchen.

Placing her teacup and saucer on the draining board, she glanced sideways at the fridge. A large piece of A4 paper was pinned to the centre.

> *Monday — bin day*
> *Tuesday — shopping day*
> *Wednesday — lunch club 12.30 p.m.*
> *Thursday — pension day*
> *Friday — indoor bowls 2.30 p.m.*

Below it were several additional Post-it notes.

> *Breakfast — 8 a.m.*
> *Lunch — 12.30 p.m.*
> *Tea — 5 p.m.*

Betty looked at the calendar clock on the kitchen windowsill. THURSDAY blinked back at her in bold letters.

12.35 p.m. Moving across to the microwave, she spied the additional Post-it note on the front.

No metal or foil

Betty smiled, taking a tin of tomato soup down from the overhead cupboard along with a china bowl. There was a further note pinned to the microwave.

Soup — 2 mins

Emptying the contents of the tin into the bowl, she slid it inside the microwave and set the timer for two minutes. While it heated, she went to fill the kettle at the sink. More notes. '*Hot*' on one tap, '*Cold*' on the other.

Her eyes then settled on a picture of her beloved Harold on the windowsill next to the calendar clock. There was a framed photograph of him in every room. She knew his name was Harold because the Post-it note told her so. It pained her that she sometimes needed reminding of so many things — along with her hearing, her memory wasn't all it used to be.

The notes were her granddaughter's idea. At first, Betty had scoffed at the very thought, saying she had no need for such things. But as time went on and she began missing meals, putting the bin out on the wrong day, getting up to make breakfast in the middle of the night — she gave in.

And it wasn't so bad really.

Most of the time she got along just fine and the notes were more of an amusement than anything else. But at other times, they really helped. The brain was a funny thing. Although she sometimes forgot Harold's name unless she looked at the Post-it note beside his picture, she could remember every last detail about him, and the sixty-six years they'd known each other.

She recalled their wedding day in 1951 in the minutest detail. Her dress had been a present from her Aunt Mabel. Mabel had been a seamstress and made Betty's ivory dress with an intricate lace bodice by hand. Betty had felt like a fairy-tale princess on her big day, walking down the aisle at the small village church. The whole day had been perfect from beginning to end. The sun had shone; the choir sang beautifully in the old seventeenth- century church set in immaculately tended gardens, and everyone had left with a smile on their face. After the war, it hadn't seemed right to put on a lavish celebration, what with rationing still in place for some foodstuffs — so they'd only invited close friends and family to the ceremony. This was followed by a very modest buffet at Betty's family home just outside Dover. Her mother and sister had done all the cooking and baking themselves, pooling their resources to put on as big a spread as they could afford.

Harold had looked immaculate in his British Army uniform, and he didn't stop smiling all day long.

The memories were so vivid to Betty, played out in her head like some 1950s newsreel, that it felt like they had married only yesterday. But ask her to recall what she'd done earlier that day, and her mind would be a complete blank.

Sighing, she heard the microwave 'ping' and set about buttering some bread.

* * *

Time: 1.15 p.m.
Date: Thursday 28 August 2014
Location: HMP Belmarsh, Thamesmead, South-East London

You're doing a good thing here, Mickey." Richie Greenwood kept his voice low. "As agreed, we'll make it worth your while."

Mickey Hatton rubbed a stubby finger across his pockmarked chin. A white scar, the jagged wound that caused it long-since healed, ran from just beneath his left eye, across his cheek and down to the corner of his mouth — continuing underneath his chin and across the neck. The slash would have ended most people's lives in a matter of minutes — but not Mickey Hatton. They didn't call him Mickey, the Mad Hatter of Croydon, for nothing.

He often used the scar's presence to his advantage, a warning to others not to take liberties. He would run a finger slowly along the scar if anyone even looked at him the wrong way. And it usually worked. He'd noticed even that low-life Jenkins was giving him a wide berth in here.

"No problem. Just doing my bit."

"As agreed, we'll take care of your mum's nursing home fees — only the best the North-East has to offer. And your wife and kid will want for nothing, too."

"Aye." Mickey kept his voice low. Although they were in a private interview room, in here you could never be entirely sure who else was listening. "Make sure that son of mine finishes college. Gets a trade behind him. I don't want him going down the same road and following me in here."

Ritchie nodded. "Consider it done."

The two men sat in silence for a while, then Ritchie got to his feet, holding out a hand. "Nice doing business with you, Mickey."

Hatton's grip was firm. A loyal member of Geraghty's team right from the very beginning, Ritchie knew the man would see it through. He didn't really have much choice — Hatton's life on the outside was effectively over. Banging on the door to indicate the meeting was finished, he turned and gave a discreet nod in Mickey's direction.

"Look after yourself in here. We'll take care of everything else."

CHAPTER ELEVEN

Time: 1.30 p.m.
Date: Thursday 28 August 2014
Location: Waverley Street, London

Jonathan Spearing stood at the corner of Waverley Street as instructed, nervously hopping from foot to foot. The sun was beating down furiously overhead, making his shirt stick to his back. He was sure anyone passing by would be able to see the sweat pouring off his face, and hear his heart hammering inside his chest. But no one seemed to even acknowledge his presence, going about their day without giving him so much as a second look.

It was a relatively busy intersection of two roads — and Spearing wasn't sure if that reassured him or not. It had crossed his mind that whoever was behind this may have already killed Katarina and was merely luring him out into the open to do the same to him. He felt sick at the thought, his legs quivering. But surely nothing could happen out here in broad daylight, could it? Not on such a busy street? This was London, for god's sake — not Sicily.

Spearing glanced at his watch for the millionth time. The message had said 1.30 p.m. sharp.

Don't be late.

Right on cue, the black taxi rounded the corner to his right and stopped at the kerbside, indicator flashing. The windows were tinted so Spearing couldn't see the driver, but he instinctively knew this was it. His stomach flipped as the rear door sprang open.

For a split second he hesitated.

He had time to run; time to escape.

Time to call the police.

But he knew with a sickeningly heavy heart that Katarina's life would be over — if it wasn't already — if he took that option. With legs like jelly, his palms thick with sweat, Spearing stepped forward and slipped into the rear of the taxi.

* * *

Time: 1.30 p.m.
Date: Thursday 28 August 2014
Location: HMP Belmarsh, Thamesmead, South-East London

The man didn't have 'criminal' tattooed on his forehead — but Jason Alcock had an eye for a villain. He'd seen him several times over the last few days, but he couldn't quite put his finger on precisely what it was that made the man stand out. Maybe it was the way he walked — a noticeable swagger that only the overconfident could pull off.

"You clocked him too, eh?" Out of nowhere, Lindsay Jenkins appeared at Jason's side, giving him the distinct feeling once again that the ex-wrestler was deliberately following him.

"Just seen him around a few times. No big deal. He's probably a visitor — or a brief."

"He's no more a brief than I am." Jenkins started following Jason towards the library. "I have it on good authority that he's the new kingpin in town, if you know what I mean." Jenkins tapped the side of his nose with a fat finger.

Jason's expression told Jenkins he didn't know and didn't particularly care.

Jenkins' face contorted into a scornful grin. "You've been spending far too much time in here, my friend — not outside in the *real* world where the real stuff happens."

Jason stiffened at the word '*friend*', but let it pass.

"That fella there has just taken over from Joseph Geraghty. The big G's fallen off the face of the earth — rumour has it someone might've bumped him off. Maybe even one of his own."

Jason had heard of Joseph Geraghty — there weren't many on the inside who hadn't. But he couldn't give two hoots about what had happened to the man, or who'd risen out of the ashes to take his place. "Shouldn't you be somewhere else?" Jason stopped outside the corridor that led down to the prison library. "You can't come down here."

"Don't you want to know who he's been visiting?" Jenkins ignored the question and gestured back over his shoulder.

"Not really. I've got better things to do."

Jenkins didn't take the hint. "Well, the first question that springs to *my* mind is what a kingpin like *him* is doing visiting scum like Mickey Hatton."

Jason considered it an odd choice of word to come from the mouth of a convicted killer, but let it go. Maybe there were different degrees of scum in Lindsay Jenkins' world.

"He's a nutcase, that Hatton. Did you hear how he forced some bloke to swallow battery acid then set his feet on fire?"

"Still not interested." Jason turned to walk along the corridor leading to the library.

Jenkins followed, clearly not finished yet. "So what about our new boy, then? You seen much of him? He been down to the library yet?"

"What new boy?"

"That new fella I told you about last week — I've found out his name now. Quinn."

Jason stopped outside the door to the prison library. "Not interested in that either."

Jenkins leaned in close behind Jason's ear, so close Jason could smell the man's breath. It wasn't pleasant. "You wait 'til I tell you what he's in here for — then you'll soon change your mind."

Jason's shoulders sagged, knowing Jenkins wouldn't leave him alone until he'd said his piece. "What then?"

"Tried to kill a copper, that's what. Shot him in his own home, he did — but the stupid bugger missed, and then fell down the sodding stairs trying to make a run for it." A wide grin stretched across Jenkins' pockmarked face. "Bloody idiot."

Jason's hand hovered over the door handle. He half-turned back towards Jenkins, who was still loitering close behind, but remained silent.

"But then again, I'm pretty sure you know all about that, don't you, Alcock? You know exactly who Quinn is." Jenkins' mouth stretched wider, revealing a row of uneven teeth. "Don't act like you don't know what I'm talking about — it's written all over your face. He's your mate, isn't he? That copper fella that got himself shot."

Jason gripped the door handle harder but continued his silence.

Jenkins carried on. "I've heard something else about him, too. This Quinn fella."

"Oh?" Jason kept his voice even. "And what's that?"

"Yeah, well between you and me, someone in here's gunning for him. And you know what I mean by that, don't you — he's a marked man."

"Why? Because he shot at a copper? I thought that would make him a hero in here."

Jenkins shook his head, eyes shining. "Nah, no one's bothered about the copper. Probably think he should've done a better job of it. No — it's something else. Word has it someone's been put in here to get rid of him. All very hush-hush though." Jenkins tapped the side of his bulbous nose with a podgy finger. "Know what I mean?"

Jason did know what he meant. It was more common than people liked to admit — prisoners being singled out for punishment by their peers. Sometimes it was just to hurt them; frighten them and let them know who was boss within the prison walls. Boiling sugar water was a favourite — a napalm bomb to those in the know. Jason had seen its effects up close — and it wasn't pretty. Other times it was just a good old-fashioned kicking.

But then there were those that would take it that bit further. Hurting wasn't enough. Disfigurement wasn't enough.

They wanted to kill.

Murders within prison were, thankfully, a rarity — but they weren't impossible.

"You mark my words. He'll need eyes in the back of his head in here. But I'm sure you know all about that already."

"Jenkins!" The door to the prison library swung open, prison librarian Louise Freeman standing in the doorway, her arms folded in a headmistress-like stance. "Twice in two days — we *are* honoured. I'm sure I don't have you down as having an authorised library session right now, but seeing as you are so keen, would you care to join us for our literacy hour? Or have you somewhere else you need to be?"

Jenkins took the hint and backed away. "Don't forget," he called back over his shoulder. "I'm watching you, Alcock."

* * *

Time: 1.35 p.m.
Date: Thursday 28 August 2014
Location: Metropolitan Police HQ, London

"The photoshopped images of the victims came back." Cassidy picked up several colour printouts from her desk and handed them to Jack. "I think they're pretty good."

Both headshots were now minus the coarse and blood-ied thread that had sewn their mouths shut, and gone were the bruises around their lips. Eyes closed, skin smooth, they looked comfortably asleep.

Jack stared at the images. "And they've gone to all the usual news outlets?"

Cassidy nodded. "Pippa put together a brief statement — facts only. Everything went out in the last half an hour."

"Well, let's keep our fingers crossed for something positive. In the meantime, I've got some more news from the doc." Jack handed everyone an A4 piece of paper showing a series of colour photographs. "After what he and Daniels saw at the post-mortem yesterday, he re-examined the first body this morning and found what he believes to be a similar marking on the first victim. He sent these pictures through earlier with his draft report, and I have already put Daniels on the case."

"Is it a tattoo?" Cassidy squinted at the images. "It's not very clear."

"Something more than just a tattoo I think. Daniels — too soon for anything on that I'm guessing?"

"Early days. They do look like some kind of lettering though — but it's not an alphabet I recognise. It's something different. I'll keep digging."

"Good man. In the meantime, Cooper — anything on our beloved Carson brothers?"

"A bit." Cooper sent the information to the interactive whiteboard, the screen flickering into life. But knowing Jack's preference for old school methods, he handed Jack a printed copy. "We have Lance Carson — elder of the two. Age twenty-nine. Records have him attending a technical college in Billericay until 2005. Minor conviction back in 2009 but nothing since. Thought to be the brains behind the operation. The second Carson is Wayne. Five years younger. Not so academically gifted but what he lacks in brain power he more than makes up for in brawn. Was on the cage fighting and bare-knuckle fighting scene in his late teens. Again, just the one minor conviction back in 2011. Nothing since."

"They've certainly learned how not to get caught," muttered Cassidy as she watched images of both brothers flicker up on to the screen.

"Indeed. What else do we know about their operation?" Jack flicked through the paperwork.

"Mostly a loan shark enterprise, money laundering and low-level drug dealing. Some cannabis farms with bit of prostitution on the side."

Jack stopped at the mugshots of both men. "How recent are these pictures?"

"About three years old. Both were under surveillance for a while but nothing came of it."

"Do we know where they live? Family? Favourite haunts?"

Cooper nodded and brought another entry up on to the whiteboard screen. "Both have houses registered to them in North London. They also have a shop on the Croasdale Road, selling second-hand goods and music memorabilia. It's long been suspected that this is how they launder their ill-gotten gains from drugs and prostitution, but every time it's been raided, it's as squeaky clean as the money that comes out the other end. Nothing seems to stick."

Once more Jack's head filled with images of Joseph Geraghty — Teflon Man. Called that because nothing ever stuck to him either. Could Dougie King be right and the Carson Brothers were moving up in the world? For some reason Jack felt that, as distasteful as the brothers were, he couldn't quite see them sewing up the mouths of their victims. Alive *or* dead.

But Jack had been wrong before.

"Let's keep an eye on them. Put their names on the board and we'll revisit them." Jack turned towards his team as Cooper added the Carson brothers' details to the second whiteboard. "Anything else?"

"CCTV from the bus companies along the main road and the bridge has come in." Cassidy shifted herself closer to her computer monitor. "I can make a start now but there's quite a bit to get through."

"Draft in some help if you need it. Then widen the search to include everywhere between the two dump sites. They're not too far away from each other, as Cooper and I found out yesterday. Our perpetrator knows both locations are a camera blind spot — he's not stupid. He's a planner. A plotter. He won't take risks unless he's calculated them beforehand."

Jack paused. He was starting to sound like Rachel Hunter — the force's criminal profiler. They'd been out a few times recently — just a couple of lunches, a drink in the pub over the road; all purely platonic and mostly work-related. But he wondered how much of her work was rubbing off on him. Rachel had provided profiles in a few of Jack's cases in the past — and he wondered if this one was destined to be heading in her direction, too. He pushed the thought from his head for the moment and continued.

"Cooper, help Amanda out with the CCTV. In particular, see if we have any vehicles that pop up in both locations. Anything that stands out. And Daniels — keep looking at that lettering."

* * *

Time: 1.40 p.m.
Date: Thursday 28 August 2014
Location: HMP Belmarsh, Thamesmead, South-East London

He supposed it was as good a deal as he was likely to get. He wasn't getting any younger, something Ritchie Greenwood had been very quick to point out. And it wasn't exactly much skin off his nose when he thought about it. He was in here for a decent stretch anyway, so what was a bit extra? Gloria would have moved on by the time he saw daylight again — so it made little difference to him one way or the other.

Mickey Hatton leaned back on the hard mattress and stared at the concrete ceiling above. Joseph had been good to him over the years — but Joseph wasn't here anymore.

Times were changing and Mickey wasn't at all sure it was for the better.

Ritchie was young and ambitious — everyone could see that. But youngsters could also be reckless. Mickey didn't trust him as far as he could throw him, but he was hardly in a position to do much about it now. Would he be as good a boss to the others as Joe had been? Time would tell, but it was clearly time Mickey no longer had. He was out of the loop, no longer a part of things. An *outsider*.

But he had no regrets — you couldn't be in this game if you lived your life by way of regret. He knew the consequences of every action he took — just ask the poor sod he'd tipped the battery acid down. Sometimes the throw of the dice just didn't land in your favour and all you could do was take it on the chin.

I'm stuck in here for the foreseeable, might as well get paid handsomely for it.

Although, it was Gloria that would be paid handsomely. He doubted there would be much left by the time he got out — if he ever did. Cocking his head to the side, he trailed a finger across the surface of the two photographs tacked to the wall. At least this way they were both looked after, her and Adam. The boy would get the schooling he needed, move on with his life without the shadow of the law breathing down his neck all the time. It was best for everyone; let them get on with their lives without him, enjoy the good times while they could.

And then there was his mother, God bless her. She was nearing the end of her days now and Mickey wanted her to be more comfortable than the current council-run home could offer. Richie assured him they'd find somewhere suitable, and he had no reason to doubt the man.

So why was he feeling so anxious? The deal had been struck; he'd made his confession; the deed was done. And he'd come out of this a whole lot better off than when he came in.

Mickey gazed back towards the ceiling. He wasn't really concerned about the deal with Ritchie.

The real problem was James Quinn.

* * *

Time: 1.40 p.m.
Date: Thursday 28 August 2014
Location: Tower Drive, London

The taxi journey didn't last long. It wasn't exactly a sightseeing trip. The instructions in the text message had been crystal clear. Ten thousand pounds in notes, wrapped in cling film and sealed in a plain brown envelope. And all Spearing had to do was leave it on the back seat of the cab like a piece of forgotten luggage.

The envelope sat on his lap. He'd thought ten thousand pounds would look bigger than it did, but the notes took up surprisingly little space. It had taken him most of the morning to gather it all together — they had some cash in the house, put by for paying the carpenter next week when he came to install some fitted wardrobes in the spare bedroom, then work on upgrading their kitchen; three thousand sitting in the top drawer of the bureau. That left seven thousand. Spearing drew what he could out of his own bank account and then raided their joint savings account. It had taken pretty much every spare penny they had, but he'd eventually managed it.

Ten thousand pounds.

A small price to pay for Katarina's life.

The taxi swung to a stop — the ride over. The Perspex glass between the front and rear of the cab was also tinted — Spearing couldn't see the driver and the driver never spoke.

With increasingly shaking limbs, Spearing pushed the rear door open and dropped the envelope on the back seat as he left.

CHAPTER TWELVE

Time: 3.15 p.m.
Date: Thursday 28 August 2014
Location: Metropolitan Police HQ, London

Jack wasn't sure how long it had sat on the top of his in-tray before he saw it. A plain white envelope — typed lettering on the front with no postmark.

Plucking the envelope from the tray, he sliced it open, pulling out the single piece of white card from inside.

One word immediately stood out.

Quinn.

Jack dropped both the card and the envelope as if they were made of hot coals.

James Quinn — the man Jack suspected had murdered his mother some forty years ago.

He read the note again — it didn't take long; there wasn't much to it.

The Ferryman Riverside Bar
8.30 p.m.
Come alone.

Regarding Quinn.
JG

If the name Quinn caused Jack's stomach to tighten, the initials JG gave it a deathly squeeze.

Joseph Geraghty.

Even in death the man wouldn't leave him alone.

Jack slotted the plain white card back inside the envelope, and tossed it back where he had found it. He could do without anything else clouding his judgement right now. He had two bodies — two *unidentified* bodies — that were clamouring, deservedly, for his attention.

And in any case, he and Rob were going for a curry later.

Intent on ignoring the envelope and the cryptic message it contained, Jack instead pulled a copy of both post-mortem reports across his desk plus enlarged crime scene images for both victims — the non-airbrushed versions.

Alive.

If the doc was to be believed, both victims had been alive when their mouths were sewn shut, before being suffocated. Jack didn't want to think too deeply as to how long that might have taken. Having the head of a rat, dead or otherwise, stuffed inside your throat can't have helped. Despite Daniels' research into mouth sewing and rodents, Jack didn't believe they were looking at some sadistic cult performing a ritual to ward off the devil.

To him the inference was loud and clear; so much so it was almost deafening.

Keep quiet.

Just then, the door to Jack's office swung open, and DS Robert Carmichael stepped inside.

"Sorry, Jack — I'm going to have to bail on you tonight." Carmichael was already shrugging into his jacket, car keys in hand. "I've got to head out and interview a witness. Apparently, it can't wait until tomorrow and I'm not really sure how long it's going to take. I'll catch you later. We'll do that curry tomorrow night, yeah?"

Before Jack could reply Carmichael was gone.

Pulling the white envelope back out of the in-tray, Jack sighed. His excuse for not showing up as requested had now disappeared along with Rob and his favourite chicken tikka.

* * *

Time: 3.15 p.m.
Date: Thursday 28 August 2014
Location: Acacia Avenue, Wimbledon

Jonathan Spearing turned into Acacia Avenue and headed towards home. He'd walked some of the way back, in desperate need of the fresh air, but the close sultry weather made him feel anything but refreshed. With legs like jelly, and a dizziness making his head spin, he grabbed hold of one of the wooden porch struts outside his front door. The sickness that had pooled in his stomach during the short taxi ride earlier had now multiplied and spread. Panic was now starting to grow.

What if they were inside?

He glanced towards the main window overlooking the front garden. The curtains were still drawn, giving nothing away.

What if they were waiting for him — just like they might have been for Katie?

Fear gripped his insides as he thought, once more, about what they might have done to her. Although nothing had looked out of place, no signs of a struggle or any violence, and thankfully no blood, Spearing couldn't help but have visions of his wife being struck and reduced to unconsciousness — or maybe even worse.

Nausea building, he gave a final check over his shoulder before forcing the key into the lock. Once inside a thick, heavy silence greeted him. He dashed as quickly as his trembling legs would allow into each of the downstairs rooms — nothing. His heart rate started to slow. He was alone.

But for how long?

Ten thousand pounds had been a lot of cash to get his hands on — but he'd do anything for Katarina. Now all he had to do was wait.

But waiting wasn't something Jonathan Spearing was good at.

Heading through to the kitchen, he flicked on the kettle — more out of habit than anything else. As he waited for the water to boil, his thoughts turned back to the kidnappers. He may not know exactly who they were, but it was becoming crystal clear to him now that it was all down to him. It had to be.

He'd had plenty of time to think about it in the forty-eight hours since Katarina had been taken. Initially he'd been blindsided, shock overtaking him at lightning speed, but then it had become startlingly obvious.

It wasn't money these people were after, despite the ransom demand. And it wasn't his wife, either. This was no random nut job just trying his luck for a bit of cash.

Katarina had been targeted. *He* had been targeted.

And he knew precisely why.

Spearing's stomach lurched. He should have known from the very moment that first text message had come through that it was all down to him. *His fault.* Hand quivering, he reached into the inside pocket of his jacket, his fingers closing around the single memory stick inside. He was acutely aware it wasn't safe to carry it around like this — but what else could he do?

Ignoring the kettle, Spearing ran for the stairs.

* * *

Time: 4.00 p.m.
Date: Thursday 28 August 2014
Location: St Benedict's Street, London

Her legs felt numb from the cramped position she'd fallen asleep in. Stretching them as far as they would go, Katarina rotated her ankles in painful circles. How long had it been now? With the crate so tightly closed she had no concept of day or night or the passing of time.

She could remember hearing voices earlier — low, gruff voices — but she wasn't able to make much sense of what they were saying. Now there was nothing but silence. She wasn't quite sure which frightened her the most. Her stomach lurched as she fought back the wave of panic threatening to overwhelm her once more — and then she thought of Jon. Tears pricked at her eyes.

What must he be thinking? Had he been taken too? Was he hurt? He must be worried sick.

The endless possibilities made her shudder. She knew her husband wasn't the most likeable person, but there was a side to him that nobody else saw. A vulnerability. A softness. He wasn't really the hard-hearted, emotionless newspaper reporter everyone made him out to be. It was just the way of the media — you had to be like that just to survive.

Thinking back to when she'd answered the door at home, she mentally kicked herself for not being more cautious. But why would she? It was the middle of the morning. There was no way she could have foreseen what was about to happen. She ordered lots of supplies online for her party business and naturally assumed it was just another parcel delivery and hadn't thought twice about pulling open the door.

She swallowed past the lump in her throat. If only they'd invested in some security cameras — then maybe none of this would have happened. Jon had told her about these new video cameras attached to your doorbell. He'd been really enthusiastic about them; saying they were taking off in the US. Katarina couldn't see them being much of a thing over here. British people were far more reserved than the Americans — she didn't think anyone would want something so intrusive right on their doorstep. Who would want to be videoed every time they knocked at someone's door?

But, right now, Katarina wished they'd had one — intrusive or not.

* * *

Time: 6.00 p.m.
Date: Thursday 28 August 2014
Location: Skyline Apartments, Canary Wharf, London

Ritchie Greenwood couldn't be completely sure the detective would be at the bar tonight — but he put faith in the man's curiosity outweighing any caution. Ritchie had dealt with plenty of people like Jack MacIntosh in the past to be able to predict what might be going on inside their heads.

The man would show up; he'd bet his life on it.

The visit to Belmarsh earlier had put Ritchie in a good mood. He hadn't really needed to show his face there again — the deal was already struck, the deed done — but he wanted to look Mickey Hatton in the eye one last time. The man had been a loyal servant to Joseph over the years, no question about that; and the old boss had sung his praises often enough. But Hatton was past his prime, and he knew it. London had changed — and it was still changing. It was a young man's game now; a young man's city. Mickey knew his days were numbered and was sensibly taking the only way out there was.

New blood was what the organisation needed — and new blood was what it was going to get. Ritchie had plans; plans which didn't involve people like Mickey Hatton.

He closed his eyes for a moment, drinking in the faint sounds below of the city preparing for the coming night. He loved it up here in the penthouse — Joseph had chosen well. Up here you were separated from all the craziness of the streets below — up here you could be free. It was at moments like these, the calm before the storm, that Ritchie would often wonder what Joseph would have made of it all — Ritchie's handling of his precious empire.

So far, he'd followed the boss's instructions to the letter and things were starting to happen.

'Keep an eye on the Carsons.'

Ritchie's eyes snapped open as Joseph's words floated in front of him, almost as if the man himself was truly there.

'*Keep an eye on the Carsons — don't give them an inch. They'll be looking to move in on our patch when I'm gone — you mark my words.*'

Ritchie straightened up and snatched at his phone, stabbing at the speed dial. He wasn't particularly bothered about Lance or Wayne Carson; the pair were a joke. But instructions were instructions. He didn't quite believe in the afterlife, or spirits watching over you once they passed — but he wasn't taking any risks where Joseph Geraghty was concerned. When the call was answered, he barked his instructions. "Get me that information on the Carsons I asked for — I need it tonight. You know where I'll be."

Without waiting for a response, Ritchie ended the call and rose from his balcony chair. Carsons or no Carsons, he had a meeting with a detective to prepare for.

CHAPTER THIRTEEN

Time: 8.30 p.m.
Date: Thursday 28 August 2014
Location: The Ferryman Riverside Bar, South Bank

There were many reasons why Jack shouldn't have even contemplated going to the Ferryman — and each one circulated his brain in a never-ending merry-go-round for the entire thirty minutes it took to get there.

The sun had already gone down over the South Bank as Jack made his way towards one of the outside tables facing the river; far enough away from the smattering of other patrons who were also enjoying a midweek evening drink. The air around felt hot and sticky — a thunderstorm was on the way according to the news, but as yet there was no sign. A nearby waiter took his order and then hurried back inside.

Jack had visited the Ferryman a few times before. It enjoyed a prestigious position overlooking the Thames, something that was reflected in its bar prices. The capital could look quite impressive when viewed from the water's edge — so long as you didn't look too closely. Behind the glitz and glamour of the welcoming lights from each waterside pub and restaurant along this stretch of the water, lay any number of darkened alleyways that nobody wanted to see — hidden parts of London that never made it into the tourist guides. It was those parts of London that Jack knew well.

The beer arrived quickly and, after slipping out of his jacket, Jack took a long mouthful, glancing at his watch as he did so. He let his gaze scour the seated customers, searching for the author of the note that sat in his pocket — but none of them paid him the slightest bit of attention. Jack had almost finished his pint when a tall figure appeared at his side, a glass tumbler then shunted across the wooden table in his direction.

"I know you like a drop of the good stuff." The man held out a hand. "I don't believe I've had the pleasure. Richard Greenwood. Ritchie to my friends. Joseph spoke very highly of you."

Jack regarded the man standing less than six feet away from him, ignoring the proffered hand. He was tall — over six feet — and despite the warm evening was dressed in an expensive Savile Row suit. His hair was swept back from his face, a little long over the ears. And then there were his eyes. Even in the darkening evening light Jack could see they were different colours. "Am I to take it you've stepped into his shoes, then — now he's no longer with us?"

Ritchie smiled, withdrew his hand and took the seat opposite. "Well, I couldn't possibly comment — but they're going to be mighty big shoes to fill, wouldn't you say?"

Jack took a sip of the whisky, wondering for the millionth time what he was doing here. He turned his gaze back out over the river, watching the water churn by.

Ritchie followed his gaze. "Funny things, tides. They're always there, but always moving. Do you know you never see the same section of water again? As soon as it's there, it's gone." Ritchie tipped a shot of whisky into his mouth, savouring the burn. "I'm no whisky connoisseur but this is pretty good stuff, don't you think?"

"Why am I here?" Jack turned his attention away from the water. "What do you want? I'm a busy man."

"Oh, I know you are, Jack — and that's why I'm here." Ritchie slugged back another mouthful. "I'm offering my services. Call it a favour from Joseph. I can help you."

Jack paused, his glass hovering in front of his lips. "Help me with what exactly?"

"Quinn."

Jack tossed the rest of his whisky into his mouth. "I don't need any help with Quinn. He's already in prison."

"James Quinn is a stain on society — you know it, I know it. He's a leech. A parasite. He doesn't deserve to breathe the same air as you and I."

"I don't necessarily disagree with that, but — as I said — he's out of circulation now."

"I can have him taken care of." Ritchie eyed Jack over the rim of his whisky glass. "Permanently, I mean. I have people on the inside."

It took a moment or two for Jack to realise what was being offered — then the penny dropped. Hard. Placing his empty glass down, he shook his head and made to get up from the table. "I don't need him 'taken care of'. The courts have dealt with him and they'll continue to do so."

Ritchie's expression changed, a hardness entering his eyes. "But will they, Jack? Will they *really*? I didn't have you down as being quite so naive. I know all about his involvement in your mother's demise — Joseph told me everything. Even if Quinn does get sent down for that eventually — what will he get? Life doesn't mean life these days, you know that as well as I do. He could be out before the end of his days, get to walk the streets as a free man. Surely you can't be happy with that?"

Jack hovered by the table, the neat alcohol swirling uncomfortably in the pit of his stomach. He shook his head to clear his mind.

"I want justice. And justice means he faces a trial by jury. I don't want him 'taken care of' as you so eloquently put it. Stay away from Quinn. And stay away from me." Jack stared Ritchie full in the face, his expression fixed. "I mean it."

103

Ritchie gave a mocking grin in return, holding both hands up in surrender. "I hear you, I hear you." His expression hardened further. "But don't forget — you owe me, Jack. Who do you think called the emergency services down in Surrey that night, waiting just long enough for you to have left the scene and put a decent amount of distance between you and Joseph? Who do you think ensured the whole plan ran smoothly?"

"I don't owe you anything." Jack shrugged back into his jacket. Coming here had been a bad idea. "I need to leave."

"If you say so, Jack." Ritchie pushed his chair out a fraction to block Jack's escape. "But you might want to reconsider your loyalties when a certain story hits the media in the next day or so. Keep an eye out. Here's my card for when you change your mind." He leaned across the table and pushed a small white card in Jack's direction.

"What story?" Jack instinctively picked up the card.

"You'll see."

Ritchie didn't get a chance to explain any further as Jack's phone began to vibrate in his pocket.

Pushing forcibly past Ritchie's chair, Jack headed out towards the boardwalk. "Cooper, what's up?" He heard Ritchie Greenwood's subtle tone calling after him.

"I'll be in touch, Jack. Remember, you owe me."

Jack didn't turn round, instead heading up a narrow street that led to the main road and the nearest Tube.

"Boss?" Cooper sounded breathless on the other end of the line. "We've got another one."

* * *

Ritchie watched the detective disappear from view. He could see why Joseph had liked the man; there was a certain something about him. Something different to all the other coppers that crossed his path from time to time. Although it was strange, a hardened criminal like Joseph Geraghty forming a friendship of sorts with a detective — someone on the other side of the fence — Ritchie could see the advantages. A detective tucked away in your pocket could be useful in their line of work. Not that Jack would ever class himself as being in anyone's pocket, Ritchie was sure of that one.

But all that was about to change — the man just didn't know it yet.

With the detective out of view, Richie turned his attention to the other thorns in his side — the Carson Brothers. Pulling out his phone, he stabbed at the handset and waited impatiently for the call to be connected.

"You get that information I wanted on the Carsons?" Ritchie downed the last of his whisky as he listened to the reply. "Good. Get me a car — I'm at the Ferryman."

Ending the call, Ritchie contemplated another drink while he waited. But when the waiter came to hover expectantly at the edge of his table, Richie waved him away. If he was going to be tailing the Carsons tonight, then he needed a clear head.

* * *

Time: 9.00 p.m.
Date: Thursday 28 August 2014
Location: Manchester Way Industrial Estate, London

It was yet another dark and dilapidated building, just like all the others — but at least this one didn't smell so bad. Stefan hadn't been brought with them, which Natalia was partly thankful for. The smell of his decaying body in among the fermenting barley turned stomachs like a rolling ship on the ocean. But, by being left behind, it meant that Stefan was now alone, abandoned like a piece of rotten meat. And the man certainly didn't deserve that.

Natalia rubbed a hand across her shoulder, wincing at the pain from yet another bruise. The beatings were coming more frequently now — letting them all know who was in charge and what would happen if you stepped out of line.

But Natalia only had to think of Stefan and what had happened to him to make her quickly silence her tongue.

She had caught snippets of hushed yet angry conversations as they were all bundled into the van and transported here — to their new 'home'. Her English was good and she could tell from their tone that they were angry. Something bad had happened. And when bad things happened it usually meant more beatings would follow. Natalia ran another hand over her shoulder, feeling hot tears begin to prick at the corners of her eyes.

She had been stupid to have believed all their lies — the offer of a better life for her and her family back home. The jobs. The money. She wasn't usually that naive. With Stefan dead and both Danika and Elina having disappeared, Natalia felt even more alone. Danika had been the one person Natalia trusted, the one beacon of hope she had that they would all, one day, manage to get out of this hell hole alive. Without her, Natalia felt her hope diminish.

Sniffing back her tears, she glanced down at her shackled feet. Crying wouldn't get herself out of here. She needed to be strong — strong and resilient. Because she was determined she wasn't going to become another Stefan.

Or another Danika.

CHAPTER FOURTEEN

Time: 9.30 p.m.
Date: Thursday 28 August 2014
Location: McSweeney Malthouses, Juniper Lane, London

Jack jumped out of the black cab and headed towards the commotion, police tape already stretching across the entrance to the darkened alleyway. A quiet corner of the city at this time of night, with no through traffic, he could already see the evidential difficulties stacking up by the second — and the look on crime scene manager Elliott Walker's face confirmed his fears.

"Before you ask, Jack — no cameras, no windows overlooking the building, and so far no witnesses. Other than the kids who called it in."

Jack ran a hand through his hair, beginning to regret both the beer and the whisky at the Ferryman Riverside Bar. "Where are they?"

Elliott glanced over his shoulder. "I think they've been taken away by some uniforms. Statements taken, that kind of thing. I was more concerned with what we found in there." The crime scene manager gestured towards the red-brick building a few metres away. "You'll need one of these."

Jack accepted the forensic suit and slipped it on. Donning gloves, overshoes and a mask, he followed Elliott towards a heavy-duty wooden door that was already pulled open.

The smell that greeted them — even through their masks — was somewhat indeterminate; a complicated, heady mixture of general unpleasantness. Jack's nasal passages had been assaulted by a variety of aromas over the years, and tonight was no exception. Elliott saw the detective's brow creasing.

"Place used to be a distillery for a local brewery many years ago, then one of those micro-breweries moved in. Looks like it's been abandoned for a while, though. That'll be the rotten barley you can smell." He beckoned Jack to follow him towards the rear of the building. As usual, metal stepping plates guided their way. Temporary lights had already been installed, and were now illuminating the dim and darkened space.

The rotten barley smell intensified the further they walked. Jack liked a pint of real ale from time to time — but festering barley was nothing short of stomach churning. And there was something else, too.

"Rats." Elliott brought them to a halt by one of the temporary arc lights. "And mice. And all the shit that comes with them. I'm told rodents love a bit of grain — the more rotten the better."

Now they were next to one of the powerful lights, Jack could see several faded and dusty sacks piled high against the crumbling brick walls, giving the impression they hadn't been moved in a while. Huge gaps in the sacks spilled out swathes of rotten and fermented grain.

Stomach heaving, Jack turned away and looked towards the rear of the building where most of the commotion was centred. A familiar, glistening bald crown told him that the pathologist had beaten him to the scene.

"Doc," greeted Jack, approaching the hub of bodies centred beneath the arc lights.

"We need to stop meeting like this, Jack," replied Dr Matthews, without turning around. "My wife will start wanting to have words."

Jack looked over the pathologist's hunched form. Still in situ, lying on yet more rotten sacks of decaying barley, the body was on full display. The harsh lighting bounced off the pale flesh, giving it a bleached white appearance. But even from this distance, Jack could see the all-too familiar blue-black bruising in varying shapes and shades decorating the torso. Again, the victim's wrists and ankles were bound.

Dr Matthews straightened up. "You don't need me to state the bloody obvious, Jack."

Jack's eyes gravitated towards the victim's head. Staring skywards, the victim's eyes were wide open and glassy; a prominent Adam's apple stood out from an otherwise slender neck. But it was the mouth that made Jack's stomach clench.

Crudely sewn shut, the dead man's lips carried the same gut-wrenching message.

Keep quiet.

Three such messages now — how many more would there be?

Jack felt himself shudder. "Any idea how long they've been here?" Jack was no pathologist but even he could see the passage of time was evident on this one. Although the body looked to be one of a relatively slender male, the torso was grossly distended, the discoloured skin hideously stretched. And then there was the smell. And the maggots.

"It's not a fresh one, that I *can* tell you." Dr Matthews stepped away, beckoning Jack to follow. "I'll know more once I get him back to the mortuary — but even then you know it'll only be a rough window. Right now, my guess would be anywhere north of a week. But more likely two."

Jack started making the rough calculations in his head, but the pathologist beat him to it. "I think we can safely put this one as your first victim of the three you have so far — before your Jane Doe from yesterday, and before the one under Southwark Bridge. This one was just harder to find." Dr Matthews bent in closer towards Jack's ear, his tone hushed. "What did you make of the tattoo?"

"We're only just starting to look at that. You mentioned it looked like unusual lettering?"

The pathologist nodded. "They're crudely made, not expertly done. Might be a symbol rather than a letter. It was quite hard to find on both victims — what with the discolouration from the bruising. But . . ." He stepped to the side to allow two further crime scene investigators to pass by. "I'll see whether there's anything similar on this one when I get him back to the mortuary."

"Anything on the thread?"

"Samples have been sent for analysis. You'll no doubt have seen from the photographs that the thread is quite coarse. It has a wax-like coating — not unlike thread used in leatherwork."

"Leatherwork?"

Dr Matthews shrugged. "Doesn't have to be, of course. But it's certainly not your run-of-the-mill dressmaking cotton."

Jack filed the information away in his head for later. Right now, he needed to get out into the fresh air before his stomach decided the next churn was one too many.

* * *

Time: 11.07 p.m.
Date: Thursday 28 August 2014
Location: Canterbury Lane Industrial Estate, London

Lance Carson instinctively felt inside his jacket pocket as he stood waiting in the shadows behind the BMW, checking that the envelope was still there. Although it was dark, and his choice of meeting place was secluded, his eyes still darted from side to side scouring the immediate area for anything out of the ordinary. He knew the industrial estate to be long-since abandoned, but you could never be too careful; not out here.

Another glance at his watch.

They were late.

Carson hated timewasters. If they didn't show up, then he would be seriously annoyed — and nobody got off lightly when they ruffled the feathers of one of the Carson brothers. He felt inside his pocket once more. Still there.

Seven minutes late and counting. He'd give them ten minutes — then he was out of here. Angry.

At nine minutes past eleven, he saw a car approaching, its headlights sweeping the deserted car park. Carson figured it must be them. No one else would be daft enough to venture out this far — not even the local low-life junkies bothered to set foot around here anymore. Carson had made sure of that.

He waited for the car to come to a stop and for the headlights to dim before stepping out of the shadows. He saw the driver's door open and a pair of feet hit the tarmac.

Carson stood his ground, jaw clenched. After making him wait, they could come to him.

The figure hesitated briefly before making their way across the car park towards the BMW, stopping some six feet away.

"You're late," barked Carson. "I said eleven o'clock."

"Traffic," came the reply, with no hint of an apology.

Carson squinted through the half-light of the pale moon. He'd considered sending one of his underlings to do the deal, keeping his own face out of the negotiations. It may have been the wiser and safer option, but did he trust anyone enough to take his place in something like this? Not really. Probably not even his brother. Wayne was good for brawn, but he wasn't the sharpest tool in the glovebox.

So, he'd decided to handle the deal himself — let them know exactly who they were dealing with.

"You got the money?"

They were getting straight to the point which, in a way, Carson admired. He nodded and patted his jacket pocket. "I do."

"Then let's make this short and sweet. I'm sure we've both got places we need to be."

Carson placed his hand into his pocket, his fingers closing around the envelope containing the notes. "You do know what happens if I find out I can't trust you?"

"Don't worry, your reputation goes before you."

"And you know what to do next?" Carson let the question hang in the air.

"I do."

Carson brought out the envelope and handed it over. "Then it's nice doing business with you," he said, a hint of a smile on his lips. "I'll be in touch."

* * *

Time: 11.15 p.m.
Date: Thursday 28 August 2014
Location: Canterbury Lane Industrial Estate, London

Ritchie considered it a good place for a meeting — maybe even a murder. The industrial estate wasn't frequented by anyone anymore — even the addicts who had once inhabited the empty warehouses had chosen to move on. Something, or more likely *someone*, had made them start giving the place a wide berth. Ritchie Greenwood placed his money on that someone being Lance Carson.

He'd followed the BMW at a discreet distance without being seen — either Carson wasn't expecting to be tailed, or Ritchie's surveillance technique had improved. He'd parked a few units away, hiding his car behind a broken fence, covering the final distance on foot. A conveniently placed skip, long-since forgotten judging by the weeds growing around the base, offered him good cover. From its shadow he could make out Carson's sleek BMW parked outside the entrance to a boarded-up unit that had once sold motor spares.

Time ticked by, but eventually a set of headlights had appeared to his left from the main road that cut through the industrial estate. Ritchie had instinctively shrunk back further into the shadows, but kept the BMW in his sight. After a few moments he saw Lance Carson himself step out of the gloom.

The exchange had been brief — over in a matter of seconds. Ritchie took a couple of snaps with his phone camera — just in case. You never knew when things like that might come in handy. And the exchange had intrigued him.

After watching both cars pull out of the deserted car park and disappear into the night, he pondered what he'd just witnessed.

It had to be cash. Or possibly drugs.

But Ritchie's money was on cash.

The only question was — who owed who; and what for?

* * *

Time: 11.30 p.m.
Date: Thursday 28 August 2014
Location: Acacia Avenue, Wimbledon

He'd handed over the ten thousand pounds some ten hours ago now. What were they doing? Spearing turned the screen on the burner phone towards him, checking once again for any new messages.

Nothing.

He'd kept his side of the bargain; got them what they'd asked for. So why hadn't they called? Or just returned Katarina home? He'd sat at the window since arriving back home that afternoon, waiting . . . but Katarina hadn't appeared.

A sickness began to spread as Spearing thought of the alternatives. Maybe Katarina had been dead all along — and now the kidnappers, whoever they were, had his life savings too.

Spearing began to chastise himself for not handling things better. Why hadn't he demanded to hear her voice, or at least see her to prove she was still alive before he handed over the money? Why hadn't he asked them for details on when she would be released — why, why, why?

It was too late now. All he could do was hope — and pray.

Spearing gripped his hands tightly together, silently pleading with God — any god, any religion — to help him. He wasn't particularly religious himself, but Katarina came from a Catholic family and still occasionally went to Mass. Surely that counted for something?

As Spearing closed his eyes and prayed, the burner phone chirped with an incoming message. His eyes snapped open, his heart instantly lifting.

Katarina was coming home!

He snatched up the handset and it took all of two seconds for his world to implode.

'£100k. 5.15 p.m. Saturday. Location to follow. No police or she dies.'

CHAPTER FIFTEEN

Time: 6.15 a.m.
Date: Friday 29 August 2014
Location: Acacia Avenue, Wimbledon

£100K.

A hundred thousand pounds.

Spearing dashed towards the kitchen sink, dry heaving all the way. He grabbed the worktop for support, as his legs started to crumple beneath him. He'd been pacing the floor for most of the night, ever since the text had come through, feeling sicker with each passing second. There had been no question of getting any sleep.

Where was he going to get a hundred grand from?

The answer was simple — he couldn't. He'd already cleaned out their bank accounts — there was simply *nothing left*. And he wouldn't be able to borrow that kind of cash — certainly not in forty-eight hours, anyway. His credit rating wasn't great, and he didn't have a long list of rich friends he could ask, either.

All he had was Katarina's family.

The thought made him retch again.

Katarina's family were wealthy — seriously wealthy — but they hated him, pure and simple. They'd made that crystal clear right from the very beginning, looking down their noses at him and his chosen career path. All they saw was a low-life hack making money out of other people's misery and misfortune. Although somewhat accurate, Spearing had always felt more than a little hard done by.

Although they would stump up the cash in a heartbeat if it meant saving their daughter's life, he just couldn't bring himself to go to them with something like this. If he did, he would then have to explain how foolish he'd been, and how his actions had put their precious daughter in harm's way. They'd end up hating him even more than they already did, if that were humanly possible.

His thoughts turned back to the £100k and where he could possibly get it from. He didn't have any close friends — didn't have *any* friends at all if he was being brutally honest about it. Spearing pulled over one of the kitchen chairs and sat down before his legs gave way completely. The career he'd forged for himself over the last fifteen years was now turning on him in the cruellest way imaginable. He was well known in the industry for being ruthless when it came to getting what he wanted, attacking people's credibility and private lives wherever possible to get that unique angle to his articles. He didn't care who he hurt or what lives he ruined in his desperate scramble to the top — *to be the best.*

The bosses at the *Daily Courier* tolerated him because, despite his methods, he got the exclusive scoops and the inside stories that no one else even got close to.

But at what price?

One hundred thousand pounds — *that* was the price.

Spearing ran a shaking hand through his hair. Karma — that's what this was. He was being made to pay for all the bad things he'd done in his life up to now, all the lives he'd ruined just to get himself on to the front page.

Karma.

Decision made, Spearing reached a shuddering hand towards his phone. This new-found insight into his faults and flaws, as many and widespread as they may be, wasn't going to help get Katarina back.

It was becoming clear to him, as the seconds, minutes and hours ticked by, that there was only one person he knew who could do that.

* * *

Time: 6.45 a.m.
Date: Friday 29 August 2014
Location: Isabel's Café, Horseferry Road, London

Isabel had told Gina all about Angus McBride — so she made sure his white coffee and two sugars was ready for him at precisely 6.45 a.m., along with a freshly baked sausage roll. She'd barely sealed the greaseproof paper bag when the bell chimed above the door to signal the arrival of the café's first customer of the morning.

"Morning, Angus," beamed Gina. "What's it like out there today?"

Angus McBride let the door close behind him and shuffled over to the counter, his Royal Mail bag falling at his feet.

"It's a bright one, hen," he replied, rubbing a hand over his greying beard. "And it feels like it'll be another warm one, but a storm isn't far off, you mark my words."

"Well, here's your coffee." She pushed the takeaway cup across the counter. "All good to go."

Angus pulled out a handful of change and began to count the coins on to the countertop. Gina glanced over his shoulder.

"You wouldn't be a love and bring those newspapers inside before you go, would you?" She nodded towards the door where she knew a selection of papers bound up with a plastic tie would be sitting on the pavement outside. "If I leave them out there much longer they'll get swiped."

Angus tipped the rest of his coins on to the counter and winked, his grey eyes twinkling. "Anything for you, hen."

Pulling the café door open, he grabbed the bundle of papers and returned to the counter to deposit them next to the till.

Gina's eyes swept the headlines.

"Aye, it's a right nasty business that." Angus nodded towards the newspaper, taking a mouthful of his coffee as he did so. "Fair makes you shiver."

Gina released the plastic tie and pulled the paper free.

POLICE APPEAL IN HUNT FOR SADISTIC KILLERS

"I was a wee boy in Glasgow when the Krays were around. They used the local city gangs to do a lot of their dirty work for them — everyone knew it, even the police. And Glasgow was ripe for it, I can tell you that. Plenty of people ready for a bit of action. There was some right nasty stuff going on back then, but this . . . ?" Angus dropped his gaze back to the headline. "This is something else."

Tucking the greaseproof bag containing his breakfast into the Royal Mail bag, he swung it back up on to his shoulder at the same time as scooping up the coffee cup. "I'll be seeing you, hen. Have a good day."

"You too, Angus." Gina waved in the general direction of the departing postman, but kept her eyes trained on the newspaper headline — and the two images displayed beneath it.

Do you know these women? the article asked.

Gina steeled herself behind the counter.

Yes.

Yes, she did.

* * *

Time: 7.45 a.m.
Date: Friday 29 August 2014
Location: Metropolitan Police HQ, London

Jack's head was pounding. As was his shoulder. Neither had allowed him much sleep by the time he'd got back to Kettle's

Yard late last night, so he'd been at his desk since sometime before six o'clock that morning.

Another beaten body.

Another mouth sewn up.

The stench of decaying human flesh and fermenting barley had stubbornly clung to his nostrils ever since the discovery in the disused brewery. With Elliott confirming the building was a haven for rats and other vermin, Jack made a mental note to call the lab to see if there was any evidence the other two victims had spent time there. It seemed too much of a coincidence with rats sewn into each victim's dying mouth. He felt his empty stomach lurch.

Ritchie Greenwood had also filled his thoughts in the early hours, despite Jack willing his brain to shut the man out. The veiled threat at the end of their meeting — '*you owe me*' — had lodged itself inside his head, refusing to budge.

Tossing a couple of painkillers into his mouth, he swigged back a mouthful of bitter black coffee, wincing at the lack of sugar. Eyeing his paper-strewn desk, Jack searched for any more anonymous white envelopes, relieved that there were none.

Abandoning the coffee, he headed for the door at the very same moment his phone began to ring. The screen told him it was another withheld number. He'd had several calls already that morning, and he'd ignored each and every one.

'*I'll be in touch*'. Ritchie Greenwood's parting words followed him out into the corridor.

Jack killed the call and went in search of his team.

CHAPTER SIXTEEN

Time: 8.00 a.m.
Date: Friday 29 August 2014
Location: HMP Belmarsh Thamesmead, South-East London

James Quinn could feel everyone's eyes stabbing him in the back as he made his way along the landing. They felt like lasers, burning through his prison-issue T-shirt into his toughened, leathery skin beneath. Eight days in to his Belmarsh stretch and everyone was still giving him the widest of wide berths. Even that Jenkins bloke who Quinn knew ran the whole wing. A formidable brute of a man, six feet five if he was an inch, and maybe almost as wide, but even he was keeping his distance. For now.

The silent treatment made Quinn nervous. Fresh meat in the form of new prisoners, was usually something the established clientele on the inside looked forward to — but, for some reason, no one was going anywhere near James Quinn.

He continued limping his way towards the servery, trying to inject a confident swagger into his walk. All he ended up achieving was a grimace as the metalwork in his leg protested. There was no reason he knew of for anyone to be that afraid to cross his path; he didn't have that kind of a reputation on the inside. Or the outside, for that matter. Not that he didn't sometimes wish that he had. In reality, he was nothing more than a small-time burglar and con artist, fencing the occasional catch of stolen goods. Not exactly crimes of the century — and certainly nothing that would warrant him such an elevated status in Belmarsh.

There was that tart back in the early seventies, though. A thin smile crept on to his lips as he limped. He'd quite enjoyed choking the life out of her — more so than he'd expected. Seeing that smirk finally wiped off her pretty little face had pleased him. But that alone wouldn't warrant the quiet treatment in here. And besides, as far as he was aware, nobody in Belmarsh even knew about Stella MacIntosh and how she really met her end.

He arrived at the breakfast queue with just a couple of prisoners ahead of him. The welcome aroma of scrambled eggs and baked beans reached his nostrils. But alongside the smell of breakfast there was a tension in the air; so heavy you could almost feel it. Quinn's stomach tightened once more as those around him seemed to edge away.

Something was about to go down. He'd seen it happen before, no end of times. A palpable electricity in the air before all hell broke loose. But being stuck away in his solitary cell meant he wasn't privy to what that something might be. He craved a cellmate — *any* cellmate. Anyone to give him that connection to the others.

For right now he felt very alone.

And alone wasn't somewhere you wanted to be in Belmarsh.

* * *

Lindsay Jenkins watched Quinn limp away with his breakfast tray, head down, his foot dragging a little behind him on the stone floor. Jenkins couldn't for the life of him think why someone would want to top him — the man looked insignificant, a tiny speck of dirt in the dark cesspit that was Belmarsh.

But maybe James Quinn wasn't all he made himself out to be. Maybe this weak and damaged look he presented was just a front for something else. Jenkins had asked around, digging for anything from the newcomer's background, but no one seemed to know anything — or at least didn't want to say. Watching Quinn continue to shuffle back to his cell, Jenkins vowed to keep a closer eye on the man.

Watching — he was good at that.

Jenkins switched his gaze to another figure leaving the servery and heading back to his cell. Jason Alcock. There was something about that cocky little runt that bothered him, too. He had this weird friendship with the copper Quinn had taken a poorly aimed pot shot at — but when Jenkins had told him Quinn's days in here were numbered, he'd barely reacted. Said he wasn't bothered — *'not interested'* had been his exact words, if Jenkins remembered correctly.

Jenkins wasn't renowned for scoring too heavily in the intelligence department, but even *his* brain cells had started making the obvious connections. It was the perfect cover, wasn't it? The quiet and unassuming library assistant? Who would suspect someone like that?

Jenkins turned away, vowing to not only keep a closer eye on Quinn, but Alcock too. He'd watch the man's every move, monitor his every breath. If he was going to be the one to top Quinn, Jenkins wanted a ringside seat. Action, however it presented itself, was a welcome spectator sport inside these walls. You had to get your kicks where you could.

As he made his way back towards his cell, Jenkins felt another pair of eyes boring into him. Without checking his stride, he clocked the other relatively new arrival on the block hovering on the top landing. Although they had yet to be formally introduced, Mickey Hatton's reputation went before him. A notorious hard man, he wasn't someone you would choose to mess with unless you had a death wish. You didn't pour petrol over someone's feet and set them alight, while then attempting to dissolve their insides with battery acid, without turning a few heads.

Hatton's eyes seemed to follow Jenkins as he made his way along the landing. A confrontation between the pair was inevitable, but Hatton could wait for now. The day would come when they'd square up to each other and see just who was the real hard man on the block but, for now, Jenkins returned his attention to the retreating back of Jason Alcock. The man had strange loyalties, that was plainly evident — but the question was, just how far would they run?

* * *

Time: 8.30 a.m.
Date: Friday 29 August 2014
Location: Metropolitan Police HQ, London

DS Cooper had already tacked a crime scene image of last night's victim to the first whiteboard and started adding the somewhat sparse details. There seemed to be a lot of question marks.

DC Daniels was up at a third whiteboard, working on a timeline. "I'm not sure this timeline is helping much," he announced, as Jack arrived. "The estimated time of death for each of them is so vague."

"You're doing a grand job." Jack hovered by Daniels' shoulder. "We don't need exact dates and times — just a rough idea of how things might have progressed. Add a map too. Pinpoint each location so we have an idea how close they are to each other. Amanda?" Jack turned round. "Anything on the CCTV and vehicles yet?"

DC Cassidy pulled her notebook towards her. "There's a lot of footage to sift through — and now we have another crime scene to add. I took your advice and called on some extra bodies to help us out, but it'll take a while."

"OK good — keep me posted. The doc thinks last night's victim died at least a week ago, probably two or

123

maybe even more. So, as far as I see it, that makes him our first victim — the first we know of, anyway. Which means they could've died around the fifteenth of August or so, as a guess." Jack watched as Daniels annotated the whiteboard with 'Vic 3' shown first on the time line. "Next in line we have our victim one — or at least the first body we discovered. Again, hard to be exact but the doc reckons they died up to three days before she was found." Daniels had already placed 'Vic 1' in the centre of the timeline. "And that leaves us with our second body — now our third victim." Daniels had placed the last victim at the end of the timeline.

"We all know that the first hour in any murder investigation is the most crucial." Jack tapped the first whiteboard. "I think we can all agree that the delay in the discovery of all three bodies makes that a little difficult, and we can kiss goodbye to our 'golden hour'." The 'golden hour' was the time immediately following the commission of an offence where the most forensic material was likely to be available. As each hour passes, that crucially important time window decreases. "Cooper, take us through the main similarities between the victims once more."

"Obviously, the main similarity is the sewing shut of each of the victims' mouths, the insertion of the head of a dead rat plus the multiple bruising. Two were female, but the one found last night was male. Neither of the first two post-mortems revealed any signs of sexual assault." Cooper stood back from the first whiteboard so everyone could see the images. "None had any forms of ID on them. All victims were bound at the wrists and ankles by what looks like the same type of twine. And something I noticed from the crime scenes photos on the first two bodies was that their feet were dirty and blistered — as if they'd not been wearing shoes for some time. And also their hands. Lots of dirt beneath their fingernails. I've checked with the lab and scrapings were taken from both hands and feet for analysis."

"Good. Follow that up with the lab. In particular, we are looking for anything that puts all our victims in the same place. My money is on that brewery. Get them to run the DNA from the first two bodies against samples taken from the scene last night."

"Do we know much about the boys from last night?" asked DS Cassidy. "The ones that found the body?"

Jack stepped away from the whiteboards and grabbed a vacant chair. "From what I've heard they were just a bunch of kids prowling the streets, as they are inclined to do these days. Their statements don't really give us much — I had a quick look this morning. They saw the door was unlocked and thought they'd have a look inside." Jack paused. "I think they got a bit more than they bargained for." He turned his attention back to DC Daniels who was still standing by the timeline. "Anything useful yet on those markings on the first two bodies?"

Daniels turned round. "In a way — I might need to look at it some more but I've a feeling it's Cyrillic."

"It's what, sorry?"

"The lettering — I think it's from the Cyrillic alphabet." Daniels stepped across to a fresh whiteboard. "Which was why I don't think anyone recognised it to begin with. The alphabet has anything between thirty and thirty-three letters, depending on the country. It was developed in the ninth or tenth century for Slavic speaking people and it's currently used in approximately fifty languages — including Russian, Ukrainian and Bulgarian." Sliding an A4 sheet of paper from his notebook, Daniels pinned it to the board. "This is the alphabet currently used in Bulgaria."

"Could our traffickers be from Eastern Europe, then?" mused Cooper. "Just thinking about the language element."

Jack gave a shrug. "It's a theory. Anything else?"

Daniels headed across to his desk, pulling out the photographs Dr Matthews had sent through the previous day. "But then I looked at the post-mortem photographs more closely, and they didn't really fit. I was convinced they looked Cyrillic but . . ." He paused, and waved the bundle of photographs in the air. "Then I realised they were numbers."

"Numbers?" Jack's stomach dropped a notch.

Daniels nodded, adjusting his glasses. "See here." Pulling another sheet of paper from his desk, he pinned it next to the alphabet on the board. "The number two here looks a lot like our letter B. A five looks like an E. From taking a better look at these photographs, I'm pretty sure the first body we found has the number twenty-two inked in, but it looks to us like the letters K and B. With the second body, I think it's the number fourteen. Looks to us like the letters I and A." He headed back to the whiteboard and tacked the pathologist's photographs next to the alphabet, plus the list of Cyrillic numerals. "See how similar they look?"

Numbers.

"Someone's marking their property," said Cooper.

Cassidy shivered. "Like branding them, you mean? Like they do with sheep?"

Jack sighed. "Fits with the illegal trafficking angle. Lord knows how many people these gangs have had in their clutches over time — numbering them seems logical. Good work, Daniels. It gives us something to work with."

But it doesn't help us find out who they are, Jack wanted to add.

"I had a look for any similar cases," continued Cooper. "Unidentified bodies with mutilated faces and such like." He made a face. "Didn't throw much up, unfortunately. Nothing about rats or sewing up mouths at any rate. Plenty of beatings, though."

Jack felt his stomach start to growl. He hadn't managed to grab much to eat before heading out to the Ferryman last night, and then the discovery of the bloated body in the disused distillery had somewhat killed his appetite. He got to his feet.

"Amanda. Keep going with the CCTV and fixed cameras. Daniels — help out with that one. Track as many vehicles as you can in the vicinity of all three dump sites. Whoever is behind this, they have to transport these bodies somehow."

Reaching the incident room door, he turned round. "Who wants breakfast?"

* * *

Time: 8.30 a.m.
Date: Friday 29 August 2014
Location: Isabel's Café, Horseferry Road, London

Danika.

Gina gripped the front page of the *Daily Mirror*, her knuckles turning white. The image was unmistakable — which was exactly what she'd told the police on the hotline number just ten minutes ago.

Now sitting upstairs in Isabel's flat, she shuddered as the memories flooded in.

Danika.

Gina could remember her vividly, even though it was some time since she last saw her. There had been something about her — a spark — something that set her apart from the other girls. She'd been so young when Gina first met her — barely sixteen, if she remembered correctly — but she had the confidence and personality far beyond her years.

Reaching for the coffee Dominic had made her before Sacha shooed her up the stairs, she sat back against the soft cushions and sighed. Livi, Isabel's tabby cat, hopped up on to the sofa, nose twitching, bobbing her head against Gina's elbow. Gina instinctively gave the tabby cat's chin a tickle, feeling the feline's gentle purr beneath her fingertips.

If only life was as simple as a cat's, she mused. She'd tried hard to lock away her memories of the years she'd spent in the Carson brothers' clutches — but they were always there, just floating beneath the surface of the new life she'd created for herself. Danika had been the only one to really show her any kind of friendship while she finally came to terms with the situation she'd found herself in; in debt up to her

127

eyeballs, trapped in a suffocating web of drugs, prostitution and worse. Danika had made it bearable — just.

But then one day she'd simply disappeared. There one minute, gone the next — just like that.

No one spoke of Danika and what had happened to her — when Gina mentioned her name all it got her was a forceful slap around the face from the younger Carson brother, enough to send her crashing to the ground, resulting in a huge purple bruise on her cheek that lasted for days.

As the weeks went by, inevitably gossip began to circulate among the rest of the girls — albeit quietly — and Gina was horrified to hear that Danika had been sold like a piece of meat. And, apparently, she wasn't the first. It was enough to give Gina the impetus she needed to finally get herself out of there.

Gina stroked Livi's head as the tabby cat settled down on her lap. Being trapped in the cruel and sadistic world of the Carson brothers had been bad enough, but the thought of being sold? Who could Danika possibly have been sold to?

That had been one of the questions the police had asked her when she'd finally drummed up the courage to call the hotline number. And she was no closer to knowing the answer now as she had been back then. The police had thanked her for the information, saying someone would come and see her, but Gina wasn't sure she'd been that much help. She didn't know Danika's surname; wasn't entirely sure how old she was, other than she'd been very young, and didn't really know where she came from. Bulgaria, maybe? Hungary? None of the girls divulged too much about their pasts — it was often the very thing they were running away from.

Hot coffee scalded her lips but she barely noticed. Thoughts were now tumbling through her head with increasing ferocity — thoughts she'd tried so hard to bury as she started to get her life back on track. She'd told the police about Lance and Wayne Carson — reluctantly at first, worried they might find out it was her that had identified Danika. She couldn't risk them finding her again. Reassurances had followed, so Gina told them all she knew.

For Danika.

Glancing back down at the newspaper's front page, she wondered just what the Carsons had done to the poor girl. The end would have been brutal, whatever it was. She shivered, despite clutching the hot mug to her chest.

Thinking about the Carson brothers shifted her thoughts to her first session with the Argyle Foundation which was later that evening. The timing couldn't be worse. She'd already been feeling the nervousness bubbling away inside even before she'd seen Danika's face staring out at her in the morning news.

Now her anxiety was off the scale.

Maybe she should cancel, tell the organisers she was unwell? She pulled her phone from her pocket and brought up the number for Howard Murphy, her contact at the Foundation. Her finger hovered over the 'call' button. But instead she put the phone to the side.

She had to do this, no matter how much it unsettled her.

She had to do it for Danika — and all the other Danikas that were still out there.

CHAPTER SEVENTEEN

Time: 9.00 a.m.
Date: Friday 29 August 2014
Location: Metropolitan Police HQ, London

Jack jogged down the stairs from the canteen, cheese and pickle sandwich for himself in one hand, a double bacon butty for Cooper in the other. As he reached the bottom, he almost collided with Jane Telford.

"Careful, Jack," the detective inspector smiled, skilfully sidestepping as Jack fumbled with his sandwiches. "How's things?"

Jack regained his footing. "Oh, you know. Same old same old."

Jane grinned. "Story of my life. How's your brother and his new wife? The wedding was beautiful by the way — such stunning surroundings. I was quite disappointed when it was time to leave." Jane had accompanied Jack to Stu's wedding in Scotland as his plus one — much to the general amusement of the rest of the team, bearing in mind Jack's legendary bachelor status.

"He's good thanks. They're both good. Just taking some time off, a short break away."

"And you?" Jane nodded towards Jack's shoulder. "I see you're out of the sling at least."

Jack gave his arm a wiggle. "Getting there. It aches from time to time." *And the rest*, he thought. "Actually, I was hoping to catch up with you — I took a call from the CPS yesterday. The Carrie-Ann Dixon case is all set. They reckon it'll be listed for trial in the new year."

"Well, that's good news. It's about time that family saw some justice for what happened to her." Jane made to carry on up the stairs towards the canteen, turning as she went. "I hear you've got an intriguing one on the go at the moment. Is it three bodies now?"

Jack nodded. "I've just heard about a call with a possible ID for one of them — in response to the pictures in the press this morning. It's a start at least."

"I'll let you get on with things, then. Keep in touch, Jack. Don't be a stranger."

As Jack turned to leave, the double doors at the end of the corridor swung open and a flushed looking DS Carmichael rushed through.

"Can't stop." Carmichael strode past. "We've a live kidnapping on the go. Keep it to yourselves though — it's the usual 'need to know' basis. Got an urgent briefing with the new DI and they're bringing in an SIO from outside to head up the command group." With that, he disappeared through another set of double doors.

"Kidnapping?" Jane raised an eyebrow as she continued to climb the stairs towards the canteen. "Not often we get one of those."

"Indeed it isn't." Jack waved his cheese and pickle sandwich in the air as he headed back down the corridor towards the incident room. He couldn't remember the last kidnapping case they'd had, but right now he had other things on his mind.

Danika.

If the caller was to be believed, they now had a name — which was more than they had yesterday. And after last night's disturbing discovery, there would be another post-mortem to attend later. As Jack pushed his way through the double doors, he wondered whether the cheese and pickle sandwich was such a good idea.

* * *

Time: 9.30 a.m.
Date: Friday 29 August 2014
Location: Hopton Court Road, London

"We're taking care of the nursing home fees." Ritchie Greenwood placed his empty mug on the worn carpet by his feet.

"The council pay those already." Mickey's wife, Gloria, sat stiffly on an armchair by the window of the Hatton family home. "There's nothing to pay."

Ritchie pulled a glossy brochure from his inside pocket and handed it over. "Your mother-in-law is going to be moved here."

The Forest Pine Nursing Home looked more like a stately manor house, with a long sweeping drive flanked by well-tended, neat gardens. Various thumbnail images of smiling staff and residents covered the inside pages.

A frown crossed Gloria's brow. "But how . . . ?"

"Like I said, it's all taken care of. The least we can do while Mickey is away from home."

Gloria flicked through the rest of the brochure, noting the onsite hairdresser, luxury pool and exercise room, gourmet dining and twenty-four-hour room service. It sounded more like a five-star hotel than a place to end your days. "I still don't understand how . . ." She bit back the rest of her words, and merely nodded. "I guess this is another of those 'don't ask' situations?" She coolly held Ritchie's gaze for a second or two before handing the brochure back. "I should say thank you."

Ritchie smiled. He'd never met Mickey's wife before — those in the organisation rarely involved their nearest and dearest in its workings. It was usually better for the families that way — better not knowing exactly what your husband, brother or son was involved in to afford the lifestyle they provided for. He glanced around the front room of the modest end-of-terrace house. As expected, there wasn't much evidence of the ill-gotten gains Mickey brought into the family. The room was dark, the mahogany furniture making it appear even darker. The carpet was somewhat worn, the sofa sagging. Faded wallpaper lined the walls, and curtains that had seen better days hung at the window. The place looked suitably shabby — but there was nothing shabby about Gloria Hatton. Ritchie noted the immaculately manicured fingernails; the tinted highlights in her hair; the healthy glow to her skin from expensive cosmetics and no doubt the odd holiday in the sun. And then there was the gleaming gold jewellery dangling from her ears and wrapped around her neck. He could instantly see where most of Mickey's hard-earned cash was being spent.

Not that Ritchie blamed her. It couldn't be an easy way of life — never quite knowing if your husband would be coming home from work that day, or if the next knock at the door would be another police raid.

"And you'll be adequately compensated yourself, of course." Ritchie pulled the white envelope from the briefcase he'd laid on the sofa next to him and handed it over. Gloria barely glanced at it before tucking it behind the cushion at her side. "There'll be a similar amount every six months." Gloria merely nodded. "Mickey said he wanted to ensure the boy went to college."

Ritchie turned his gaze towards the only photograph to grace the mantelpiece — a lanky teenager sitting astride a 125cc motorbike, an awkward grin on his face.

"Adam." Gloria's eyes flickered towards the same photograph. "Wants to be a mechanic."

"Get him into a good college. There'll be enough money to set him up in a trade of his choosing afterwards. Mickey doesn't want him to follow in his footsteps."

Gloria scoffed. "There'll be no chance of that, I can assure you."

Ritchie didn't doubt it. Gloria Hatton looked like a strong-willed woman, hardened due to the lifestyle she'd been forced to endure — and there was no question in his eyes as to who ran the household here. Would she miss her husband? Mickey was unlikely to get out of prison in the foreseeable future, possibly not ever, and maybe there was a small part of Gloria that was glad; glad it was all over and her husband wasn't coming home. Ritchie got to his feet.

"I'll leave you in peace."

Gloria walked him to the hallway. "Thank you," she said, pulling the front door open.

Ritchie noted the variety of deadlocks and bolts fastened to the inside. He wouldn't be surprised if the panels had armoured plating beneath them. The perils of being part of the biggest crime gang in the country.

Stepping out on to the pavement. Ritchie nodded his goodbye and turned towards the street. He'd noted Gloria hadn't asked what her husband had done to warrant such recompense. Maybe she didn't want to know — which was probably best in the long run. She looked to be a smart woman.

Glancing at his watch, he jogged towards the car while pulling out his phone. What he'd seen the night before was still playing on his mind. It wasn't like the Carsons to pay people off — *if* it was money that had been in the envelope, which he was pretty sure it was. Usually, it was the other way around.

He pulled up one of the photos he'd snapped of last night's clandestine meeting and attached it to a quick message:

'*See if you can find out who that is with Carson. Pronto.*'

* * *

Time: 9.35 a.m.
Date: Thursday 28 August 2014
Location: Metropolitan Police HQ, London

Becky strode as confidently as she could towards the first whiteboard. This had to go well. She couldn't afford to mess it up now. At least she'd managed to commandeer a halfway decent incident room to use — a step up from the box-like office she now temporarily called home. The whiteboards were all empty, a fresh stash of marker pens standing by.

A flurry of butterfly wings fluttered inside her stomach. It was silly really — she'd been in the job long enough to know what she was doing and she'd run complex investigations before at her old station, so it shouldn't be any different here. But it *was* different — these were new people, new voices, new personalities. And there was a lot riding on this case.

"Right, listen up." She turned towards three expectant faces all looking in her direction. "We have an ongoing crime in action — a kidnapping that needs our fullest attention. Drop anything else you have for the time being." Turning back to face the first whiteboard, she grabbed a pen and wrote '*Operation Crow's Nest*' across the top. "This investigation has to be treated with the utmost sensitivity and discretion — a woman's life is at stake."

She'd met her new team two days ago now, but wasn't yet at the stage where she could say she knew them well. DS Carmichael came across as a hardworking, diligent officer — and even in the short time she'd been here, she'd noticed he was the first one to arrive in the morning and the last one to leave at night. The other two officers on the team, DC Paul Ashford and DC Malcolm Sullivan she knew much less about, but she hoped that would change as the investigation progressed. If she was going to pull this off she needed them on her side — and quickly.

I can't muck this up.

"Carmichael — Robert." She forced her best smile, trying to quell the queasiness she still felt inside. "I'd like you to be my second in command for this case. It's going to be fast-paced and there's little room for error. The Gold Command Group is being set up as we speak and a specialist kidnap SIO is coming in from Essex. All records are to be kept secure and closed as is usual practice. For now, everything is run from this room — and everything you hear within this room stays within this room."

Carmichael nodded. "What do we know so far?"

Becky snapped the lid back on the marker pen but kept it in her hand to give herself something to fiddle with; her nerves still jangling. If truth be told, she'd never handled a kidnapping before; not that she was telling anyone that golden nugget right now. She needed to come across as competent and composed — that she *knew what she was doing* — even if inside her nerves were creating merry hell.

"The call came in earlier this morning. From the victim — the husband. The subject is a Mrs Katarina Spearing. Age thirty-five. Works from home as a party organiser. On Tuesday twenty-sixth August, she was taken from the family home in Wimbledon by a person or persons as yet unknown. The husband found a burner phone in the property which the kidnappers have been using to contact him."

"Spearing?" Carmichael's brow hitched.

Becky caught his eye. "That name sound familiar?"

"What's the husband called?"

Becky glanced down at her notepad. "Jonathan. Newspaper reporter."

Carmichael began to nod. "With the *Daily Courier*."

"Problem?"

"Not especially. Just surprised, that's all. What else do we know?"

"The first message was received at around two o'clock the same day." Becky read from the brief notes she held in her hand.

'We have your wife. If you call the police, she dies.'

"This was followed with a second message around seven-thirty the following morning, asking for ten thousand pounds in cash. Mr Spearing paid this sum at an agreed rendezvous point around one-thirty that afternoon." Becky wrote '£10k' on the whiteboard together with Katarina's name. "But instead of releasing their hostage, the kidnappers upped their ransom demand to one hundred thousand pounds. This demand was received by the victim at eleven thirty last night." She added '£100k' to the whiteboard. "Needless to say, this was beyond the husband's capabilities and he's now turned to us."

"Do we have the phone?" Carmichael began jotting various points down in his notebook. "Be useful to take a look at it."

Becky nodded. "We do. It's being analysed for fingerprints, DNA and suchlike. We're also trying to trace where it might have been recently." She paused. "I'm not holding out for much on that front though — it's clearly a burner, unregistered. And I have a feeling that we're dealing with a very well organised gang here — I doubt they'd be stupid enough to leave their fingerprints on the handset. We're obviously checking the numbers they messaged from — but I'm expecting a dead end there, too."

"CCTV? Anyone in the street have private cameras?" Carmichael continued scribbling.

"Being looked at as we speak. But I must stress we need to be discreet on this one. It's very clear that Katarina's life is in danger and the kidnappers were very explicit in their warnings about involving the police. Mr Spearing came to us at his wit's end, in fear for his wife's life. We do not want to make that a reality. Our involvement must be kept under the radar."

"Do we know why the subject was targeted?" asked DC Ashford.

"That's a little unclear at this stage. As I said, she works from home and her husband is a journalist. They're not known to be wealthy."

"I guess house-to-house will be tricky?" DC Sullivan chewed the end of his biro. "If we're keeping a low profile?"

"Indeed, it will be. For all we know the house may be being watched. We're advising Mr Spearing to go about his normal daily activities so as not to arouse undue suspicion."

"Where is he now?" asked Carmichael. "Here or at home?"

"He's in an interview room at the moment. But the idea is to return him home as soon as possible, taking the burner phone with him. Everything must be as it was. We'll go and chat to him before he leaves."

Becky felt the butterflies beginning to settle. She felt good — strong and confident.

I can do this.

* * *

Time: 10.00 a.m.
Date: Friday 29 August 2014
Location: HMP Belmarsh, Thamesmead, South-East London

"It's you, isn't it?" Lindsay Jenkins injected enough force into his tone to show Jason Alcock it wasn't really meant to be a question that needed an answer. "You're the one."

Jason bristled, but bit back the response poised on his tongue. Jenkins wasn't someone you ordinarily picked a fight with. He was becoming quite tired of the man following him around lately, always seeming to be one step behind him in the shadows. You couldn't exactly hide in prison, so it was blindingly obvious Jenkins was keeping tabs on him.

He turned, eyes fixed on the ex-wrestler standing in the doorway of the prison library. "I'm the one doing what exactly?" Jason's own tone was laced with just enough ice to show his irritation.

"You're the one who's gonna top that Quinn fella." Jenkins' eyes were dancing with his own amusement. "Go on, admit it. Everyone knows you're best pals with that copper — the one he shot at and missed. Stands to reason it'd be you." Jenkins leaned up against the door frame, arms folded, looking pleased with himself. "Tell me I'm wrong."

Jason held the man's gaze for a second longer than necessary then turned away. "Right little Miss Marple aren't you, Jenkins." He pulled a stack of books across the table towards him. "I don't know how you cope with being so sharp."

Jenkins sniggered. "Didn't think you had it in you, mind. You being such a goody-goody these days." He cast a glance around the library shelves. "But I guess I underestimated you."

Jason stepped around the table and faced Jenkins, a cool look on his face. "Well, you know what they say — it's the quiet ones that you need to watch out for. We finished here?" Jason gestured towards the doorway that Jenkins was currently blocking with his six feet five inch frame. "Only I've got things to be getting on with and I'm pretty sure you should be somewhere else."

Jenkins hesitated for a moment, a steely look entering his eyes, replacing the previous good humour. "Sure. I'm just on my way to the gym as it goes." He stepped to the side, allowing Jason to pass by. "But I'm watching you, Alcock. I'm watching you very closely."

Jason took in the ex-wrestler's flabby frame, seriously doubting much gym work would be done. "Suit yourself."

CHAPTER EIGHTEEN

Time: 11.00 a.m.
Date: Friday 29 August 2014
Location: Metropolitan Police HQ, London

Jack took hold of the marker pen and wrote 'DANIKA' in capital letters next to the digitally enhanced photo of their second victim tacked to the first whiteboard.

"It's a start." He turned back to face the rest of the team. "This is the name we've been given for the body found on Wednesday morning at Bankside. No surname, but the caller believes she could have been Bulgarian, or maybe Hungarian. Or at least from that part of the world. And young — maybe no older than sixteen the last time she saw her — which would fit with our estimated age range from the post-mortem."

Jack stepped across to the second whiteboard and tapped a marker pen against the name 'Carson'.

"The caller also identified our good friends Lance and Wayne Carson as running the prostitution and drugs ring that our victim Danika was a part of." Jack could almost hear the Chief Superintendent's words drumming inside his head.

'As soon as you think this case is gang related, you let me know.'

Ignoring it, Jack pushed on. "Anything else new for this morning?"

"Post-mortem bloods are in for our second body — Danika." DS Cassidy pulled the details up on to her screen. "Evidence of drugs in her system. Same as for the first body."

"Any conclusions with that?"

"If we're thinking our victims are part of an illegal trafficking ring, then maybe it could be a way to keep them subdued? Drugged to keep them quiet?"

Jack slumped into a vacant chair. The seed of disquiet that had been sown by Dougie King earlier that week had now taken root. None of the victims screamed drug addict to him — so Cassidy's conclusion looked to be the most obvious.

"That would fit with the people-trafficking angle." Cooper swallowed the last of his second bacon roll of the morning, wiping a blob of tomato sauce from his chin. "They're otherwise young and fit — there has to be some way they're coerced and kept under control. Abrasions on the wrists and ankles suggest restraints but drugs would help too."

Jack's thoughts, as they often did, strayed to Joseph Geraghty. If the man was still around, then this kind of thing would be right up his street. Two years ago, Jack and the team had managed to put away several people associated with Geraghty's gang on charges of people trafficking, although never quite getting near the top man himself.

But Geraghty was dead.

Jack's thoughts swiftly turned to Ritchie Greenwood and whether he could be handling such a set up in the boss's absence. Anything was possible and, if he *was* involved, then three bodies turning up in quick succession like this meant someone had clearly upset him. Upset him enough to shove a dead rodent down each victim's throat and sew their mouths shut.

It wasn't a great way to go.

"Cooper, chase up those results from the lab — we need to know where our victims have been kept all this time."

Cooper wiped his hands on a paper napkin before pulling his keyboard towards him. "Whoever's behind it, something spooked them to move out of that distillery pretty sharpish. Something or somebody." He paused, then added, "And careless enough to leave a body behind."

"I guess moving a dead body, and a decaying one at that, would be time-consuming." Jack thought back to the bloated body inside the old distillery, and the crawling flies and maggots and goodness knows what else lurking inside the poor man's decomposing tissues. Leaving it behind was probably best in the long run. "But you're right. Something happened to make them run. We need to find out who or what that was."

Jack got to his feet and started heading for the door. "Today we've got the post-mortem on the third body, but before that I'd like to go and see our witness Gina Simmonds and go over what she knows about Danika. Cooper, when you've finished with the lab come and find me. You'll remember Gina from the Narelle Williams case earlier this year." Jack pulled open the incident room door. "We'll head out to the mortuary after."

Although tempted to delegate the post-mortem visit to the ever-eager Daniels, Jack was aware that Daniels was knee deep in CCTV footage — and, in any event, Jack thought it high time he showed his own face at the mortuary. It had been a while.

"Keep at it everyone. There must be something somewhere."

* * *

Time: 12.15 p.m.
Date: Friday 29 August 2014
Location: HMP Belmarsh, Thamesmead, South-East London

Louise Freeman busied herself tidying away the materials from the literacy class that had ended a few moments ago. As she filed away the workbooks some of the prisoners had been working on, she kept one eye on her assistant.

Jason had been quiet for most of the morning. Not necessarily unusual for him — he wasn't a particularly gregarious individual at the best of times — but there was something about his manner that morning which lingered with her. Usually laid-back with a good sense of humour, it was often difficult to reconcile the man's past crimes with the person that presented himself the library each day.

She knew the details of why he'd been locked up in Belmarsh for the last six years. The man had violent tendencies, of that there was no doubt. But Jason portrayed another side — he was intelligent, charming even — not your usual take on a murderer. But Louise was also no fool — she knew just how manipulative prisoners could be, often portraying a completely different persona to the one that landed them in here. Sometimes it was all smoke and mirrors.

Although with Jason, what you saw was usually what you got.

Except for today.

Today there had been a dullness in his eyes; he'd lost the impish grin and cheekiness that was usually so in abundance. He'd been polite enough, going about his daily routines in the same way he did every other time he was helping out in the library, but there was definitely something different about today. Something was clearly on his mind — she could see it as clearly as she could see the tattoos inked on to his skin.

"You OK over there, Jason?" She'd asked the same question several times that morning already, and expected the same answer.

She got it.

"All good."

Even his voice sounded flat.

"If you say so." Louise finished filing the literacy paperwork and headed towards the door. "Time to lock up then, if you're done? You'll be needing to get back to the wing for lunch."

Jason placed the last book from his trolley back on to the shelves and followed Louise towards the door.

She decided to try one last time. "You can talk to me — you do know that, don't you? If there's something bothering you?" She felt Jason hesitate by her side, his body tensing. "It's not that Jenkins causing trouble again, is it?" She heard Jason give a quiet, throaty chuckle. "Because if it is . . ."

"I can handle that clown, don't you worry."

I'm sure you can, Jason, she mused, watching him disappear along the corridor. *I'm sure you can. But it's what else you're handling that worries me.*

* * *

Time: 12.30 p.m.
Date: Friday 29 August 2014
Location: St Benedict's Street, London

Jimmy Neale looked at the photo again. Lance Carson was plain to see — he'd recognise that man a mile off. But the other one? He squinted closer towards the phone screen. It was a decent enough picture but he just couldn't be sure he knew who it was. It certainly didn't ring any bells.

His brother, Bobby, had sent the photo through to him earlier that morning.

'*You any idea who that is with Carson?*' had been the question.

Jimmy had spent much of the morning looking at it — it wasn't like he had much else to do with his time. But the face was still unfamiliar.

And now Jimmy was bored. He'd sat in the same place for three days now and was getting itchy feet. He felt like a babysitter — and an underpaid one at that. To begin with he'd felt quite sorry for the woman cooped up in the box, but now his feelings were indifferent towards her. If he could, he'd up sticks and get the hell out of there, leaving her to fend for herself. But the fire in his belly was always quietened when he thought about what the boss might do to him if he left his post.

Jimmy wasn't a pushover and could more than easily look after himself — but even he didn't relish the thought of what might happen if he disobeyed his instructions. But surely whoever it was in that box couldn't last much longer, could she? She'd had some water yesterday — and then there was the bottle of urine — but he hadn't fed her anything else. How was he meant to? He'd been told to keep the lid bolted shut. She'd been quiet for much of the morning. There had been some moaning earlier, maybe a foot kicking at the sides, but then she'd fallen silent again.

Jimmy turned his attention back to the photo on his phone. The more he looked at it, the more he wondered if he did know them after all. Maybe not *who* they were exactly, but he had a feeling he might know *what* they were.

Smiling, he dashed off a reply.

CHAPTER NINETEEN

Time: 12.30 p.m.
Date: Friday 29 August 2014
Location: Metropolitan Police HQ, London

"There's no way I can get my hands on that kind of cash." Jonathan Spearing's hand trembled as he placed the burner phone back on the table. "Absolutely no way. That's why I came to you."

Becky turned the phone screen towards herself. "It is a significant sum. Substantially more than they asked for initially."

"The ten thousand I could just about get my hands on. Our savings, mostly. But this?" Spearing buried his head in his hands. "There's just no way. I just don't know what else to do."

"We'll come up with a plan." DS Carmichael looked expectantly across the table at DI Yates. "Won't we?"

"Do you have any idea who might be behind this?" Becky turned the phone screen back round to face Spearing. "It's a different number than before. No doubt a new burner phone at their end. We'll do our best to trace it."

"This is just going to make it worse." Spearing continued to bury his head. "I should never have come to you."

"Mr Spearing, I appreciate how distressing this is, but time really is of the essence here. You definitely did the right thing in bringing this to us, but I need you to think. Do you have any idea at all why you might be being targeted?"

Spearing merely shook his head, remaining silent.

"A hundred thousand pounds is a lot of money. Why do the kidnappers think you have that kind of cash? In my experience, kidnappers target specifically — if they are asking for this amount then they must think they have a reasonable chance of getting it."

Spearing didn't reply, muffled sobs coming from behind his hands.

"Mr Spearing, I can't help you if you don't cooperate. Is there any reason why the kidnappers think you have this kind of money?"

The reporter sighed and raised his head from his hands. "It's Katarina. She has the money — well, her parents do. They're loaded."

"Your wife's parents?"

Spearing nodded. "They're in the construction business back in Croatia. Own a multi-million-pound company. The pair of them are worth a fortune."

"And why am I just hearing about this now?" Becky flashed a look in Carmichael's direction.

"No one asked," replied Spearing.

Becky took another look at the message on the phone screen. "Well, my guess is that the kidnappers know only too well who your wife is, and which family she comes from. *This* is where they believe the ransom demand will come from." She paused and looked up. "I think you need to contact them."

Spearing's eyes widened. "Contact Katarina's parents? Why would I do that? I thought we were keeping this whole thing under the radar?"

"We are. But I still think you should contact them and bring them into the picture. They're already intrinsically involved. The kidnappers must know that this is the only avenue you have of raising that kind of money. They will be expecting you to make contact with them. We can still keep things discreet — we have protocols that we're adhering to."

Spearing gave a strangled laugh. "I work for the media, remember? Nothing is kept discreet for long."

"We've done this before, Mr Spearing. We can contact Katarina's parents and no one needs to know." Becky tried to keep her tone firm and authoritative — this was not the moment to reveal exactly how out of her depth she felt.

"I'm not so sure. They hate me. Always have. They'll blame me for what's happened, I know they will."

"But they love their daughter, surely?" Becky's tone softened. "Their feelings towards you will be immaterial. Your wife's life is on the line, and by the looks of it her parents could very well be the next target if we don't move fast. We at least need to alert them and offer them some form of protection."

Spearing's face paled, eyes wide. "You think the kidnappers will go after her parents?"

"I've no idea, but we need to stay one step ahead. If they feel that targeting you isn't working, then what's stopping them going direct to the organ grinder? Cut out the monkey completely?"

Spearing's eyes widened even further. "I hadn't thought of that."

"Well, it's a good job we have." Becky got up to leave. "I suggest you put a call in to your in-laws. Use a different phone in case they're tracking yours. And we'll need a full list of friends and family, plus both of your movements over the last three to four weeks. Robert, can I leave that with you?"

Carmichael nodded.

As Becky reached the door, she turned. "And when you speak to your wife's parents, Mr Spearing, keep calm. Reiterate that we have everything under control but we need them to cooperate fully. Katarina's life could depend on it."

* * *

Time: 12.30 p.m.
Date: Friday 29 August 2014
Location: HMP Belmarsh, Thamesmead, South-East London

"Time to go."

James Quinn gathered up his sparse belongings and followed the two prison officers out of his cell. As they walked, he felt numerous pairs of eyes watching on, burning like hot pokers into his back with every step he took. It was lunchtime; everyone was back on the wing and meant to be heading to the servery — but instead many were stopping to watch the procession.

Why was he being moved?

The question had crossed his mind several times since he'd been given the news earlier that morning — and he had yet to come up with a credible answer. It wasn't a particularly unwelcome move — sharing a cell with another inmate was something he'd thought about almost constantly since his arrival some eight days back. But, now it was a reality, another thought crossed his mind — who would he be sharing with?

Quinn had seen Jenkins loitering on the landing as they passed — relief flooded in that at least it wouldn't be him. Although the two of them had yet to exchange a single word, harsh or otherwise, Quinn didn't relish sharing a cell with the man.

The journey was a short one. Before too long, they came to a stop outside an open cell door. "Here we are — home sweet home."

Quinn paused outside the cell, his mouth turning a little dry. Taking a deep breath, he clutched his belongings to his chest and stepped inside.

* * *

Jason Alcock stood by the side of the two bunk beds, gesturing towards the bottom bunk. "You're down there." He watched Quinn inch closer, caution oozing from the man's every step. "I don't bite," he added, listening to the prison officers' retreating footsteps on the landing outside. "Despite what you might have heard."

Jason had had a few cellmates over the years — people that came and went as they paid their debt to society and moved on — but he'd been on his own for a while now and was starting to get used to it. So, it had come as a surprise when he'd learned exactly who his new cellmate was going to be. Jenkins had been bending his ear about the man relentlessly for the last few days, and here he now was — sharing a cell with the man who'd aimed a gun at Jack MacIntosh and pulled the trigger. He tried to hide a curious smile from breaking out on his face, wondering what Jack would make of it all if he knew.

Quinn moved towards the bottom bunk, depositing his meagre bundle of possessions on top of the thin mattress. "Thanks," he said, a gruff edge to his tone.

Jason edged out of the way as Quinn bent over to sit down on the edge of the bed. Up close, the man wasn't what he'd expected. He looked like he might have been handy in his day — but what muscle there might have been back then had clearly turned to fat, most of it collecting around his belly. His hair was cut short, an area on top shaved to show a healing scar from the recent head injury.

Jason thought about how close Jack might have come to a more serious injury, maybe even death, at the hands of the man now sitting in his cell. He swallowed the sense of distaste that was building. Jack was a decent bloke — for a copper. "I'm Jason," he announced, keeping his voice low and even. "Alcock if you prefer."

"Quinn."

I know who you are, thought Jason, as he watched the man straighten himself out and lie down on his new bunk. *I know exactly who you are.*

* * *

150

DS Cooper's eyes lit up as the plate of chocolate brownies was placed in front of them.

"Knock yourself out." Jack had already noticed the detective sergeant's hungry gaze. "But don't forget we're heading to the mortuary for the post- mortem later."

Cooper swiftly lifted a large brownie from the plate and stuffed it into his mouth, grinning. "Doesn't bother me, boss."

Gina placed the tray of coffees next to the brownies and settled into the armchair opposite. A copy of the *Daily Mirror* sat on the table in front of them.

"How well did you know her?" Jack gestured towards the picture in the front-page article. "Danika, you said her name was?"

Gina clasped her hands together in her lap, her nails biting into her skin. "I wouldn't say I knew her well — none of us did really — but she was a sweet girl. Young, but streetwise."

"How did she come to be there — part of the Carsons' set up?"

Gina could only shrug. "I don't know. I don't know how any of us ended up there really. We didn't talk much about our backgrounds — where we came from, what drove us to end up where we did. I guess we all knew it wouldn't be pretty. She was running from something, or someone, that's all I understood. But we all were, in our own way."

Jack reached for his coffee mug. "When do you think you saw her last? I appreciate it might be quite difficult to pinpoint."

"It was just before I got out — before Hughes bought my debt from the Carsons. It would be around the spring of last year."

"And you've no idea where she went?"

Gina nursed a coffee she didn't *really* want. "No. Like I told the officer on the phone, we eventually found out she'd been sold. But I don't know who to, or where. And then after

I got out . . ." Gina fixed her gaze on the cooling coffee. "I'm ashamed to say I didn't really think that much about her."

"Understandable." Jack sipped his plain white coffee while eying Cooper reaching for a second brownie. "I know it's difficult, but do you recognise the second image?" He nodded back down towards the folded newspaper.

Gina's eyes strayed towards the front-page news article. She'd instantly recognised poor Danika, but she wasn't so sure about the other one. "I'm not sure. I don't think so. There were so many girls, but Danika was the only one I really spent any time with." She looked back up at Jack, her voice cracking. "What did they do to her?"

Jack put his half-drunk coffee back on to the table. "I can't really divulge that while it's part of a live investigation, but . . . it wasn't nice."

Gina nodded, slowly. "I hope you catch them."

So do I, thought Jack. "Did she ever talk about her family?" Gina shook her head in response. "Never talked about where she came from? Where she grew up?"

Another shake of the head. "No. Not that I remember. None of us really talked about our past. But I think she came from somewhere like Bulgaria. I can't remember why now."

"What about the other girls that you remember from back then? Did any of those suddenly disappear like Danika?"

Gina gave a sad smile. "Girls came and went all the time. It's impossible to know what happened to them. But there was always gossip — some said maybe Danika wasn't the only one to be sold." Gina felt herself shiver at the word. "But that's all it was — gossip."

Jack nodded. "OK. How about the Carsons? What can you tell me about them?"

Gina shuddered. "They were horrible. Sadistic individuals that took great pleasure in inflicting pain whenever they could. We were all frightened of them — especially the younger brother. He was huge — he thought nothing about dragging you by the hair and slamming you into the ground if you didn't bring in enough punters." Gina placed her unwanted coffee back on to the table. "Makes me feel sick even thinking about them."

"Was there anyone else involved in their enterprise? You ever see anyone else other than the brothers?"

Gina gave a firm shake of the head. "No, just them. I never saw anyone else."

Jack got to his feet. "Nice to see you again, Gina. I just wish it was in better circumstances. If you think of anything else that might help, then give me a call." Shrugging back into his jacket, he turned to Cooper. "Pack the rest of those up, Cooper. We need to be off."

As Cooper placed the remaining brownies into a folded napkin, Jack made his way to the counter, fishing a twenty pound note out of his wallet.

"Oh no, it's on the house," smiled Gina, slipping back behind the till. "It's the least we can do."

Jack folded up the note and slipped it into the Macmillan charity box next to the cutlery tray. As he did so, he spotted the pile of flyers for the Argyle Foundation.

Gina caught his eye. "Should be a good night, if you fancy it? Good for the community."

Jack pulled an identical but crumpled flyer from his wallet. "Already going," he replied, holding it up.

"I'm doing a talk," added Gina, her smile slipping slightly. "And I'm really nervous. I've never done anything like this before, standing up in front of people. Just thinking about it makes me feel sick."

"You'll be fine, I'm sure." Jack waved the flyer in the air as he and Cooper headed for the door. "Like you say — it's good for the community. I'll no doubt see you there."

* * *

Time: 12.45 p.m.
Date: Friday 29 August 2014
Location: HMP Belmarsh, Thamesmead, South-East London

"That's him." Jenkins nodded towards Jason Alcock's cell. They'd both stopped to watch the small parade as Quinn was led towards his new home, Jenkins' eyes narrowing when he realised exactly which cell the man was destined for. "Goes by the name of Quinn. You heard about him?"

Mickey Hatton merely shrugged. "What's it got to do with me who he is?"

Jenkins continued. "I just heard a rumour, that's all."

Mickey raised an eyebrow. "What kind of rumour?"

"Move along now. You know not to loiter." Jenkins felt the presence of two prison officers by his side. "Move along."

Reluctantly, Jenkins started to shuffle along the landing in the direction of the servery, taking Mickey Hatton with him. The show was over anyway and he was feeling hungry. This was the closest the two of them had got; the first words they'd exchanged. But Jenkins felt like digging deeper. As they walked, he inclined his head towards Hatton and lowered his voice a notch. "That Quinn's on borrowed time, that's the rumour. Someone wants him gone."

Mickey's jaw tensed. "That'll be prison talk. I don't take much notice of it. It's usually something and nothing."

Jenkins snorted. "You don't know this place very well, do you?" He edged even closer. "Or me. I *know* things in here, mate. This is *my* nick. If I say something's going down, then it's going down." He tried to fix Mickey with a hardened stare, but the man refused to catch his eye.

"I see." Something that looked like a smile twitched at Mickey's lips. "So what's going to happen to him then? This fella Quinn?"

Jenkins gave a shrug, switching his gaze towards the servery and the queue building in front. "That I can't tell you — but mark my words, he's about to get a very special welcome, if you know what I mean. Or maybe it'll be a more permanent exit."

Mickey gave another non-committal shrug and wandered off to join the back of the queue. Jenkins watched the man go, frowning at his retreating back. He'd heard all about Mickey Hatton — meant to be some hard nut from Joseph Geraghty's old firm — but what he'd seen of the man so far didn't exactly live up to that reputation. And the few words they'd just exchanged supported that. Bloke seemed soft, well past his best at any rate.

It had crossed Jenkins' mind more than once that he might have to challenge Mickey Hatton for the superiority of the wing — working himself up in anticipation of a fight. But Hatton hadn't shown any interest in being the top dog. Jenkins would keep an eye on the bloke — anyone who came from Geraghty's set up would no doubt be a bit handy with his fists, able to look after himself, but Jenkins no longer saw him as a threat.

He joined the queue, keeping one careful eye trained on Mickey Hatton — but his thoughts soon returned to James Quinn. He knew prison whispers were notoriously unreliable, but Jenkins thought this one rang true. The rumour had come from a much more reliable source than the other prison noises that often echoed around the thick walls of Belmarsh. Quinn was a marked man, that was abundantly clear.

The cell move intrigued him, though.

He knew Alcock had spent more years inside prison than he had on the outside. Almost hacking a taxi driver's head off earned you a degree of notoriety in here, so he wasn't exactly a bloke you wanted to get on the wrong side of, even if he did give everyone this butter wouldn't melt, model prisoner vibe. But it didn't wash with Jenkins. Once a killer, always a killer. It never left you, that murderous streak. You could hide it, bury it, mask it in good deeds all you wanted — but once you'd crossed that line there was no coming back from it.

* * *

Time: 12.45 p.m.
Date: Friday 29 August 2014
Location: Metropolitan Police HQ, London

Carmichael sat back in his chair, stretching his neck from side to side. He'd been sitting in the same position for the last three hours, poring over the Spearing kidnap case, and his muscles were now protesting in earnest.

He'd been through every word of the investigation so far, several times over — it wasn't as if they had a lot to go on. Spearing had been asked for a list of his friends, family and work colleagues — and the list was uncomfortably short. He'd also been asked for an account of his and his wife's movements over the last three weeks — and, again, there wasn't much to tell. They didn't go out much socially, kept themselves pretty much to themselves. Just the usual shopping trips and commuting to and from work.

Carmichael rubbed his eyes and started to gather up the meagre paperwork. He'd asked Spearing for some recent photographs of Katarina, to which he'd eventually obliged and sent through a few headshots and another of them both at a barbecue in the back garden of their home.

Carmichael had then asked Spearing for details of the clothing he thought his wife would have been wearing the last time he saw her. He couldn't be too certain but guessed it would be a pair of dark blue jeans and a cream sweater. He'd then mentioned a distinctive Swarovski watch she usually wore on her left wrist and a silver bracelet on her right. Plus, a favourite necklace which she rarely took off. As he couldn't find any of these items in their bedroom, he assumed Katarina must have been wearing them at the time she disappeared. The necklace was a unique piece she'd commissioned from a local jeweller for their wedding anniversary the previous summer. Carmichael had asked for a photograph, which Spearing duly provided having recently taken photographs of their most valuable possessions after a spate of burglaries in the area.

Carmichael pinned the photograph of the necklace to the outside of the case file. He wasn't sure it would lead them anywhere but he'd get it valued and make some discreet enquiries with local pawn shops and jewellers — if they were desperate for cash, it was just possible the kidnappers might slip up and try and sell it on.

Stomach grumbling, Carmichael reached to switch off his computer monitor. As well as following up on Spearing's close contacts, he'd been ploughing through the last two years' worth of newspaper articles the man had penned — trying to find any hint of who could be behind the kidnapping. Spearing definitely pulled no punches when it came to his style of reporting — frequently stepping close to the mark and even leaping across it on occasions. Compiling a list of those he might have offended could take some time.

But Carmichael wasn't entirely sold on the 'enemies' angle. The whole case reeked of money to him — not revenge. If he was a betting man he'd stake his reputation on the only motivation behind the kidnappers' actions being cold hard cash, especially now they knew Katarina's family had serious money. Unable to quell the hunger any longer, he grabbed his jacket and headed for the canteen. Although he was meant to be taking a curry round to Jack's later, he wasn't sure his stomach could wait that long.

CHAPTER TWENTY

Time: 3.50 p.m.
Date: Friday 29 August 2014
Location: Westminster Mortuary, London

Jack was glad he hadn't partaken in a chocolate brownie at the café when the familiar cloying stench of the mortuary assaulted his nostrils, even beneath his mask. Both he and DS Cooper had pulled on their protective aprons and rubber boots, and were now heading through the double doors into the examination room.

"Greetings, gentlemen." Dr Matthews was already standing next to the steel examination table in the centre of the room, a mortuary technician by his side taking a series of close-up photographs. "Good timing. We're just about to begin."

Great, thought Jack, edging slowly closer but letting Cooper lead the way. *Just great*.

He'd been to enough post-mortems to know the drill by now, and by and large they didn't affect him too much — not as much as they did DS Cassidy, anyway. His very first had been an eye-opener though — almost literally, as the poor sod's face had been caved in by such a brutal beating that his eye sockets were smashed to smithereens and his eyeballs were suspended on bloodied stalks.

Tuning out much of the preliminaries as the pathologist conducted the external examination, Jack focused his gaze on the victim's face. And, especially, the man's mouth — which was crudely sewn shut, just like the others. Just who would do this to another human being — and if the doc was to be believed, a *living* human being? Organised crime gangs were vicious beasts at the best of times but this took things to a whole new level.

"If that's OK with you, Jack?"

At the sound of his name, Jack turned his attention back to Dr Matthews. "Sorry? I must have zoned out for a second there."

A smile crept on to Dr Matthews' lips. "I was just telling young Cooper here that I wouldn't be surprised if this poor chap's blood work shows a similar set of results as the others — with evidence of drug use. There's evidence here of puncture marks on both forearms. I can also see some outward signs of malnutrition. I can rush through the blood results if that would be of assistance?"

Jack nodded. "Thanks, doc."

With the external examination complete, the pathologist moved towards the victim's head, selecting a fresh scalpel. "Let's get this bit over and done with first, shall we?"

Jack found himself stepping closer, standing shoulder to shoulder with Cooper. He kept his eyes trained on the victim's face — willing himself not to let his gaze stray to the grotesquely bloated torso beneath. Bile bubbled within him as the smell intensified. Shooting a quick look at Cooper by his side, he noted the detective's face was full of wonder, eyes gleaming. How he could stand there, with lord knows how many sickly chocolate brownies swirling around in his stomach, not to mention the two bacon rolls he'd devoured earlier, Jack couldn't fathom. The man must have a stomach made of steel. Jack's own stomach lurched uncomfortably as he watched the pathologist start to pull away the coarse thread running through the victim's lips.

"Here we have a similar type of material as seen with the previous two victims." Dr Matthews snipped a small section off, dropping it into a waiting test tube held by the technician. Focusing the overhead light closer, he began to carefully unpick the rest of the thread. "So, gentlemen — any guesses as to what we might find inside?" He gestured with the end of his scalpel towards the left-hand corner of the victim's mouth and glanced up.

Jack stepped a little closer. *Was that a tail?*

A short section of what had initially looked like another piece of coarse thread, or maybe a maggot, was poking out between the victim's teeth.

"Jesus," breathed Jack, swallowing and taking a step back. Cooper remained where he was — if anything, he inched closer.

Dr Matthews continued to tease the thread free of the man's lips, then slowly forced the jaws apart. He beckoned the mortuary technician forward to take a picture of what now faced them. Photographs completed, he carefully pulled the head of the dead rodent from the victim's mouth, plus its tail, dislodging a maggot or two in the process. "And here it is. Another deceased rat's head by the looks of things — plus the severed tail for good measure."

Even though he was wearing a mask, Jack covered his nose and mouth with his hand. The smell from the rat's head was so intense, Jack almost succumbed to the bile waiting to spew from his mouth. Even Cooper sported an uncharacteristically pale green tinge to his cheeks.

"A decaying rodent is not something you'd want to have in your mouth for any length of time, gentlemen. I do apologise for the aroma." Dr Matthews placed the rat's head into a stainless-steel kidney dish. "Decomposition rates for rodents vary, but this one looks like it's been dead for more than three weeks as a rough estimate." The pathologist then turned his attention to the man's bloated torso and began the internal examination.

With the scalpel about to cut through the victim's flesh, Jack knew from experience the vile stench that would soon be released from the man's decomposing tissues and decided it was probably time to call it a day. Rob was meant to be bringing a curry round to the flat later — at this precise moment that was feeling like a distinctly bad idea.

"You carry on here, Cooper. I'm going to step out for a while. Places to be."

Dr Matthews raised a hand as Jack headed for the door. "I'll be in touch, Jack. Report will be with you first thing in the morning."

Jack headed for the small changing room a short distance down the corridor, ripping off his apron and stepping out of the rubber boots. From the sink tucked away in the corner, he splashed cold water on to his face, dipping his head down to drink from the tap. Post-mortems didn't usually get to him like this — but this one was different. As he straightened up, his phone beeped. A quick glance showed him it was a reminder message from his calendar.

"Shit." It was later than he'd realised and he was now going to have to go to the Argyle Foundation talk straight from the mortuary. There was no way he'd be able to fight his way through the rush hour Friday afternoon traffic to go home and get changed and then make it to the Freemason's Hall on time.

Sighing, he just hoped he didn't smell too much of dead rat.

* * *

Time: 4.30 p.m.
Date: Friday 29 August 2014
Location: Abandoned warehouse, South-East London

Natalia rummaged in her jacket pocket, bringing out a wedge of less than fresh bread and a small square of waxy cheese. "Here. Have this." She held the paltry offering out towards the small girl shivering at her side. "It's not much but . . ."

The girl hesitated before taking the bread and cheese, her wide eyes blinking in the dim light.

"Eat it now, before they come back." Natalia nodded towards the closed door on the far side of the workroom. She had no idea where they were — somewhere in London was as specific as she could be. It wasn't far from their new base — she refused to call it 'home' — but wherever it was, it was just like all the other places they were taken to. Huge empty spaces, abandoned and neglected.

Today's task was lacing trainers. Tomorrow it might be electronics. The day after, packaging medicines. It was tedious, monotonous work. Fourteen-hour shifts with only a fifteen-minute break for stale bread and cheese. There was no noise, no talking allowed. The only sound would be the regular whippings dealt out for substandard work.

Natalia's back ached from sitting in the same position since early that morning. Her arms felt like lead, her fingers beginning to bleed. She wiped the blood on to her jeans — she daren't get any on the trainers. It would earn her another whipping — or worse.

Boxes of counterfeit trainers lined the walls of the workroom; all displaying a well-known designer logo but made at a fraction of the cost. Once laced up and boxed they would be shipped out and sold throughout a multitude of street markets and online shops.

Natalia knew the small girl at her side was called Ana, but that was it. They'd exchanged a few words at the beginning of the shift, when Natalia had been instructed to show the newest arrival how to lace the trainers and box them up — all under the watchful eye of two of the gang's hardest henchmen. She'd explained the process to the girl in English first of all, but was unsure if she'd really understood. Now their captors had slipped out, leaving them alone, Natalia took the opportunity to find out more about her companion.

"Where are you from?" she asked, watching the girl hungrily devour the stale bread. The question elicited no response.

Natalia tried again, this time in her native Romanian. This time the little girl looked up and blinked.

"Near Lasi," she replied, her voice little more than a whisper.

Natalia nodded. "I'm from close to there, too," she smiled. "Not far at all. How old are you?"

Ana swallowed the last of the bread, wiping stray crumbs from her lips. "Ten."

Natalia's eyes widened. "Are you here alone?" She couldn't fathom how a ten-year-old girl from Lasi could end up somewhere like this, all alone.

Ana shook her head, her bottom lip beginning to quiver. "My parents — they were with me when we left home. But . . ." The girl faltered, shoulders heaving. "We got separated across the border — they said we would all meet up here, but . . ." The girl glanced around her. "I don't know where they are."

Natalia could see the girl was fighting back tears and quickly shuffled across, putting an arm around her shoulder to pull her close. "I'm sure they're on their way. Don't worry." Natalia had no idea if what she was saying was true — she suspected it wasn't — but she couldn't bear to see the little girl so distraught. It was bad enough for her at twenty-three, she couldn't imagine going through an ordeal like this at just ten.

"Hurry — eat the rest of that cheese before they come back."

Natalia glanced towards the door. They were never usually left on their own for long — there was always at least one guard monitoring their every move. Not that it wasn't a welcome relief, to be alone. There was only one of the men who showed any sort of kindness towards them — at least, he did to Natalia. The odd bottle of water, an extra slice of bread.

"I'm frightened," whispered Ana, swallowing the cheese. She wiped her watery eyes with the back of a dirty hand. "I don't want to be here."

You and me both, thought Natalia, giving the girl another squeeze before scooting back to her own workstation and picking up another box of trainers. "You'll be fine. Just stick with me and you'll be fine."

* * *

Time: 4.30 p.m.
Date: Friday 29 August 2014
Location: Metropolitan Police HQ, London

"So, none of their movements or contacts over the last few weeks is any cause for concern?" Becky directed her question at DS Carmichael. He shook his head.

"They seem to live very normal lives. Neither have that many social contacts, which is borne out by the list Spearing gave us. They don't seem to go out much unless it's together."

"Any family members likely to be holding a grudge? Any fallings out apart from the one with Katarina's parents?"

Again, Carmichael shook his head. "Nothing. Spearing has a brother, but from what I can tell they have a cordial if not terribly close relationship. The brother lives in Gloucestershire, works as a web designer. Their parents live just outside Exeter, and again — nothing seems unduly out of place with them. There's been no contact between them for some time, evidenced by the phone records — but there's nothing particularly unusual in that. Last call was over four months ago."

"Friends?"

Carmichael shrugged. "Spearing doesn't seem to have any — which if you knew what he was like isn't that much of a surprise. Not terribly close with any colleagues from work either. I checked with the newspaper — he rang in sick on Monday and is still on leave."

"He rang in on Monday?" DC Ashford looked up from studying Spearing's meagre contact list. "That's the day *before* the kidnapping. Does that not sound a little odd to you?"

Becky considered it for a moment then said, "Make a note. What about the financials?"

DC Ashford pulled several sheets of paper towards him. "It's still early days but it looks like they have a number of credit card debts. There was a decent amount sitting in their savings account, but Spearing used that for the first ransom demand. We're checking for any other accounts and loans. The house is mortgaged up to the eyeballs."

"OK, so it looks like the kidnappers somehow got wind of Katarina's family money and took their chance."

Carmichael tapped his biro against his notepad. "Do you think he's kosher?"

Becky raised an eyebrow. "Who? Spearing?"

Carmichael nodded. "You think he's telling us the truth about the kidnappers? The ransom demands? He wouldn't be the first person to stage a kidnapping and play at being the victim."

Becky hesitated, mind racing. "True," she eventually replied, brow furrowed. "But do we really think that's the case here? Do we have any evidence of that?"

"Well, no — not exactly. But we don't have a lot of evidence of anything right now." Carmichael gave another shrug. "I'm just asking the question."

"It's a good question to ask and we won't rule it out. Let's look deeper into the state of the Spearings' marriage — discreetly, mind — and dig further into the financials."

"What do we do with him in the meantime?"

"Let's leave him at home. If he's being watched, they need to see him acting normally. We've issued him with another phone to communicate with us from, but let's check in with him before the end of the day."

"Spearing told me what he thinks Katarina was wearing when she was taken — her clothes, jewellery and watch. He's sent photos in." Carmichael nodded towards the paperwork in front of him. "I've made copies — the originals are in my office."

"Good. Anything from CCTV or fixed cameras in and around Acacia Avenue?"

DC Ashford pulled up a still CCTV image on to his monitor. "No cameras on Acacia Avenue itself, but there was a dark coloured van seen at some traffic lights on an adjoining street at midday on Tuesday — the day of her disappearance. Spearing says he left the house at around half past ten, and when he returned just before one o'clock she was gone. As the van was seen at midday it fits in that three-hour window." Ashford indicated towards the image of a van waiting at a set of lights. "The picture isn't clear enough to see anyone inside — the registration plate is partially obscured. We only have a partial index."

Carmichael peered at the image over DC Ashford's shoulder. "Has Spearing told us where he was going that morning? Have we even asked him properly?"

Becky frowned. "Let's ask him now, using the new number we've given him. Ask him where he was going, and also why he rang in sick the day before. But let's not lose sight of the ransom deadline — I feel that is the only chance we have of getting to these people."

Carmichael grabbed his jacket and headed towards the door. "I'll call from my office."

CHAPTER TWENTY-ONE

Time: 4.55 p.m.
Date: Friday 29 August 2014
Location: Freemason's Hall, Wellingborough Street

Although there were still a few vacant seats at the front, Jack opted to stand at the rear, close to the tea urn and custard creams — and also, more importantly, the exit. He wasn't a great one for forced gatherings. Or speeches for that matter. Or whatever it was this evening turned out to be. As a young probationer he'd made the rookie mistake of tagging along to an environmental activists' meeting one drab Monday evening in Hounslow and spent the best part of an hour being harangued and then accused of contributing to the world's poor environmental state by merely being alive. He'd come away, ears ringing and pockets stuffed with brochures and leaflets — which, ironically, must have been the equivalent of a tree or two.

He already gave to charity — ticked the Gift Aid box when asked, supported the local homeless shelter at Christmas. It wasn't enough, though — he was well aware of that. He ordered far too many takeaways in non-biodegradable plastic cartons, and used his car when he could probably walk. But it was better than nothing.

Despite feeling like a fish out of water, Jack knew he couldn't say no when the invitation landed on his desk some two weeks ago. And he'd barely been there thirty seconds, eyeing up the biscuit choices, when he caught the eye of Jason Alcock.

The convicted murderer strode confidently across the floor of the Freemason's Hall, a broad grin on his face. Jack recognised him instantly.

"Good to see you, Jack. I wasn't sure you'd make it."

Neither was I, Jack felt like saying, but instead nodded towards the chairs that were rapidly filling up. "Looks like you've drawn a decent crowd, mate." A steady stream of people continued to pass through the door to their left. "It'll be standing room only soon."

Jason's grin widened. "You should've seen the last one we did in Tottenham. It was insane."

Jack continued to watch the room fill. He surreptitiously sniffed his hands, wondering if the dead rodent smell from the mortuary was still clinging to his skin. So far so good. "Well, you must be doing something right — good on you."

There was a gentle hum of conversation as the new arrivals found their seats and, while Jason left in the company of a prison officer to greet those streaming through the door, Jack leaned up against the wall at the rear and glanced down at the leaflet thrust into his hand as he'd entered.

Living in a Gangster's Paradise? Do you have the power to say no?

As the time edged towards five o'clock, the door to the hall was closed and a short, stocky man sporting a pair of round-rimmed spectacles and a faint moustache bounded up on to the stage. "Ladies and gentlemen. My name is Howard Murphy, organiser of this evening's event. Thank you so much for coming here today. It means so much to all of us at the Argyle Foundation that you've taken time out of your busy lives to be with us. This Foundation was set up by the family of Thomas Argyle — a young lad, just fifteen years of age, who died as a result of a street stabbing four years ago. Our mission here is not to preach — it is merely to inform and to educate. What you then choose to do with that information is largely down to you. Not to delay things any longer, I'll hand you straight over to our main speaker for the event — Mr Jason Alcock."

While Jason threaded his way through the plastic chairs towards the stage, Jack let his gaze wander across the assembled audience. The first few rows were made up of youngsters — mid to late teens by the look of them; all puffa jackets and low-slung jeans. For the moment, at least, they appeared to be listening. Jack was secretly glad he'd been born when he was — growing up in today's society, today's London, was a vastly different beast to his own experience. Kids got sucked into the gang lifestyle at such an early age it was often too late to help them claw their way back out again. With knife crime on the rise in the capital, as in most other towns and cities in the country, Jack wasn't sure how much impact a few speeches from a bunch of reformed criminals would have. But he'd reserve his final judgement — at least until after his first custard cream.

With the introductions out of the way, Jack watched the slight, but powerfully, built frame of Jason Alcock take to the stage. A mix of emotions rippled through him. Jason had been part of his brother Stu's gang, back when they were living at St Bartholomew's Home for Boys — and, by all accounts, was the instigator behind the fateful robbery that cost Stu and the rest of them their freedom as teenagers back in 1982. There was no question Alcock had deserved every single one of the days he'd subsequently spent in prison — the man was a killer, after all.

But, despite that, Jack liked Jason Alcock.

And, in the handful of times they'd met, Jack could see that the man had changed. Gone was the cocky attitude that he would no doubt have had in abundance as a younger man — the disrespect for authority, the indifference as to how his actions harmed others. Jason must be pushing his early forties now, so it'd taken some time.

Usually a sceptic when it came to criminals turning their lives around, Jack was forced to admit that here was living proof that maybe, *just maybe*, rehabilitation was possible.

As Jason began to speak, Jack edged towards the refreshment table, spying a freshly opened packet of chocolate digestives. After swiping a handful, he settled back to listen.

* * *

Time: 5.00 p.m.
Date: Friday 29 August 2014
Location: Acacia Avenue, Wimbledon

Jonathan Spearing's throat felt so parched that he glugged down the glass of water far too quickly, making himself choke. Going to the police had been the wrong thing to do, he was sure of that now. He no longer had control, and it wasn't a feeling he particularly enjoyed. But what other choice did he have?

The officers seemed nice enough, trying to make him eat a sandwich and drink their foul-tasting coffee when he'd been at the station. And they seemed to know what they were doing, assuring him that they'd handled things like this plenty of times before. They'd quizzed him about his personal relationships, his friendships, his family and work colleagues. It hadn't taken long. Apart from Katarina he didn't really have anyone close. They'd offered to contact his parents for him — but he'd merely waved the offer away. He didn't need them — not unless they had a spare hundred thousand pounds knocking about.

In the end he'd given them the number for Katarina's parents, unable to bring himself to make the call. What would he say? There were no words for the unholy mess he'd landed them all in. Then they'd simply sent him home, reassuring him once again that everything was in hand and he shouldn't worry.

Shouldn't worry? How could he not worry when Katarina's life was hanging by a thread? Maybe she was already dead? The thought turned his stomach once again and he turned back towards the sink, bringing the undigested water back up.

They said they would be trying to trace the phone numbers the kidnappers had used, and accessing any CCTV in the local area overnight. Spearing knew they would come up with nothing, before they'd even started. The phone numbers wouldn't be traceable and the kidnappers wouldn't get picked up on camera. He'd covered enough crime stories in his time to know how this worked. These were professionals — they wouldn't be stupid enough to leave clues like that behind.

DS Carmichael had rung to ask him where he was going that day, bearing in mind he'd rung in sick at work the day before. Spearing had been momentarily struck dumb — realising for the first time how much digging the police must be doing into his own background. They must have rung the paper, found out about him ringing in sick. Of course, they would be digging — Spearing knew how these things worked. He just hoped they didn't dig too deeply.

He hadn't lied, not exactly. He'd told them he was going out to get some paracetamol for his killer headache — which he *had* done, but that wasn't the main reason for leaving the house. For the moment, he wasn't ready to explain exactly where he'd been going.

Spearing collapsed on to a kitchen chair, his legs feeling weak. A glance at his watch told him they had just over twenty-four hours left. Twenty-four hours to bring Katie home.

He started to sob.

What have I done to you, Katarina?
Just what have I done?

* * *

Time: 5.05 p.m.
Date: Friday 29 August 2014
Location: Freemason's Hall, Wellingborough Street

"As Howard has already said, thank you for coming along tonight." Jason's voice was strong. He wasn't a natural at public speaking and had physically baulked at the idea when

Louise had suggested he get involved with the foundation some six months ago. He'd dutifully taken the leaflets back to his cell — intending to bin them soon after — but the very next morning he'd signed up.

For this outreach programme wasn't like any of the others on the circuit. It wasn't made up of do-gooders who thought they were best placed to preach to the masses — the ex-probation officers, social workers, or even ex-police who thought they knew what it was like to be part of a gang, to be a part of that sub-culture.

The Argyle Foundation was different.

And it was different because it was largely run by criminals — or *ex*-criminals, to be more precise. But every person who stood on the stage at the Freemason's Hall tonight had, at one time or another, been part of a gang, committed crimes, taken drugs or served a prison sentence.

For some, like Jason Alcock, they'd done all four. And some were even still serving their time.

So, when speakers from the Foundation took to the stage, they spoke from the heart. They spoke from experience. They weren't just telling you how it was; they were *showing* you how it was. Nothing hidden. Nothing dressed up or watered down. They showed you what it was really like — warts and all.

And from the growing number of young people turning up at their events, it seemed like they might actually be making a difference; that they might actually be getting through.

"I can see some of you here tonight sitting in the front row are what . . . late teens? Mid-teens?" Jason fixed his gaze on the seats in front of him. A smattering of murmured responses drifted around the hall. "Anyone here under sixteen?"

Three hesitant hands were raised.

"And how old are you? If you don't mind me asking?" Jason locked his gaze to where three boys were sitting in the middle of the second row.

"Fifteen," replied one boy, dressed in an orange parka.

"Fourteen," said another.

"Thirteen," added the final boy.

"Thirteen." Alcock fixed his gaze on the youngest attendee. The boy looked small for his age, his hair closely cropped, his pale skin just starting to break out with pre-pubescent spots. The defiant look in his eyes was one Jason recognised. "You know — I was around the same age as you — thirteen — when I first got involved in crime. And I was locked up less than two years later."

A flicker of what could have masqueraded as a smile crossed the youngster's face, a glimmer in his eyes. Jason hardened his stare. The smile disappeared.

"Be under no illusion. No matter what you might hear out there on the street, or what your so-called mates might say, or what graffiti tags you see daubed on the walls around your neighbourhoods — prison isn't where you want to end up. Not at this age — not at any age. It doesn't earn you respect. It doesn't make you a hero or a hard man. All it does is destroy you — and those around you."

Jason switched his gaze to the rest of the room. "I've spent more time behind bars than I have on the outside. Am I proud of that? No. Do I wish I'd taken a different path?" He paused, his gaze coming to rest on Jack at the back of the room. "Every day."

For the next thirty minutes, Jason spoke fluently and eloquently. What he had to say wasn't dressed up in fancy language — he told it as it was, in all its brutal glory. There were snippets of humour in among the stark reality of gang and prison life, but mostly it was a dark and torrid account of a life wasted. By the end, most people in the room wore an expression close to shock — including the teenage trio on the second row.

It was an unusual concept — getting criminals to talk about their crimes, their time spent in prison, their life within gangs. It ran a real risk of glorifying that lifestyle, making them out to be heroes, people to look up to and emulate. The exact opposite of what they were trying to achieve.

Jason was well aware of the fine line they were walking. "If I can leave you with one thought — just one thing to take away with you tonight." He paused, pulling his prison shirt loose and lifting it to expose his chest. "I came within an inch of losing my life inside prison — another inmate taking umbrage at something I said or did. There are no *mates* inside prison walls. There's no one watching your back in there. It's the loneliest and most frightening experience you will ever know. You don't want this." He stabbed a finger at the two-inch white scar in the centre of his chest. "You don't want to be me. Have the courage to say no. Have the *strength* to say no. Be the person you were put on this earth to be."

* * *

There wasn't the huge surge towards the biscuits at the break that Jack had anticipated, and he managed to swipe another handful of digestives before anyone else even began to get up from their chairs.

After a while, Jason arrived at Jack's shoulder flanked by a prison officer. "Enjoying the show?"

Jack took a bite out of his second biscuit. "You spoke well. Really well."

"Didn't he just." A slightly built woman stepped forward, smiling warmly towards Jason.

"This is Louise Freeman," explained Jason, starting to pour hot water into two mugs. "She runs the library at the prison." He passed one to the librarian. "She's the reason I'm here tonight. I'd never have done anything like this without her help."

"Pleased to meet you," replied Jack, picking up the plate of digestives. "Biscuit?"

Louise's smiled widened as she took one off the plate. "Don't mind if I do."

"And this here is Gina." Jason passed the second mug to the woman hovering by his side. "Tonight's her first night."

"We've already met." Jack once more gestured towards the plate.

Gina tried a smile but shook her head. "No thanks. I feel a bit sick actually."

Jack knew Gina hadn't had it easy. She'd given Isabel a very condensed version of how she'd managed to get sucked into the Carson brothers criminal empire, and Jack was pretty sure they hadn't heard the half of it — the look in her eyes tonight told him that much. He'd seen enough damaged people in his life to recognise them a mile off. Pain etched into your soul like nothing else. But Gina had dragged herself out of the gutter that the gangs had pulled her into, and things like that went a long way to impress Jack. He admired the triers in life.

"You'll be fine — they're lucky to have you." Jack didn't really know what else to say so he stuffed another chocolate digestive into his mouth.

"How about you?" Gina sipped her coffee as Jason drifted over to chat to the boy in the orange parka. "Why are you here tonight? Is this about Danika?"

"Not exactly. Jason and I go back a little — thought I'd come and see what he was up to now." Recognising they were possibly heading towards shakier waters, and fully conscious that the prison librarian was still within earshot, Jack steered the conversation to safer ground. "How are you finding working in the café?"

Before Gina could respond, Jason reappeared, taking her by the elbow. "You're on next," he grinned. "Show time!"

Jack watched as Gina was led up on to the stage.

"I admire anyone who can get up and speak like that." Louise Freeman edged back towards the refreshments table, picking up a chocolate wafer.

"You and me both." Jack hated public speaking as much as it was possible to hate anything.

"The Foundation has transformed Jason. It's been so good for him to get involved in something like this. How do you two know each other again?"

Jack hesitated, concentrating on swallowing the remains of his chocolate digestive. "Let's just say we share a common history." Thankfully, before Jack felt the pressure to enlighten her any further, Jason took to the microphone.

"If you'd all like to take your seats again — we have one more speech for you tonight."

Handing the microphone to Gina, he gave her a wink. "They're all yours. You'll be great."

After a few moments, during which time the remaining audience returned to their seats, Gina cleared her throat and willed her stomach to stop churning. She tried a smile. "Hello everyone. I'm Gina — and I'm really *really* nervous."

Pausing for a second, she caught sight of Jack still leaning up against the wall at the back — he gave an encouraging thumbs-up. Cheeks pinking, she looked back across the seated audience and took a deep breath. "The reason I'm here tonight isn't because I've been to prison — because I haven't. But I have lived in one — a prison of my own making. And it robbed me of some of the best years of my life. It also robbed me of my daughter. I'm not looking for sympathy — I did what I did because I chose to. I ended up where I did because I wasn't strong enough to take a different path. I want you to know that I understand — that I've been where you are, that I've walked in your shoes. I know first-hand that when you hit rock bottom, it feels like you can't fall much further. But let me tell you — you can. For the next twenty minutes or so I'll tell you my story — all I ask is that once you've heard what happened to me, you don't let it happen to you."

And for the next twenty minutes, Gina did exactly that. She spoke from the heart, surprising herself how much she enjoyed telling her story. Not that it was a story — this was real life. It even felt cathartic in some strange way — putting into words how she'd taken the downward spiral that she had. Twenty minutes flashed by in something more like twenty seconds.

"I wish I'd had someone like me to listen to when I was your age — and when I was older, too. For I made some of my worst mistakes as a fully grown adult, so there's no age bias here." Gina paused, holding on to the gaze of as many people as she could in the audience before her. "Be strong. Take a different path. You *can* do this."

Applause filled the hall, some people even getting to their feet, hands raised above their heads as they clapped. Gina found herself welling up, a broad smile across her face.

"She wasn't bad, was she?" Jason rejoined Jack and Louise at the back of the hall. "She won that lot over in a heartbeat."

Jack found himself clapping along with the rest of the room. "She was excellent, Jason. It's been a great evening. I'm really impressed with what you're doing here."

While Gina stepped off the stage to be surrounded by well-wishers, Jack started to make for the door, his stomach rumbling. With memories of the mortuary and its decaying rodent aroma now firmly in the past, he had a welcome date with a curry.

Jason followed on behind. "Before you go, Jack. Can I have a quick word?"

CHAPTER TWENTY-TWO

Time: 7.30 p.m.
Date: Friday 29 August 2014
Location: Kettle's Yard Mews, London

"Crap day?" Carmichael handed Jack the chilled bottle of Peroni.

Jack accepted the bottle and instantly took a mouthful. "Pretty much. Feels like we've hit a proper brick wall. We've got one ID of sorts — a first name anyway — but the other two? We haven't a clue where they've been, where they came from, or what happened to them."

"Nothing from Missing Persons?"

Jack shook his head. "Not a sniff. Something tells me these poor souls won't be on any registers anywhere. I don't think they wanted to be found when they were alive, so . . ."

"Illegals?"

Jack shrugged and swallowed another mouthful of his beer. "Ticks all the boxes, mate. Which makes it a damned sight harder to get an identification. Once you disappear off the grid like that . . ." He left the rest of the sentence unfinished. "Anyhow, what about your kidnap? I know it's all hush-hush but you know me — I'm the soul of discretion."

Carmichael tipped another mound of pilau rice on to his plate and forked in some lamb bhuna. A flicker of a smile crossed his face as he caught Jack's eye.

"Well, there is something you might find interesting. Our subject — Katarina — you'll never guess who her husband is."

Jack picked up his plate of half-eaten chicken tikka. "Who?"

"None other than your favourite journalist."

Jack almost choked. "Spearing?"

"The one and the same."

Jack gulped down another mouthful of Peroni to wash away the chicken that had lodged in his throat. "While I don't exactly like the guy, that must be tough on him. What's the story behind it?"

Carmichael gave Jack a brief run down on what they had so far — which wasn't much.

"So Spearing already made a payment to the kidnappers? That's bold."

Carmichael nodded. "Yesterday, apparently."

"Where did he get the cash?"

"Took most of it from their joint savings account."

"And you say the parents are rich — the in-laws."

"Loaded. But they're estranged from Katarina — cut her off as soon as she shacked up with Spearing — which makes things a little tricky."

"They don't like him?" Jack couldn't help but let a small smile cross his lips. "I can't think for the life of me why not."

Carmichael mirrored Jack's smile and sunk the last of his beer. "Let's just say I don't think there's much love lost between Katarina's side of the family and our dear crime correspondent. They even made him sign a pre-nuptial agreement so he couldn't get his hands on the family fortune. She's from a pretty good family."

"You think he's for real? He hasn't just got her hidden in a cellar somewhere and all this is a sham?" Jack mopped up the last of his curry sauce with a chunk of naan bread.

"I'll admit — it had crossed my mind. But the DI isn't convinced. Why would he send the ransom demand to himself? It doesn't make sense. And he's put ten grand of his own money in."

"What was the state of the Spearings' marriage?" Jack couldn't imagine being married to the reporter would be a picnic for anyone.

"The team are going through the Spearings' financials as we speak — and speaking to friends and family to try and find out about their marriage. But it's complicated. You know how it is. We can't run the investigation like we normally would — it's all cloak and dagger. And that includes speaking to their friends and family. Everything's on a need-to-know basis, all records closed to prying eyes. There's a specialist SIO drafted in to head up the investigative unit, but so far no one's seen him. No one but the DI. It's all a bit of a closed shop. Anyhow, here's the good bit." He grinned at Jack from behind his forkful of bhuna. "I rang Spearing earlier this evening. He's told me he wants to speak to you — and only you."

Jack didn't hide the surprise from his face. "Me? Well, tough. I've got enough on my plate." His thoughts flickered towards the three bodies lying in the mortuary, mouths sewn shut. "Too busy for his crap at any rate."

"Which is exactly what I told him." Carmichael shovelled a forkful of rice into his mouth. "He's not happy though, starting to clam up on us. He told me that before coming to us, he tried to call you — a couple of times I think he said — maybe more. But apparently you never answered."

Jack thought back to the calls he'd thought had been from Ritchie Greenwood. "Maybe he did."

"There is something fishy about him though," added Carmichael. "I just can't put my finger on it yet. We discovered that he called in sick at work *before* the kidnapping — almost as if he knew it was going to happen."

"So, he *could* be stashing her away somewhere . . . ?"

They continued to eat, clearing their plates of the deluxe Indian banquet for two. Jack retrieved two more cold beers from the fridge, handing one to Carmichael.

"Happy birthday for tomorrow, mate."

"Cheers." They clinked bottles. "I gave my mate down in Surrey a ring about the Bancroft murder earlier this week. It's all gone really quiet. They seem to accept Quinn didn't pull that trigger but don't seem too bothered about looking for anyone else. It was quite an odd conversation. Seemed not to want to talk about it."

Jack pushed the remains of his chicken tikka around his plate. He hadn't told Rob about his rendezvous with Ritchie Greenwood — and the offer to deal with Quinn in prison — deciding it was probably better that way. The poor bloke had been dragged into enough of Jack's shit over the last couple of years, and he didn't need to wade in any deeper.

But quite what Ritchie had meant about Jack reconsidering his loyalties after a certain news story hit the headlines, Jack still couldn't work out. Other than what had really happened to Joseph Geraghty that night, Ritchie had nothing on him.

Nothing that he knew of anyway.

Jack drank deeply from his beer bottle. He had a feeling he wouldn't sleep much tonight.

* * *

Time: 8.30 p.m.
Date: Friday 29 August 2014
Location: Central London

Ritchie Greenwood pulled out into the light evening traffic, following at a distance. The Carson Brothers intrigued him. He wasn't too concerned that they would ever stray on to his patch — *Geraghty's* patch the others still liked to call it — despite what the boss himself had thought. The Carsons might not be the brightest pair but they weren't stupid either. However, they were certainly up to something — that was plain to see — and Ritchie intended to find out just what that something was.

He'd kept tabs on the pair of them for most of the day after leaving Gloria Hatton. They hadn't done anything out of the ordinary — calling in a few debts by the look of it, and stopping at a fast food place for a burger. Nothing to raise much by way of suspicion — until now.

At half past eight the traffic was thinning out, but Ritchie didn't think Lance Carson was looking too hard in his mirror. They crossed through several sets of traffic lights, eventually turning down a street to the left. Ritchie knew this part of the city well — it was a relatively wealthy area, which you could tell from the brand of cars parked in the resident-only bays, of which there were only a few — the rest being a no-parking zone. The houses had mostly grand-looking Georgian frontages — or maybe it was Victorian; Ritchie wasn't too hot on his history. But they stretched skywards sometimes four storeys high, most divided up into individual flats. Ritchie let Carson pull ahead a little, not wanting to be spotted. He already knew that neither Carson lived in this area, which intrigued him further.

Wherever Lance Carson was going tonight, it wasn't home.

He saw the BMW pull to a stop outside a row of terraced houses, lights extinguishing as soon as the engine died. Ritchie chose to hang back, pulling in behind a conveniently parked white Mercedes van. Even from his vantage point some distance away, he could tell Carson was agitated. There was something in the way he jumped out of the BMW and slammed the door behind him, then wrenched his phone from his pocket.

Ritchie watched as Lance Carson placed the phone to his ear. Several seconds later the door to the terraced house in front of him opened, and Carson disappeared inside. Not long after, a light flickered on in the first floor flat above.

Just then Ritchie's own phone began to buzz.

"Got that information you wanted, boss," the voice got straight to the point. "For that photo. I'll send it through now."

Ritchie felt a smile touch his lips as he closed the call and waited for the message. It arrived almost instantly. Opening it up, he saw the same photograph he'd taken yesterday of Lance Carson handing over the mysterious package in the dead of night. Beneath it was a suggestion for who the receiving party might be.

Ritchie's smile flickered some more. "Well, well, well. Naughty, naughty."

* * *

Time: 8.45 p.m.
Date: Friday 29 August 2014
Location: Manchester Way Industrial Estate, London

Bobby Neale prepared each syringe with the required amount of the drug.

He approached the group nearest to him. The three of them always sat together but rarely talked. Numbers seventeen, nineteen and twenty-one they were known as — the numbers inked into their skin when they arrived. They never usually gave him any trouble, and as he neared he saw they were all dutifully sitting up against the wall, bare arms ready to accept the syringe.

But there was another one with them now, too. A girl no older than ten by the looks of her. Bobby hesitated, a feeling of disquiet prickling. This wasn't what he'd signed up for — children. But he felt powerless to do anything about it. Look what had happened to Stefan when he'd tried to step in and help.

Number seventeen was closest to him. He knew her name was Natalia — but he was never allowed to use it. To him and everyone else she was merely 'seventeen'. As he approached, she looked up at him with her huge, mournful-looking eyes, already holding out a quivering arm in readiness. Something close to shame started to prick at Bobby's conscience as he showed her the needle. But in the end he did as he was told. Maybe that made him as much a prisoner as the ones kept shackled in chains.

Many Natalias had come and gone during the time he'd been here, and he knew he couldn't afford to get attached. But there was something engaging about number seventeen, so when he'd found an old book in Romanian in a second-hand thrift shop a while ago, he'd bought it for two quid and quietly given it to her. He wasn't sure if she'd read it, but could see it tucked away beneath her blanket by her feet.

It wasn't much, he knew that. But it was something.

Kneeling down on the dusty floor, he sank the syringe into number seventeen's waiting arm.

Bobby didn't know too much about the drugs they were using — he was more involved in the acquisition and distribution side of things. He wasn't so stupid as to actually use any of the merchandise himself.

He knew it was heroin of some description — most probably cut with something else — but he could see the way they craved their nightly doses that most of them were clearly hooked already. It disturbed him a little, the way they looked up at him with a mixture of both fear and longing.

Bobby would put his hands up to being a rogue — to being on the wrong side of the law more times than he was on the right side. It was the way he and Jimmy had been brought up — it was the only way of life they had ever known. But none of this was Bobby's style. He didn't agree with how they were kept, how they were treated — which was partly why he'd agreed to help Stefan. But that plan had backfired in the most spectacular fashion. He couldn't risk it again.

Despite his misgivings, he needed to do as he was told. The boss had a sensitive nose — he could smell a rat a mile off.

* * *

Natalia felt the sharp scratch of the needle, then the effect of the drug coursing quickly through her veins. She rested her head back against the crumbling brickwork and closed her eyes, pulling Ana closer. For a moment she could forget where she was, who she was, and what was happening to her. For now, she could escape. It was the one chink of happiness she could look forward to at the end of a very dark day.

She felt her muscles relax, a feeling of calm washing over her. It was the only time she ever felt at peace — with that dirty, stinking stuff flooding her body. She hated it, but yet she loved it at the same time.

Back home, she would never have gone near the stuff — but here? Here it kept you going. Here it at least allowed you to sleep in relative comfort and forget the nightmare you were otherwise living in.

Through heavy-lidded eyes she gazed across to the other side of the dilapidated building that was now their home. For a moment she thought she could see Stefan — see his cheery, smiling face grinning back at her.

And then she saw his mouth change.

The needle.

The blood.

The rat.

The screams that filled the air.

And then Stefan was no more.

Natalia closed her eyes and pushed the thoughts from her head. She needed to take back control, do as she was told, and above all keep quiet.

If you didn't keep quiet, they shut your mouth for you. *Permanently.*

CHAPTER TWENTY-THREE

Time: 8.00 a.m.
Date: Saturday 30 August 2014
Location: Metropolitan Police HQ, London

Jack pushed open the door to the incident room to see DI Rebecca Yates standing in front of the row of whiteboards, her head cocked to the side. He cleared his throat.

"Can I help you?"

She swung round at the sound of Jack's voice. "Sorry — I'm new here. I don't think we've met. DI Yates. Rebecca, Well, Becky." Her cheeks coloured and she sounded flustered. She turned back towards the whiteboards. "Apologies for barging in like this — but DS Carmichael said I might find you in here. And I'm fascinated with this case of yours. It looks like a minefield."

Jack let the door swing shut behind him. "It is."

"Any leads at all? What's with the mouths being sewn shut like that?"

Jack joined her at the whiteboard. "I wish I knew. At the moment we think it's some kind of message. A warning. Keep quiet or else." He gave a shrug.

"Gangland?"

"More than likely."

"People trafficking? Illegals?"

Jack hesitated. "Again, more than likely."

"You infiltrated that people-trafficking gang a while back, didn't you? Got a number of the top-flight sent down?"

Jack hesitated. "You wanted to see me about something?"

"Ah, yes. Sorry, I got distracted. You've no doubt heard of the live kidnap case we've got at the moment?"

"Rob's mentioned it, yes."

"And that the victim — Jonathan Spearing — has been asking to speak to you?"

"I heard something along those lines, yes. But I'm afraid I've got too much on with this." He gestured towards the whiteboards. "As you will no doubt appreciate."

"Of course. I'll not keep you. But what's he like — this Jonathan Spearing? How well do you know him?"

"I wouldn't say I know him at all. He's no buddy of mine, let's just say that."

"But he's trustworthy?"

"He's a reporter — what else do I need to say?"

"I'm just trying to get a handle on him. He won't say much and has withdrawn from us a little. I guess he's traumatised, worried about his wife. You know he didn't come to us straight away? Tried to deal with it himself?"

"Rob said. Until the kidnappers upped the ante and demanded more money?"

Becky nodded. "He's done the right thing, though. We're keeping it under the radar at the moment, as is usual procedure, so we don't spook the kidnappers. I was just after some background, that's all. We need to know who we're dealing with."

Just then, the door opened and DS Carmichael approached. He looked harassed.

"Boss? You're needed. We've got Katarina's parents on the line — and they're not best pleased."

* * *

187

Time: 8.15 a.m.
Date: Saturday 30 August 2014
Location: Skyline Apartments, Canary Wharf, London

With the early morning sun warming his skin, Ritchie Greenwood sat outside on the balcony of his penthouse apartment and watched the world waking up to the news. He'd had the nudge that the story would be running that morning — an enterprise like the one built by Joseph Geraghty didn't get to where it was without an insider or two where one was needed. And that included the media.

He scrolled through his phone for the latest headlines.

BANKER'S MURDER — MAN CHARGED

A smile crept over Ritchie's face. The story had knocked Ebola off the front pages, relegating the tragedy unfolding in Africa to page four. A feeling of satisfaction mixed with anticipation bubbled inside him. The next step in the downfall of Detective Inspector Jack MacIntosh was starting to take shape. It really had been too easy.

But as much as the morning's headlines thrilled him, and made him wish to be a fly on the wall in the detective's office the minute he found out, Ritchie had other more pressing things to deal with. What he'd seen last night after trailing Lance Carson had intrigued him — as had the identification of who had been on the other end of the payoff on Thursday evening.

He wasn't sure what the man was up to, but whatever it was, it sure as hell wouldn't be legal.

Ritchie plucked his car keys from the table and rose from his chair. He'd give Jack MacIntosh a while to catch up with the morning's news before starting to put the next stage of the plan into action. The man didn't know what was coming next. Ritchie grinned.

He couldn't wait for the fireworks to start.

* * *

Time: 8.45 a.m.
Date: Saturday 30 August 2014
Location: Metropolitan Police HQ, London

Becky exhaled a long breath as she put the phone down. Katarina's parents were not exactly happy — DS Carmichael had been spot on with that one.

She'd spent the best part of the last thirty minutes explaining to them both that the Metropolitan Police were well positioned to take care of this — that they were in control of the situation. All they needed to do was trust her. It was a big ask — Becky knew that. But she needed to get them onside if this whole plan was going to work out the way it was meant to. There was a lot riding on it — not least Katarina's safety.

But Becky had never felt as out of control as she did right now. The enormity of what she was doing, and of what could go wrong, wasn't lost on her.

Katarina's mother had been tearful at first, letting her husband do most of the talking. He'd been quite the opposite, bullish and accusatory, but what they both had in common was an intense dislike of their son-in-law.

Even with over a thousand miles separating them, Becky got the picture quickly enough. She had no idea where this deep-seated loathing came from and didn't have the time nor the energy to ask. Pulling a caffeine-laden energy drink from her desk drawer, she cracked it open and drank deeply. Just a few more hours and it would all be over, one way or another.

Mentally ticking off the 'to-do' list in her head, she finished the rest of the can and got to her feet. Leaving her shoebox office, she made her way towards the incident room. As she pushed open the door she could see everyone hard at work, an electric buzz in the air.

DC Ashford glanced up as she entered. "Looks like the marriage may have been in trouble. We've looked into Katarina's bank statements and there's a payment to Waterman and Co solicitors — they specialise in family law."

Ashford swapped his gaze back to his computer screen. "We then found a series of emails — all asking about the grounds for a divorce and requesting an appointment to discuss. We found an appointment in her email calendar for two weeks' time. If Spearing found out about it, maybe that was enough for him to try something like this?"

Becky pursed her lips as she headed in Ashford's direction. "But he wasn't going to get a bean out of any divorce — he'd signed a pre-nup, remember? Divorce wouldn't have made him any worse off than he is now."

"Maybe that's why he might have cooked up an idea to hold her to ransom?" added DC Sullivan. "Maybe he's in with the kidnappers on this — they're all in it together?"

"That's not a bad shout," added Carmichael. "Makes even more sense now he's decided to clam up on us. When I spoke to him yesterday he was very much on edge. Even more than you would expect. Wasn't happy about being left at home, keeps wondering if the kidnappers will come back for him."

"Did he sound genuine?" Becky turned away from Ashford's desk. "Like he really feels in danger?"

"Hard to tell," shrugged Carmichael. "He could just be a really good actor. And we still haven't had a decent account of where he went on the morning Katarina was taken. I don't buy the 'I went out to buy paracetamol' line. He was gone too long for that. When I spoke to him last night, he maintained that story. But there's a shop a five-minute walk away, so why was he gone so long? There has been no activity recorded on any of his bank cards for that entire day. And no evidence he caught a bus or a Tube anywhere. In addition, he is still being cagey about why he called in sick the day before — sticking to the story of having a headache. He doesn't come across as looking particularly unwell to me. The newspaper disclosed to me his sickness record — hasn't had a single day off in the last three years."

Becky felt hot around the collar, slipping off her jacket, and heading over to the only window to push it open. "I still don't see it. If that was his ploy, why not go direct to the parents in the first place?"

Carmichael pressed on. "Like I said, maybe that was to make it look genuine? Send the ransom demands to himself, raid the joint account. Surely, it's worth looking into, right? Even if it's just to discount it?"

Becky sighed, rubbing her temples as they throbbed with an impending headache. This wasn't going the way she wanted it to. She was meant to come in, all guns blazing, solve the case, get the girl back safe and sound. Instead, she felt the case slipping away from beneath her, spinning off on an unexpected tangent.

"All right," she said eventually. "See if you can find out where he was that morning. Try local CCTV, shop cameras, anything. But don't waste too much time on it. We need to focus on getting the money drop sorted — the SIO agrees that it's the only way we're going to get Katarina back safely while potentially luring the kidnappers out into the open, whether Spearing's involved or not."

"Isn't that risky?" frowned Carmichael. "Shouldn't we just focus on getting Katarina to safety? Use the negotiators?"

"We *are* focusing on that." Becky was aware she sounded a little terser than she intended. "But going ahead with the money drop is the best way to achieve that, and also if we're going to stand any chance of finding out who's behind it."

Carmichael gave a reluctant nod. "OK. How did it go with the parents? Are they on board with everything?"

"The parents are on board, yes. Obviously shocked at what's happened — and don't have too many positive words to say about their son-in-law, but they're fully supportive in whatever we need to do to get their daughter back."

"What about the cash? They're really going to stump up the hundred grand themselves?"

"They insisted. They don't want anything to go wrong and will do anything in their power to ensure Katarina is returned safely. They have kidnap and ransom insurance because of their business interests."

Carmichael's frown deepened. "I'm not sure I'm too comfortable with us handing over cash like this. What if something goes wrong? Do we trust Spearing not to bottle it? It's a lot of money. If he *is* in on it — what says he won't just do a runner?"

"Nothing will go wrong. I've dealt with cases like this many times before." Becky held her nerve as the lie escaped her lips. "The money will never be in any danger; it will always be within our sight. It's established protocol."

"I was more concerned about Katarina than the money." There was a hardened edge to Carmichael's tone.

Becky's face flushed. "Yes of course. That's what I mean, too. Sorry. Katarina is our priority." She felt her cheeks darken further. She needed to get a grip if she was going to see this case through. What was she thinking? She needed to engage her brain before she opened her mouth. She headed for the door. "With any luck we'll have Katarina home by the end of the day."

* * *

Time: 9.15 a.m.
Date: Saturday 30 August 2014
Location: Metropolitan Police HQ, London

"Lab results are in." DS Cooper pulled up the latest information on to his computer monitor. "I don't think it's of much surprise, but DNA from our first and second bodies has been found at the disused brewery. Plus, foot and toe nail scrapings show traces of fermented grain, rat droppings and pieces of straw on both of them."

"I think it's pretty clear all three had been in there at some point." Jack glanced at the three headshots on the first whiteboard. "The brewery must have been their main hub, for a while at least. But something made them move out — we need to find where they are now."

We need to find another body.

192

It wasn't a pleasant thought and Jack didn't voice it out loud. But another body might divulge more clues, which in turn could crack the case wide open.

"We don't know how many people may have been inside that brewery building — but people need transport. Flag up any vans or large people carrier vehicles around Juniper Lane and the surrounding area. They must have used something. And I want to know where they went." Jack headed for the door. "I'll be in my office for a while if you need me. Cooper — I need you to run an errand for me sometime today. Pop in and see me when you have a spare moment. It won't take long."

* * *

Time: 10.15 a.m.
Date: Saturday 30 August 2014
Location: Canterbury Lane Industrial Estate, London

Lance Carson pulled on a pair of black leather gloves and grabbed the keys to the BMW. He'd sent Wayne out on his own to collect the day's loan repayments. Wayne had his uses — sometimes just the sight of his brother's sheer bulk sent people scurrying inside to get the cash together, suddenly deciding they did have it to hand after all. He was more than capable of handling the outstanding business for the day on his own.

Which left Lance time to deal with Dion Fuller.

The pimp's time was up — and this time Lance needed to see some cold, hard cash. No more excuses.

He wasn't due to call on Dion until later that afternoon, but maybe he'd make an exception and surprise the weasel. Lance didn't trust many people — and he certainly didn't trust Dion Fuller. He knew the man's regular haunts — it wouldn't be hard to track him down.

He ran a gloved finger around the inside of his shirt collar. He prided himself on being as cool as the proverbial cucumber, unruffled even in the face of the most trying of circumstances. Appearances were everything in this game, but even he was starting to feel the heat. The air was close and sticky, a vague hint of a coming storm on the non-existent breeze.

Sliding into the driver's seat, he gunned the engine and turned the air conditioning up to maximum. Reaching across the passenger's seat, he pulled open the glove compartment and selected a fresh set of pliers. He placed the tool within easy reach.

He had a feeling he was going to need them.

* * *

Time: 10.30 a.m.
Date: Saturday 30 August 2014
Location: Metropolitan Police HQ, London

Jack heard his office door open then saw DS Carmichael's head appear around the door jamb.

"Good, you're alone." Carmichael stepped in, closing the door behind him.

"Problem?"

Carmichael approached Jack's desk and tossed a copy of the *Daily Mail* on to the mass of paperwork covering it. The headline was visible for all to see.

BANKER'S MURDER — MAN CHARGED

Jack unfolded the front page. "What the . . . ?"

The article took up every inch of available newsprint. Surrey detectives investigating the murder last September of retired banker Roger Bancroft confirmed that a fifty-one-year-old man, Michael Hatton, currently serving fourteen years for grievous bodily harm, was arrested at HMP Belmarsh last week and subsequently charged with murder. Hatton appeared at court yesterday morning and the case was immediately transferred to the Crown Court. Sources at Surrey Police refused to elaborate further on the case, but confirmed no one else was being hunted in connection with the retired banker's murder.

Jack looked up, words sticking in his throat.

"I know." Carmichael grabbed a chair and sat down. "I rang my contact down in Surrey again. This is strictly off the record, but they got a full and frank confession from Hatton several days ago, signed and sealed in the presence of his solicitor. He's even admitted to planting evidence to try and set up Quinn for it. It's watertight, so I'm told. I think this might be why they were a bit tight-lipped with me when I enquired about the case the other day." Carmichael noticed Jack's concerned look. "But this doesn't necessarily have to be a bad thing, Jack. If this Hatton guy puts his hands up for this, then the heat is automatically off you. They won't pursue the ballistics report, and they won't look more closely at the DNA evidence. It could be good."

Jack had to concede there was a positive side to someone being convicted over Roger Bancroft's — and therefore Joseph Geraghty's — demise, but his thoughts instantly turned to Ritchie Greenwood.

'You might want to reconsider your loyalties when a certain story hits the media in the next day or so.'

Ritchie's involvement in the case left a bad taste in Jack's mouth. There was something far too convenient about it.

"I don't like it, Rob. Something's not right. Why would this guy confess to something we know for a fact he didn't do? It makes no sense. Hatton is one of Geraghty's most loyal gang members — up until he got banged up."

"Maybe that's why."

"Stretches loyalty a bit to the extreme, don't you think?"

"It's unusual, I'll give you that." Carmichael watched Jack as he reread the front-page article one more time. "He's still asking for you, by the way. Spearing. I spoke to him again this morning. He's jittery. Turned up at the station ten minutes ago, asking for you."

Jack folded the newspaper and tossed it into his out-tray. "And it's still not my case."

"*I* know that — and *he* knows that."

"I've got more than enough on my plate right now, Rob. I don't need anything extra."

"Again, noted. But he's insistent. He won't talk to anyone but you. Not even the DI."

Jack got to his feet, pulling his jacket from the back of his chair. "You still think he's for real? That his wife really has been kidnapped and this isn't just some absurdly intricate ploy for him to twist us all up into knots and then expose us for being an incompetent bunch of twats?" Jack didn't bother to hide the scorn in his voice. "He isn't top of the trustworthy table."

"I won't lie. I don't trust him as far as I can throw him. He's lying about something — I'm just not sure what that something is. We've found some emails — Katarina recently engaged a solicitor wanting information and advice about the grounds for a divorce. We're unsure if he was aware of that or not."

"What does your new boss say about it all?"

"I think she's this close to throttling him right now. He's uncooperative. Won't engage. Obviously hiding something." Carmichael followed Jack to the door.

"Sounds like the pompous, self-assured git we all know and love. But what do you think I can do? We're not exactly best mates, are we? I'd go so far as to say he hates my guts. Any opportunity he has, he twists the knife. Takes some perverse pleasure in it. Why on earth would he be asking for my help?"

"Because, mate, as much as he loves to backstab you in glorious newspaper print, my guess is he knows what a bloody good copper you are. And if his wife is going to get out of this alive then a bloody good copper is exactly what he needs."

CHAPTER TWENTY-FOUR

Time: 11.00 a.m.
Date: Saturday 30 August 2014
Location: Metropolitan Police HQ, London

"The money is sorted." Becky kept an eye on her office door and her voice low. "Everything as agreed."

The voice on the other end of the line hesitated. "All of it?"

"All of it," confirmed Becky, nervously biting the corner of a fingernail. "One hundred thousand, as asked."

"And you're not fobbing me off with Mickey Mouse money, are you? Or a bag full of paper?" The voice paused. "Because you know what'll happen if you do."

"The money's real. The parents are stumping up the cash. It's ready to be collected. They want their daughter home safe and sound and if it costs them a hundred thousand pounds then that's what they're prepared to do. They've got kidnap and ransom insurance in any event — goes with their business."

"Maybe I should have upped the ante and asked for a quarter million." The voice laughed. "By the way, I'm changing the location of the handover."

Becky's voice caught in her throat. "You're changing the drop-off? At this late stage? Why?"

The voice hesitated again. "Because I'm not sure I wholly trust you, that's why."

Becky's heart missed a beat. "*You* don't trust *me*? I'm breaking so many rules here you have no idea. My whole career is on the line."

"For which you are getting paid." The voice remained calm. "Rather handsomely, I might add."

"Where's the new drop-off location? I'll need to know the details soon if I'm to lay a false trail for the back-up teams."

"You will be informed in due course. *When* you need to know. Just make sure everything is ready."

"Why not tell me now?"

"Like I said — I don't necessarily trust you. I don't generally trust many people that I don't know. And we've never done business before. Call it a foible of mine."

"What have I done to make you feel you can't trust me? Haven't I answered all your questions so far? Haven't I kept you up to speed with the investigation and where it's going? I've done everything you asked of me."

"That may be so," the voice conceded, "but with a hundred thousand at stake I need to be sure."

"When do I get my share?" Becky's eyes fell to the photograph of herself and her mother with the turquoise blue sea behind them.

"You'll be paid as agreed — *after* the transaction has been completed to my satisfaction."

"I could just take my cut from the money before it's dropped off."

"You will do no such thing," thundered the voice, an edge entering their tone. "If I find so much as a single pound is missing from that bag, you'll suffer the consequences. And the woman will never be found."

Becky bit the inside of her lip, the metallic taste of blood reaching her tongue. "Like I said — you can trust me."

"We'll see. I'll be in touch."

The call ended and Becky put the phone down with a trembling hand. Not for the first time, she asked herself the same question.

Could she pull this off?

* * *

Time: 11.55 a.m.
Date: Saturday 30 August 2014
Location: St Benedict's Street, London

He killed the car's engine and glanced out of the side window. Everything was quiet, even though the hustle and bustle of the city was merely streets away. Only a handful of cars were parked at the side of the road, but nobody was watching as far as he could tell.

He waited a few minutes, just to be sure, then with a final glance up and down the street, he quietly exited the car and jogged across to a small step leading to the front door of number seven. A selection of door buzzers was situated to the side. He felt his eyes hitch up towards the window of the flat above. Heavy drape curtains were pulled tightly closed, masking whatever was within.

With his finger hovering momentarily over the buzzers, he pressed the one for the ground floor flat. A frosted glass panel in the centre offered little by way of a view into the interior. Squinting against the sunlight, he leaned in more closely and pressed the buzzer again. Eventually he noted a slight movement ahead.

He waited while the door was pulled open, hearing the safety chain rattling. Placing a well-practised and suitably pleasant smile on to his face, he left one hand in his jacket pocket, his fingers wrapped loosely around the small knife within. The old woman looked harmless enough, but you could never really tell.

"Yes?" enquired the elderly lady, peering over the top of her spectacles.

"Sorry to bother you, ma'am, but I have a delivery coming for the flat above — unfortunately their doorbell doesn't seem to be working." He stepped a little to the side so the old woman could see the Hungerford Removals van parked opposite. "Would you be good enough to let me in so I can go up and check that they're there?" He nodded towards the set of stairs in the background leading to the flat above. "It'd be a shame to have a wasted trip."

"I'm sorry . . ." Betty Thompson bent in closer, a frown on her forehead. "My hearing isn't what it used to be — can you say that again?"

The man drew in a deep breath and repeated the question a little louder this time — but not too loud; he didn't want to draw even more attention to himself than he may already be doing. The street might look quiet but even the quietest places had ears. He moved a foot towards the threshold and maintained his plastic smile.

The old woman looked the man up and down for a moment before stepping back and unhooking the safety chain. "So sorry," she repeated, a small laugh following. "I can't find my hearing aids anywhere and I'm as deaf as a post without them!" Betty pulled the door fully open and glanced over her shoulder towards the stairs. "Upstairs, you say?"

The man nodded, keeping a grip on the knife in his pocket as he stepped into the hallway. "We'll try not to make too much noise."

Betty gave another chuckle and headed towards the door leading back to her ground floor flat. "You do what you need to, my dear. I'll not get in your way."

He watched the old woman disappear before signalling to the van parked outside.

* * *

Time: 12.00 p.m.
Date: Saturday 30 August 2014
Location: Metropolitan Police HQ, London

Carmichael pulled his chair next to DC Ashford's. "Let's see what you've got."

Ashford navigated his way through the CCTV footage on his monitor, the grey images on fast-forward.

"This is Hawthorn Road. Where we see that dark coloured van at a set of lights." He paused the image. "Time stamp is just after midday." Clicking the mouse, he reactivated the screen. "Half an hour before that, at eleven thirty, we see our victim — Jonathan Spearing — walking along Sedgefield Avenue. That's one street away from where we see the van."

Carmichael inched in closer, watching the unmistakable figure of the newspaper reporter crossing from one side of the street to the other. "Do we know where he's headed, or what he does?"

Ashford clicked on another file. More CCTV images filled the screen. "We pick him up again about ten minutes later, heading west on Brompton Gardens. Time stamp is now eleven-forty."

A frown crossed Carmichael's brow. "Where the devil are you going?" he muttered. "Spearing told us he headed out to buy paracetamol. I didn't believe him then and I don't believe him now. Do we pick him up calling into any shops on his travels?"

Ashford tapped the screen. "We catch him on the shop CCTV — the shop that's a five-minute walk from his house. But it's not until twelve-fifteen. It does look like he buys a packet of paracetamol though — with cash."

"So, he leaves his house at ten-thirty but doesn't get to the shop until almost two hours later. A shop that's five minutes from his own front doorstep." Carmichael's eyes narrowed. "He's clearly not just '*popping out to buy paracetamol*' as he'd like us to believe. What the hell has he been doing?"

"This is the final shot of him — still on Brompton Gardens. We lose him after this." Ashford found the final image then let it run in slow motion. Carmichael watched as Spearing came to the end of the street and then stopped, looking around him.

"What's he waiting for?" Carmichael didn't need to wait long to find out. From the top of the screen another figure made his way across the road, heading in Spearing's direction. The two met on the corner, spent twenty seconds in each other's company before seeming to shake hands and go their separate ways.

Carmichael flashed a look at DC Ashford. "Can you print me off some copies of that frame there? In particular, that fella he's meeting. We need to find out who that is."

In the meantime, Carmichael took a snap of the image on his phone. What the hell was that man up to?

CHAPTER TWENTY-FIVE

Time: 12.05 p.m.
Date: Saturday 30 August 2014
Location: St Benedict's Street, London

Jimmy Neale crushed the Coke can in his hand before tossing it into the corner of the room. The clattering sound was
a welcome distraction. He was bored — *really* bored. He'd
now spent four days cooped up in this one room, without so
much as a decent meal or a change of clothes. Or a shower.
He sniffed his armpits and recoiled.

The boss popped in now and again, but never stayed
long. And whenever Jimmy questioned how much longer he
would be here for, or what they were going to do with the
woman in the box, he got the same stony look in response.

'*Not your concern, Jimmy. Just keep watch.*'

Just keep watch.

It was easier said than done. But what exactly was he
watching for?

He pushed himself up out of the wooden chair and
headed for the window. He kept the curtains closed as
instructed, but on occasion curiosity got the better of him
and he'd part them a little to take a look outside. Anything

to relieve the boredom. He'd asked the boss if he could have a TV — even a small portable one — or maybe a radio — but received the same stony stare in reply.

Turning away from the window, he headed back to the chair. As he did so, his ears pricked.

Footsteps.

It would no doubt be the boss again, hopefully with some food for his dinner this time. Jimmy's stomach rumbled. Maybe there was some news on when he might be able to get out of this godforsaken room. He slumped back in his chair — the boss could let himself in; the door was never locked.

Hearing the door swing open, Jimmy kept his eyes staring straight ahead. "I hope you've brought some decent grub — I'm starving."

The boss didn't reply, but Jimmy heard his footsteps on the bare floorboards as he approached from behind. "And maybe another six pack of Coke. It's hot up here without the window open. Or something stronger if you've got it."

"Apologies, I've come empty handed, I'm afraid."

Jimmy stiffened. The voice didn't belong to the boss. He snapped his head around in time to see a familiar face grinning at him.

"Greetings, Jimmy. I was in the area so I thought I'd drop by." The man quietly shut the door behind him. "And your brother Bobby sends his regards, by the way."

Jimmy gripped the arms of the wooden chair, about to spring to his feet, but the man was by his side in a split second.

"No need to get up on my account, Jimmy." The man's eyes slid sideways towards the crate. "What's in the box, if I might be so bold as to ask?"

Jimmy's jaw tensed. "Nothing that concerns you."

The eyes slid back. "Well, I think I'll be the judge of that, don't you? Maybe I'll just go over and take a look for myself, eh?"

Jimmy scrambled to his feet, but again the man was too quick for him. He saw the gleam of the blade only moments before he felt it slice into his throat. He staggered backwards, his weight pulling him over the back of the chair sending him crashing to the floor.

Hot, pulsating blood spurted from his neck. Instinctively Jimmy clamped his hands to the gaping wound but he already knew it was too late.

* * *

Time: 12.10 p.m.
Date: Saturday 30 August 2014
Location: HMP Belmarsh, Thamesmead, South-East London

Jason felt a heavy thud in the small of his back.

"Move along, Alcock." Lindsay Jenkins shoved Jason once again, more forcibly this time, causing him to stumble forwards almost into the back of Mickey Hatton. "I'm starving."

Mickey half-turned, a stony look on his face. "Watch where you're going."

Jenkins grinned. "Sorry mate, didn't see you there. Me and my boy here are just proper hungry, that's all."

Jason bristled. He wasn't and never would be Lindsay Jenkins' *boy*.

The lunch queue inched forward, the welcome sound of metal against metal as the prisoners' food was dished out at the servery. Several prison officers stood close by, monitoring the queue and watching for any signs of trouble. Normally, lunch on a weekend was a relatively peaceful affair on the wing — with more recreation time and no work to go to, many prisoners were in a good mood, grateful at not being locked up for the day. And lunch meant time to feed their bellies. But it wouldn't always necessarily be that way, with grievances yet to multiply, so the prison officers kept a watchful eye for trouble which could often be sparked in the blink of an eye.

As the trio passed by, a tall officer with a neatly trimmed beard inclined his head towards his colleague but kept his beady eyes fixed on the advancing queue. "We've got that Quinn on authorised bedrest today — he won't be out of his cell today, maybe not for the rest of the coming week either."

Jenkins leaned in as the queue moved forward, tapping Jason on the shoulder with a stubby finger. "What's up with your new cell buddy then?"

Jason didn't bother turning round, stepping closer to Mickey as the queue reached the first food counter. "Dunno. Think it's his leg. Where he busted it before."

"So he'll be getting room service, eh? Lucky bugger." Jenkins started to snort at his own joke. "Guess it makes sense, though. Saw him limping like an old woman yesterday on his way to your cell. Doesn't do much for his hard man image though, does it, eh? Might need one of them Zimmer frames before long." Jenkins carried on snorting.

Jason ignored him and proceeded to collect his lunch in silence. He looked down at the packet of sandwiches and bag of crisps sitting on the tray. Although his stomach rumbled, suddenly he didn't feel so hungry anymore.

* * *

Time: 12.10 p.m.
Date: Saturday 30 August 2014
Location: St Benedict's Street, London

Even in such a confined space, Katarina had managed to curl herself up into a tight ball, hands clamped around her ears. Only moments earlier the endless silence had been broken by the door opening and footsteps crossing the creaking floorboards . . . and then there had been the voices. She recognised one — belonging to the man who'd held her captive for however long she'd been inside this box — but the other one she hadn't heard before. She heard the word 'Jimmy' mentioned several times, followed by a series of grunts and raised voices. Then there was the sound of something crashing heavily to the floor.

Followed by silence once more.

Katarina wasn't sure which was worse — the voices or the silence.

She worked hard to control her breathing — inhaling the stale air around her, holding it in, then exhaling slowly. She repeated the process several more times — but it wasn't working.

Her ears strained through the quiet. Was she alone?

As if in answer to her unspoken question, another straw appeared through one of the holes by the side of her head. Instinctively, she recoiled, remembering with far too much clarity the foul taste of the concentrated urine from before.

But her throat felt as rough as sandpaper, her tongue swollen and dry. She hadn't had anything to drink for hours now — maybe even days. Her head felt groggy, pain pulsating at her temples. Right now she would gladly drink anyone's urine — even her own, had she not already emptied her bladder inside the crate several hours ago.

Compelled by thirst, she dipped her head towards the straw and sucked. Glorious cool water filled her mouth. She drank deeply and quickly, not caring if it made her choke. When the bottle was empty, the straw disappeared.

Whoever was on the other side of the crate said nothing.

And then there was the sound of the door opening and closing once again, more silence following on behind.

She was alone.

* * *

Time: 12.45 p.m.
Date: Saturday 30 August 2014
Location: Metropolitan Police HQ, London

What the hell am I doing?

Jack loosened his tie and headed into the interview room.

Jonathan Spearing looked up, his face haggard and drawn. Jack kicked the door closed behind him and grabbed hold of the only vacant chair in the room, dragging it across the floor to sit opposite the reporter.

"You came! God, am I pleased to see you!"

Jack held up a hand and avoided Spearing's gaze. "You've got three minutes, Spearing. Believe me, I have better things to be doing with my time than sitting here with you."

"But . . . ?"

"But nothing. I'm doing this as a favour to DS Carmichael. Apparently, you won't cooperate unless you speak to me first." Jack paused, leaning forward with his elbows on the battered wooden table that separated them. "So, let's hear it. What do you want to say?"

Spearing's Adam's apple bobbed as he swallowed, his chin trembling. "You have to believe me. I had nothing to do with any of this. I'd never hurt Katarina. Never in a million years."

"I don't have to believe anything." Jack's voice remained steady. "This isn't my case. I don't have any authority in this investigation at all. You should be talking to DI Yates and her team. As I said, I'm only here as a favour to DS Carmichael. So, why don't you tell me what this is really all about and we can both get on with our day?"

Spearing dropped his gaze to the table. "I know you think I hound you."

"Think?" Jack bit back the bitter laugh bubbling beneath the surface. "You go out of your way to attack me. You make my life a merry hell sometimes. It's your life's work. Tell me, why should I suddenly bend over backwards to help you now?"

"Because I need the best." Spearing looked up. "I need the best police brain to solve this one — to get me out of this massive hole, this unholy mess I've landed myself in. And to save Katarina."

"Where is she? Where is Katarina?"

At the mention of his wife's name, Spearing's eyes moistened and the muscles in his neck tensed. "I . . . I don't know. Truly I don't."

"Forgive me, but I'm a little confused here. Tell me what you think I can help you with. I really do have other things I need to be doing." Jack glanced at his watch. "You have two minutes left."

"They know Katarina comes from money. The kidnappers."

"I think DI Yates and her team have already established that. All the relevant protocols are in place — it's being handled."

"But this won't be the end of it. I don't think it's just about the money."

"What do you mean it's not just about the money?" Jack locked eyes with Spearing, watching the man fiddling nervously with a thick rubber band around his wrist. Silence filled the stuffy interview room until realisation quickly followed. "My God, it's *you*. It's *you* they really want." Jack sank back in his seat. "Tell me everything. What have you done?"

Spearing continued to fidget in his chair, twisting the wristband some more while dropping his gaze to the table.

"You've ninety seconds left." Jack made a show of checking his watch. When nothing but more silence followed, he made to get up. "I told you, I don't have time for this. You need to start talking to DI Yates when you get re-interviewed. Come clean about whatever it is you think you've done." With a final exasperated look at the reporter he pushed himself to his feet and headed for the door, anger bubbling that he'd allowed himself to get sucked in so easily.

"I need you to go to the house." Spearing's voice was steady. "My house — mine and Katie's."

Jack's hand rested on the door handle, his back still to the reporter. "And why would I want to do that?"

"I've hidden something — but I can't say where." Spearing looked furtively around him, keeping his voice low. "I think it's what they're really after. They don't want Katie — they never did. But I can't go back there — they might be waiting for me."

Jack turned around to face Spearing once more. "Just tell DI Yates what this is all about and have done with it. Why all the cloak and dagger?"

Spearing swallowed, his voice little more than a whisper. "I don't trust her. Not like I trust you, anyway."

"*You* don't trust *her*?" The sarcasm in Jack's tone was clear. "That's a bit rich coming from you, don't you think?"

"Look, I . . ."

Just then the door sprang open, Jack taking a step back as DI Yates entered. A look of surprise crossed her face. "DI MacIntosh? What are you doing in here?"

"I heard your guy wouldn't talk — I thought I might try and loosen his tongue a little."

"Oh?" DI Yates' eyebrows lifted. "And did you?"

Jack locked eyes with Spearing once more, seeing sheer terror mirrored back at him. Terror and something else. Something that looked a lot like hope. "No, sorry. Complete waste of time — he won't say a word."

Jack stepped through the doorway, the reporter's voice following in his wake.

"Have a nice day, Inspector."

CHAPTER TWENTY-SIX

Time: 1.30 p.m.
Date: Saturday 30 August 2014
Location: Metropolitan Police HQ, London

DS Cooper jogged up the two flights of stairs and headed along the corridor towards DS Carmichael's office. Jack's instructions had been decidedly vague. A decent single malt, not too cheap but not too expensive either. Not being much of a whisky drinker, Cooper hoped he'd made the right choice.

The door was unlocked, but the office itself was empty. Crossing over to Carmichael's paper-strewn desk, Cooper deposited the off-licence bag containing the bottle of whisky on top of a small stack of files. He thought about leaving a note but wasn't sure it would be seen in among the paper carnage. And he needed to get back to carry on with the search for that van.

As he turned away, his hand brushed the corner of a pile of papers, sending them crashing to the floor. As he bent down to scoop them back up, Cooper noticed a colour photograph on the top. Frowning, he gathered the papers together and placed them back on the desk, leafing through them as he did so.

He recognised the contents as being related to the current kidnapping case Carmichael was working on. Although meant to be kept under wraps, most of the station was aware of what was going on, even if not officially.

The paperwork described what the subject had been wearing the last time she was seen. Cooper's frown deepened as he switched his attention back to the photograph that had originally caught his eye. The picture was one of a necklace; a necklace that he'd seen before.

Cooper dashed for the door.

He knew *exactly* where that piece of jewellery was right now — and it wasn't around the neck of Katarina Spearing.

* * *

Time: 1.40 p.m.
Date: Saturday 30 August 2014
Location: Acacia Avenue, Wimbledon

Once again, Jack questioned his judgement; something he'd been doing a lot of lately.

He'd parked the Mondeo around the corner, just in case the house was under surveillance, and made his way steadily behind the row of spacious detached houses. He again toyed with the idea of turning around. Cooper would have been to the off-licence by now and Rob might fancy cracking open his bottle of birthday whisky. Jack glanced at his watch.

An early afternoon tipple.

Sighing, he continued picking his way along behind the row of houses.

This isn't even my case.

After leaving Spearing in the interview room, DI Yates had quickly caught Jack up in the corridor.

"Thanks for trying," she'd said, following him down the stairs. "He's not easy to get much out of right now."

"I guess he's still in shock," muttered Jack. "As much as I despise him, it can't be easy with his wife missing."

"He's worried about the house — says he's too nervous to go back in case the kidnappers are waiting for him. Idiot leaves a key under a flowerpot in the back garden, so it's not exactly secure. I've told him he needs to be seen to be acting normally. But he isn't a great one for taking advice."

Jack found a gap in the fence and slipped unnoticed towards the back of the Spearings' house. He should probably have told Rob where he was going; should have told his team too, to be fair. But he didn't plan to be long — and if he didn't do this now, he probably never would.

So, before he could talk himself out of it, Jack tipped over the solitary flowerpot and grabbed the spare key from underneath.

Stepping inside, the house had a deserted feel to it — the curtains were closed, all lights were off. No sound could be heard over and above a faint tick-ticking of a clock on the kitchen wall. Pausing on the threshold to the hallway, Jack listened to the silence — he was as sure as he could be that the house was empty. No lurking kidnappers, at least.

He looked down at the clue he'd quickly scribbled for himself on a crumpled piece of paper.

'V Festival 2002'

If it even *was* a clue — which was entirely debatable. Spearing had been fiddling with the festival wristband non-stop when Jack had tried speaking with him in the interview room. If it wasn't meant to be a clue, then Jack had just jumped feet first down the wrong rabbit hole.

"This is bloody insane," he muttered as he approached the darkened hallway. "Utterly bloody insane."

His hunch took him upstairs. If he was right, this would be where he would find whatever it was Spearing wanted him to find. If he was wrong, then this whole escapade had been a glorious waste of time and energy. And he would have achieved nothing more than hammering yet more nails into his own career-ending coffin.

Jack found the Spearings' bedroom at the front of the house, a three-door wardrobe running along the side wall. It looked like a solid piece of kit, made from thick pine with ornate-looking metal hinges and door handles. This was not your average flat-pack job from IKEA.

Jack pulled open the left-hand door. A series of skirts, dresses, tailored trousers and jackets hung neatly from a multitude of hangers. Katarina's side of the wardrobe. As he moved to the right-hand side, Jack cautiously peered out between the curtains at the window, seeing nothing but the deserted street below. Pulling open the right-hand side wardrobe door revealed a tangled pile of jeans in a heap on the floor, plus a variety of trainers, shoes and belts. Jackets, jumpers and T-shirts hung from the hangers.

His hunch steered him towards the T-shirts. Whenever Spearing appeared at a press conference, he was always dressed in some faded band T-shirt or other — something advertising a tour or album cover. Jack took another look at the crumpled note.

V Festival 2002

* * *

Time: 1.45 p.m.
Date: Saturday 30 August 2014
Location: Metropolitan Police HQ, London

The holdall sat in the middle of the desk.

A hundred thousand pounds.

It didn't take up a lot of space in the end.

Katarina's parents had authorised the cash withdrawal immediately and, after various high-level conversations back and forth between the Gold Command Group and the bank, the funds had been made available and duly collected under a discreet armed escort.

And now here it sat — a hundred thousand pounds — on her desk.

Becky glanced at her mother's photograph, feeling the lump growing in her throat. Life could be so cruel sometimes.

Next to the holdall sat a bundle of the morning post she'd scooped up from her father's house earlier that day — the topmost envelope being another reminder from the nursing home about the outstanding fees. She'd slipped it from the doormat before he'd had a chance to see it; he didn't need the additional worry right now. She picked up the envelope and slid it into the desk drawer, along with the others.

Glancing at her watch she felt her stomach clench. She needed to prepare for the final briefing — and then get the operation underway. There was just a little over three hours until the agreed ransom drop-off time.

Not long to go now.

I can do this.

CHAPTER TWENTY-SEVEN

Time: 1.45 p.m.
Date: Saturday 30 August 2014
Location: Metropolitan Police HQ, London

"How sure are you?"

Carmichael studied the photograph DS Cooper had taken from his office.

"I'm convinced it's the same one." Cooper edged his chair closer to Carmichael's. They were alone in the incident room, Cassidy and Daniels having gone for some lunch. "It looks so unique. I can't see there being two of them."

Carmichael nodded. "Spearing said it was a one-off piece commissioned by his wife for their wedding anniversary."

"It has to be the same one. I saw the old woman wearing it when she called round for a cuppa a couple of days ago. I'd just nipped back home. I'd forgotten my phone. I remember Jenny commented on how lovely it was. I think she was hinting. It's her birthday soon."

* * *

Cooper rummaged in the suitcase, eventually retrieving his iPhone. "Gotcha. Right, I'd better be heading back." Slipping the phone into his pocket he headed for the door. "Nice to see you, Mrs Thompson."

As he passed the old woman, he caught sight of the necklace she was wearing. "That's an unusual necklace, Mrs Thompson." Cooper gestured towards the piece of jewellery. "Really catches the eye."

Betty's hand went to her neck. "It is, isn't it? I wasn't sure if it was really me."

"Well, I think it suits you." Jenny handed Cooper the selection of flapjacks and shortbread wrapped in a napkin. "Wherever did you get it?"

"Oh, it was a gift," beamed Betty. "One of the nice gentlemen from the flat upstairs gave it to me. As a way of saying sorry for the noise, I think. And all their comings and goings. I didn't have the heart to tell them I couldn't hear anything — not with my ears!"

* * *

"You're sure she said it was someone from upstairs that gave it to her? A man?"

Cooper nodded. "Yes. I thought at the time it was extremely generous, especially from a virtual stranger. It looked expensive."

"And you've never seen the man or men she was talking about?"

"No. We don't have anyone above us at the moment, and we haven't really been there long enough to see much of anyone else in the street."

Carmichael tucked the photograph of the necklace into his pocket and headed for the door. "Wait here. I need to go and find the boss."

* * *

Time: 1.50 p.m.
Date: Saturday 30 August 2014
Location: HMP Belmarsh, Thamesmead, South-East London

He'd made the makeshift shank in his cell some time ago — it hadn't taken much. He'd used an old toothbrush, whittling it down over time into a sharpened point at one end. Maybe it wasn't as good as a blade, but it'd get the job done right enough — just so long as you put enough force behind it.

Knowing James Quinn was confined to his cell for the day made things a lot easier — the man would be a sitting duck.

Making his way along the wing, he tucked the sharpened toothbrush inside the sleeve of his prison-issue sweatshirt. All it would take would be one quick flick of the wrist — and bang. Lights out.

Was he concerned about ending the life of a man like Quinn? He'd asked himself that question once, and once only. *No,* had been the resounding response. Quinn wouldn't be missed. Was he capable of doing the deed? The question had brought a smile to his lips. He'd killed before, that was no secret — and he could certainly kill again.

The cell door was open, just like he knew it would be. He walked briskly towards it, no one standing in his way. The other prisoners were all out enjoying their recreation time, not cluttering up the landing; which was just as well. But he knew he couldn't afford to hesitate, though — hesitation bred mistakes. He would have one shot at this, and one shot only.

With the open doorway now before him, he strode confidently into the cell without even so much as a pause in his step, feeling the shaft of the homemade shank in the palm of his hand. He saw Quinn was lying on the bottom bunk as expected, his body huddled beneath a mound of scratchy blankets. The man was facing the wall — he wouldn't see it coming.

Pulling the shank out of his sleeve in one quick move, he lunged towards Quinn and began stabbing at his torso. It was a hurried and frenzied attack, the sharpened point of the homemade weapon slicing through the thin blankets as if they were made of nothing but air. He placed all his bodyweight behind the attack, each blow from the shank penetrating Quinn's upper body.

CHAPTER TWENTY-EIGHT

Time: 1.50 p.m.
Date: Saturday 30 August 2014
Location: HMP Belmarsh, Thamesmead, South-East London

He'd expected there to be more blood.

Pausing mid-stab, Mickey Hatton straightened up and focused on the body beneath the blankets.

Except it wasn't a body.

Sensing a movement behind him, Mickey half-turned to see four prison officers blocking the doorway dressed in full protective clothing and with riot shields thrust in front of them.

"Why don't you drop the blade, Mickey? Then we can deal with this nice and calmly."

Mickey's gaze flickered back towards the mound beneath the blankets. The frenzied attack had dislodged the top covering, showing him that he'd been stabbing at nothing more than a series of folded up pillows. Mickey let the sharpened toothbrush fall to the floor with a clatter.

"Good choice, Mickey." One of the prison officers took a step forward. "Now, turn around and face the wall, hands above your head. We're coming in."

* * *

"What do you mean, we wait?" DS Carmichael was already shrugging into his jacket. "What could we possibly need to wait for?" He searched the other eyes in the room. "Why wait?" he repeated.

Becky was still looking at the photograph of Katarina's necklace. She cleared her throat. "I'm not saying we don't go and check it out — I'm just saying we need to make sure we're following all the correct protocols." She glanced up. "And not just jumping in with both feet on a whim."

"On a whim?" Carmichael's expression bordered on the incredulous. "How is this possibly a whim? Cooper's pretty much identified the necklace as being worn by his neighbour. Given to her by some shady fella moving heavy furniture around in an empty flat upstairs." He shook his head. "I don't get it. We should be round there now. Katarina could be up in that flat."

"Which is precisely why we need to tread carefully." Becky placed the photograph down. "We don't want to do anything that might alert the kidnappers that we have this information. Or that we're targeting that address. If she's there, Katarina's life could very well depend on it."

Carmichael sighed and shrugged back out of his jacket. "OK," he conceded. "Maybe you're right. But we still need to get round there fast."

"And we will," reassured Becky. "I have done this before, you know. We need to follow established protocol. I'll make some calls and get the ball rolling. I'll need to update the Gold Command Group and it'll be their call what happens next. We can't just go off on our own little tangent here. We'll need tactical support and extra back-up as a minimum." She saw Carmichael about to groan. "It won't take long, I promise. But we really do need to do this safely. For Katarina's sake if nothing else."

"What about the deadline? Has Spearing heard anything more from the kidnappers?"

"All in hand." Becky tucked the photograph of the necklace into her jacket pocket. "The money is sorted. I'm just about to go and check that the surveillance teams are ready to go when we need them to. Give me an hour or so and we'll have that final briefing. Bring Spearing along too — he'll need to hear what we've got to say."

"Before you go — what do you think about this?" Carmichael brought out his phone and showed the detective inspector the image of Spearing on Brompton Gardens at the time his wife was being abducted. "This is what our man Spearing was doing that day — not going to buy painkillers as he suggested."

Becky frowned towards the screen.

Carmichael continued. "Looks to me like a pre-arranged meeting — they didn't just bump into each other by chance. They shake hands but — I've a feeling there was more to it than that. Maybe something passed between them."

"Who is he?"

"I was going to ask you that."

"This isn't my patch. He's not a face I'm familiar with. Have you circled it anywhere else yet?"

"Not yet." Carmichael returned the phone to his pocket. "It might be wholly innocent, but why's he lying? He's hiding something. He's definitely not telling us the whole story."

* * *

Time: 2.00 p.m.
Date: Saturday 30 August 2014
Location: HMP Belmarsh, Thamesmead, South-East London

The sound of slamming cell doors and raised voices reverberated along the wing — recreation time was being abruptly cut short and all prisoners ordered back to their cells.

Everyone, that was, except James Quinn.

Teams of prison officers stood in line along the whole length of the landing, braced for whatever else was yet to come.

There had been the expected grumbling, shouting and swearing among the inmates, even the odd scuffle, as the usual Saturday afternoon routine was interrupted. Quinn had been ordered to stay out of the way — and stay out of the way he did.

But it didn't stop him watching. He'd thought it odd at the time — being pulled from his cell earlier, without so much as an explanation why. But it hadn't taken long for the details of what had happened — or what had almost happened — to spread across the wing. News travelled at lightning speed in here — especially news like this.

Someone had wanted him gone. Cut to pieces. Dead. And Quinn wanted to know just who that was. The list couldn't be very long — he'd only been in here five minutes.

Quinn's eyes slanted to the side where another figure had been told to hang back.

Jason Alcock.

Was it him?

They hadn't spoken much yet — but Quinn had got the distinct impression the man wasn't all that thrilled to be sharing a cell with him, although he hadn't quite come out and said it. He was a sly one — the librarian's assistant. Quinn could tell there was more to the man than the quiet demeanour he presented.

And then there was Mickey Hatton.

Quinn might be new to the prison but he wasn't so naive that he didn't know who the man was. And the company he kept on the outside. Has Quinn really come to the attention of Geraghty's old gang? Somehow, he doubted it. He knew better than to tread on toes that were that big and nasty.

"Move along, now. Nothing to see here."

Quinn found two prison officers by his side, gesturing for him to make his way along the landing, presumably to a different cell. Reluctantly he limped along, wondering where he would be taken to this time — and, more importantly, who he might have to share with.

With one attempt on his life already, he didn't relish another.

* * *

Time: 2.00 p.m.
Date: Saturday 30 August 2014
Location: Acacia Avenue, Wimbledon

Jack left Spearing's house the same way he'd entered — carefully replacing the key beneath the flowerpot as he exited through the back door. Retracing his steps, he pulled himself back through the gap in the fence and jogged back to where he'd left the Mondeo.

Jumbled thoughts circulated his head as he slid into the driver's seat and fired up the engine.

Spearing.

The reporter could be the key to everything — and not just the kidnapping.

He needed to get back to the station — Jack knew he'd been off-grid for too long already. What he'd just found in Spearing's house was about to turn *everything* on its head — *Operation Scarecrow* included.

As he turned the car north-east, he contemplated the other problem that had reared its ugly head that morning — and it was a problem he knew would only fester if he didn't deal with it head on.

Glancing at the dashboard clock, he decided one more detour wouldn't hurt.

CHAPTER TWENTY-NINE

Time: 2.20 p.m.
Date: Saturday 30 August 2014
Location: The Hanged Man Public House

Jack pulled the Mondeo into the car park of the Hanged Man. Long-since closed for business, weeds were already taking over the block paving and creeping around the sides of the red-brick building. A rusting pub sign was attached by equally rusty hinges above the door.

The Hanged Man.

Jack wondered just how apt the name would turn out to be.

Killing the engine, he glanced at the faded Stereophonics T-shirt on the passenger seat.

'Have a nice day, Inspector.'

Spearing was good, Jack would give him that. It had taken him a while to find the right T-shirt — initially looking for a V Festival one. It was only after an exasperating ten minutes searching that Spearing's last words floated into his head.

'Have a nice day, Inspector.'

A quick Google search on his phone had confirmed the line-up for the 2002 V Festival. There was a whole host of decent acts that had made the trip to Essex — Manic Street Preachers, Nickelback, Elvis Costello, Elbow, and the Chemical Brothers to name but a few.

And then there had been Stereophonics.

'Have a Nice Day' wasn't a bad song, but Jack preferred something like 'Maybe Tomorrow' or 'Dakota'.

However, Spearing and his eclectic music choices, and even Katarina's kidnappers, would have to wait a while. Jack turned his attention to the folded newspaper on the passenger seat next to Spearing's T-Shirt — with its headline in full view.

BANKER'S MURDER — MAN CHARGED

Jack felt himself bristling once more and kicked open the door of the Mondeo. There was no sign of anyone else in the car park — but Jack knew they'd be there. The card Ritchie Greenwood had given him at the Ferryman bore no contact details other than the address of the abandoned pub. The door was unlocked, as he expected, admitting him into a musty smelling hallway. Stale beer reached his nostrils. One of the walls opposite still sported a rack of rusting hooks — a solitary umbrella hanging from one; left behind by the last departing customer before the pub had closed its doors for good.

Jack pushed through the door with a brass plaque above saying 'bar'.

The bar was just as musty smelling as the hallway — but it was lighter. Recessed wall lights were flickering on low and behind the bar stood Ritchie Greenwood, beaming from ear to ear.

"Welcome to my humble watering hole, Jack my friend. What can I get you?" Ritchie swept his arm along the length of the bar. "No pumps working but we do have a fine array of your favourite tipple."

Jack eyed the range of whisky bottles. There was a decent looking Macallan but he wasn't tempted. "What do you mean by this?" Jack slung the newspaper up on to the bar.

Ritchie Greenwood merely smiled wider and poured a shot of whisky into two glass tumblers. "Now, now, Jack. Let's not fall out. Just a simple thank you will suffice."

Jack ignored the tumbler and took a step closer to the bar. "Thank you for what, exactly?"

"For helping you out with that little bit of trouble down in Surrey." Ritchie sipped his whisky. "Joseph left strict instructions on how to get you out of that particular hole, if such a hole presented itself. You're off the hook, so to speak." He nodded towards the newspaper. "Looks like there's been a timely confession — I very much doubt anyone will come looking for you now."

"I didn't ask you to do that."

Ritchie grinned behind his glass. "You didn't need to ask, Jack. What are friends for, eh?"

"You're no friend of mine. Let's be clear."

"Oh, don't be so ungrateful, Jack. The deal is done. You can enjoy your freedom and we can leave it at that. Just remember that you owe me, that's all."

"I don't owe anybody anything, and definitely not you."

"I think you might want to reconsider that, Jack. I mean, you don't want the papers to hear about how such a well-respected detective inspector staged a murder scene, do you? Maybe even had a hand in the poor man's demise? Not to mention trying to set someone else up to take the fall — planting evidence and such like. Tut-tut — it doesn't look good, does it? Just think what that might do to your reputation — and your career. And not to mention your police pension. Then there's that little conundrum you've got going on at the moment. I hear you have a kidnapping underway?"

"How do you know about that?"

"Walls have ears, my friend. Didn't they teach you that at police training college? There's not much I don't get to hear about, one way or another." Ritchie gave Jack a sickly smile. "Anyway, here's a titbit for you — if you're finding that one difficult to crack. My advice is to take a look a little closer to home. And you can have that little nugget for free."

Ritchie grinned some more. "But all in all, on balance, I think you'll agree that you owe me."

"If you think I'm in any way indebted to you, somehow in your pocket, then you're wrong. You're very, very wrong." Jack turned, intending to head for the door. The exit was blocked by five well-built hulks dressed in smart suits. He turned back and scowled towards the bar. "Get your guys to move."

"Like I said, I think you might want to reconsider your position, Jack. I wouldn't want to have to force you into submission." Ritchie's eyes lost their gleam, replaced with a hardened, steely gaze.

"You think you can force me to be your puppet?" Scorn loaded Jack's tone.

"Given time, I think we can probably persuade you, yes."

Jack took another look at the five men blocking his escape and gave a scornful chuckle. "What, you and the Backstreet Boys here? Don't make me laugh."

Ritchie's face darkened, and Jack felt the wall of muscle behind him tense and start to inch closer. Within seconds, Ritchie's face broke out into another wide grin. "Oh my, we have a joker in the pack, lads. How refreshing!" Downing the rest of his whisky he waved a hand towards the door. "Let our friend here be on his way. I'm sure we'll be catching up again real soon. You can tell me all about that brother of yours — and his pretty new wife."

Jack's jaw clenched. "You leave Stu out of this."

Ritchie winked and again waved Jack on his way. "Just jesting with you, my friend. Off you pop. But you'll come back and see us again soon, won't you?"

Jack slammed the door of the Hanged Man behind him and strode across the weed-strewn car park back to the Mondeo. As he did so, his phone chirped with an incoming message. It was Carmichael.

'We've got a lead on the necklace. Could do with your help.'

* * *

Time: 3.00 p.m.
Date: Saturday 30 August 2014
Location: Metropolitan Police HQ, London

"Trev? How many countries did you say used that Cyrillic alphabet again?" DS Cassidy peered closely at her computer screen.

"Mostly Slavic countries — there's about fifty languages that use it in some form. Why?"

"Take a look at this." Cassidy angled her monitor towards DC Daniels. "After looking for vehicles popping up in all three locations, I had another look at the bus CCTV." The image was a face from one of the countless CCTV reels they'd been looking at during the past couple of days. The black and white image was relatively sharp, taken from the inside of one of the buses that ran along the main road close to Southwark Bridge.

Daniels pulled his chair across while Cassidy let the image play on.

The man had boarded the bus alone, his face caught in full by the on-board cameras. A nondescript face, closely shaven, nothing out of the ordinary.

"Here." Cassidy paused the reel and pointed at the screen. "See what he's carrying?"

Turning to walk down the aisle of the bus, the camera caught the man side on to reveal several books being carried underneath his left arm. Daniels cocked his head to the side. "I see what you mean," he murmured.

"Do you think it's relevant? It's just over a week ago. But some of the lettering on one of those spines looks an awful lot like the Cyrillic alphabet you pinned up on the whiteboard."

Daniels pulled his chair in closer. "Can you enlarge it a bit?"

Cassidy dutifully tapped the keyboard making the image expand to fill the screen.

"That one in the middle is definitely some form of Cyrillic. Could be Bulgarian. I can't be sure of course but . .

229

." Daniels pulled out his phone and took a snapshot, using it for a Google search. "And that other one is in Romanian — a translation of *Dracula*, by the looks of it."

The pair stared at the screen in silence for several moments before Daniels said, "Where does he go after this?"

Cassidy resumed the playback of the images. "He gets off a few stops later, halfway along Clearwater Road."

"We must have other cameras along there, surely? It's a busy enough area."

"Can you check it out for me? Look for any more cameras along Clearwater Road. And if he paid by Oyster card or bank card then we might be able to trace him that way. While you're doing that, I'll see if our friend here pops up in any of our other locations."

"I've had some hits looking for that van." DS Cooper tapped the screen of his computer monitor with the end of a biro. "Vans big enough to transport a decent number of people seen in the vicinity of the disused brewery over the last week." Cooper sighed. "It's a pretty long list though."

"Have you mentioned it to the guv yet?" Cassidy scooted her chair over to Cooper's side.

"Mentioned what to me?" Jack pushed open the door to the incident room just in time to hear the end of the detectives' conversation.

Cooper looked up. "Ah, you're back. Got some results for the vans in and around the brewery — just about to run some of the plates through ANPR to see where they go."

"And we're following up a face seen on one of the buses," added Cassidy, nodding towards her screen.

"Good. Let me know if you find anything worth following up. Cooper — I need you with me." Jack waved Jonathan Spearing's Stereophonics T-shirt in the air. "I've something to show you. My office in ten."

"Carmichael's looking for you too, boss." Cooper got to his feet. "It's about a necklace belonging to Spearing's wife."

CHAPTER THIRTY

Time: 3.15 p.m.
Date: Saturday 30 August 2014
Location: Metropolitan Police HQ, London

Jack placed the photograph of Katarina's necklace down on to his desk, then turned to DS Cooper. "You're sure you've seen your neighbour wearing this?"

Cooper nodded. "A hundred per cent. There can't be two of them, right?"

Jack had to concede it was unlikely. "What does your new DI say about it all?"

"That's just the thing, Jack." The exasperation in Carmichael's voice was plain for all to hear. "She wants us to wait."

"Wait? Why would you wait?"

"That was my reaction. She said something about not jumping in with both feet, needing to go through the correct procedures with back-up, blah blah. That it's the Gold Command Group's decision on what to do next." Carmichael paused. "I know she has a point but it just doesn't seem right to me. Something is off."

Jack remembered Spearing's words from earlier.

'*I don't trust her.*'

"OK, let's deal with the necklace in a minute. First, I've got something you both need to see." Jack angled his computer monitor towards Cooper and Carmichael while inserting the memory stick. "I found it sewn into the hem of a Stereophonics T-shirt in Spearing's bedroom wardrobe."

Carmichael opened his mouth to ask the inevitable question, but Jack raised a hand to silence him. "I'll fill you in later, Rob — but right now, you need to see this."

* * *

Time: 11.30 a.m.
Date: Sunday 10 August 2014
Location: Acacia Avenue, Wimbledon

"I'm recording this on my phone, but also from a camera set up behind me." Jonathan Spearing gestured back over his shoulder to the hastily erected video camera behind. "I trust you're happy with that?"

Stefan nodded.

Spearing thought he looked older than the twenty-three years he claimed to be — but maybe that was down to the terror so clearly evident on his face. Fear had a way of ageing you. Spearing peered more closely at the screen of his iPhone. The FaceTime connection wasn't ideal, but it was the best they would get. Face to face wasn't an option here.

He tried to make out where the man was — but all he could see in the background was crumbling brickwork and what appeared to be piles of dusty sacks.

"I don't have long," the man said, his eyes darting from side to side. "They'll be back soon."

Spearing pulled his reporter's notepad closer. Although the interview was being recorded, old habits die hard. "Noted. To begin with, Stefan, in your own words — tell me how you ended up where you are."

232

Keeping his voice low, the man started to speak. His English was good, clear and precise. "Some weeks ago, I boarded a lorry in Bucharest which took me through Hungary and Austria to the border with Germany. For thirty-five-thousand Leu I was promised a job, a flat to stay in, and enough money to send back to my family in Romania. In time, they would be able to join me, too. I was told I would be working in hospitality — in a good hotel. I have hospitality experience back home. They promised access to further education if I wanted to study, and access to free healthcare."

"And what was the reality?" Spearing had a feeling he already knew, but asked the question anyway.

"I'm work fourteen-hour shifts, locked up for the rest of the time. We are chained by our ankles." Stefan moved his legs, and Spearing was able to hear the clink of metal chains over the phone connection. "I don't see the sky. At night we all sleep on the floor. It stinks. Everything is rotten. They give us stale food, dirty water to drink. We are all ill. There is no sanitation. When we go to work, we are taken in a windowless van to the workshops — dark, abandoned buildings. We have no idea where we are. We get beaten if we talk out of turn or ask questions. The work is monotonous — sometimes sewing, sometimes packing. Every time we make a mistake we are whipped."

"And the money you were promised?"

The man shook his head. "We get nothing. They tell us that our wages go towards our accommodation and food. If we question it, we get beaten again. They say they are saving part of our wages for our families — but I don't believe them."

Spearing could only see the man's face and upper body — but he could still see evidence of the blue-black bruising across his chest and upper arms.

"And you have no means of escape?"

Stefan shook his head again. "We are beaten. We are drugged. People are killed if they disobey. We are not allowed any contact with our families back home — no phones."

"How many of you are there?"

The man shrugged. "It changes. Sometimes there are as many as twenty of us locked up in here — other times it is less. People are moved on."

"Do you know the identity of those who are behind it? Any names of those involved?"

The man hesitated, his eyes once more darting from side to side. "No. No names. The ones that brought me here were Bulgarian. But the ones that deal with us here speak English. Good English."

"And you have no idea where you are?"

The man shook his head, but leaned in closer to the phone screen. "No, not for sure. But we're close to the river. And this whole place smells of rotten beer."

Just then, Spearing heard another voice out of camera shot. Stefan looked sideways.

"I have to go," Stefan said, just as another face edged into focus. "They're coming."

* * *

Time: 3.25 p.m.
Date: Saturday 30 August 2014
Location: Metropolitan Police HQ, London

Jack reached forward to pause the recording, the man's face frozen on the screen. "Face look familiar to you, Cooper?"

"He's our victim number three — the one found in the disused brewery on Thursday night."

"Indeed, he is." Despite the decomposition process having distorted and bloated the man's appearance when they'd seen him lying on the rotten sacks of fermenting grain, the likeness couldn't be ignored.

"I'm guessing someone found out he'd been speaking to the press," added Cooper. "Hence the mouth being sewn shut. Keep quiet."

"But how did he get in touch with Spearing?" questioned Carmichael. "And get hold of a phone?"

234

"My guess is he had help." Jack used the mouse to hover the cursor over the second face on the screen. "Him. Goes by the name of Bobby Neale."

"Wait a minute . . ." Carmichael pulled his phone from his pocket. "Do we think this is the same guy?" He turned the phone screen towards Jack, pulling up the CCTV image DC Ashford had found. "Spearing went to meet him on the morning his wife was abducted. Told us some cock and bull story about going to get painkillers."

Jack squinted at the somewhat grainy image. "Looks like Bobby Neale to me. Are they exchanging something?"

"No idea." Carmichael ran a hand over his unshaven chin, the stubble prickling his fingers. "But are we now saying Katarina's kidnap is connected to your people trafficking case? And it's all connected to Spearing's story?"

"Spearing told me he thinks that the kidnappers were after *him* — not his wife. How it wasn't all about the ransom — that they were after something else. Maybe it's this." Jack nodded towards the memory stick. "But as far as I know, this story hasn't been published yet. The rest of the memory stick has copies of the research he's been doing — quotes from other sources, photographs. But, as yet, none of it is in the public domain. So, it still doesn't quite add up."

"Well, my guess is *someone* found out about it." Carmichael gestured towards the screen. "I'd better let the boss know what you've found. This changes things slightly. The drop-off for the 100K is scheduled for later today — but if the motive behind Katarina's abduction isn't just the money, then this might put a different spin on things."

"In the meantime." Cooper picked up the image of the bespoke necklace. "What are we going to do about this?"

CHAPTER THIRTY-ONE

Time: 3.30 p.m.
Date: Saturday 30 August 2014
Location: Metropolitan Police HQ, London

"Gotcha." Daniels gave a small involuntary whoop and flashed a grin across towards DS Cassidy. "I've tracked our guy as far as I can along Clearwater Road from when he steps off the bus." Cassidy came to peer over his shoulder. Scrolling back through the footage he pressed play. "See him there? That's the same guy as on the bus for definite. He's heading west towards the Tube."

Cassidy agreed. "Definitely him. And I've just found him in the street on CCTV close to that disused brewery on Monday just gone. No books this time, but I'm sure it's him. Can you track him any further and see where he goes?"

Daniels played the footage on until the man disappeared from the screen. "This is where we lose him. He turns down that small side street on the right." Using the computer's zoom button, he enlarged the image to bring up a somewhat blurred street sign. "Weighbridge Lane. That's the last we see of him. No cameras down that way — I checked."

"Maybe no cameras, but . . ." Cassidy hopped back to her own desk and brought up Google Maps on her screen. Logging Weighbridge Lane into the search bar, she selected Street View. "Let's have a closer look."

With Daniels looking on, Cassidy used Street View to look both ways along the entire stretch of Weighbridge Lane. Mostly they saw brick-fronted buildings opening directly out on to the one-way street, with a smattering of roll-top garage doors in between. Further along the lane, several side roads branched off— their man could have disappeared down any one of them, or even into one of the buildings. But it didn't take long for Cassidy to focus on one building in particular.

"Cobblers," she said, a look of triumph on her face. "They're shoe makers, right?"

Daniels nodded. "But technically, cobblers were shoe *menders*. Shoe *making* was a more skilled job — carried out by cordwainers. Not many of them left now, I shouldn't think. And that one there looks like it shut up shop sometime last century."

The building did, indeed, look a little on the unloved and shabby side. Even from the Street View images, the former shoemakers shop looked long-since abandoned. Each of its three windows — one downstairs, two upstairs — were boarded up, decorated with a variety of colourful graffiti tags. A door stood to the side; it looked battered, with faded paint peeling off in strips to reveal the aged wood beneath. Above it a metal sign was bolted to the crumbling brickwork — '*Cornhill and Sons, shoemakers of distinction 1712–1952*'.

"Are you thinking what I'm thinking?" Cassidy let her eyes stray towards the first whiteboard where images of the victims with their sewn-up mouths stared back out at them.

Daniels followed her gaze and nodded. "I think we might just have found the source of the thread that sewed those poor souls' mouths shut."

* * *

"The kidnappers have sent another message to Mr Spearing's phone. The drop-off is now due to take place on the corner of Flanagan Street at five-fifteen. But the routine will be the same as before." Becky eyed Jonathan Spearing seated towards the back of the incident room, his face a ghostly white. "Mr Spearing will wait at the designated spot for the taxi to arrive. He will then enter the taxi, like he did before, leaving the ransom money on the back seat as arranged."

Spearing shifted nervously in his seat.

"Surveillance teams will be on stand-by in two locations." Becky pointed at the large street map tacked to the wall, identifying two side streets close to the ransom drop-off. "After Mr Spearing vacates the taxi, they will continue to follow the vehicle to its destination where we will then gather the intelligence to unveil the identity of the kidnappers. Further surveillance teams are waiting on all major routes and will be activated where necessary."

"Are two surveillance teams enough?" Carmichael raised an eyebrow in Becky's direction. "It's a busy part of the city. I'd be more comfortable with more units in place. What about aerial support?"

"Two is sufficient for the drop-off location. As I mentioned, other units are at strategic positions on all major arterial routes out." Becky's voice was steady. "But I have also asked for two unmarked motorcycle units to be on stand-by in addition."

Jack caught Carmichael's eye and the pair exchanged a look.

"I have to say I echo Rob's concerns." Jack was sitting close to Spearing at the back of the incident room. "Surely you'll need more than just a couple of surveillance cars and motorbikes if the taxi leads you to where you think it will — to where Mr Spearing's wife is being held?" He gave a shrug. "Clearly, it's not my case — I'm just shoving my two pennyworth in."

"Everything is in hand," repeated Becky, a slight pink tinge entering her cheeks. "Tactical have been briefed in addition to the surveillance units. I'm confident we have enough boots on the ground to make this a success. I'm staying behind to coordinate things from this end along with the Gold Command Group. Everything is being covered." She paused, seeking out Jack at the back of the room. "Don't let us keep you if you're needed elsewhere, Detective Inspector."

Another look passed between Jack and Carmichael. "That's me told," breezed Jack, getting to his feet. "Let me know if you need my help at all, Rob."

Becky raised her voice a notch. "And it goes without saying — nobody, and I mean *nobody*, is to set foot anywhere near any of the locations I've just mentioned. The only personnel authorised to be in the vicinity are the surveillance teams and additional covert backup teams. Is that clear?" She paused, flashing a look at everyone in the room. "This is not a free for all."

Jack heard various murmured assents float around the room as he made his way towards the door, noting Jonathan Spearing's wide eyes following him as he did so. Slipping the memory stick from his pocket as he passed, Jack held it up so Spearing could see it. The reporter's eyes widened further as Jack disappeared out through the door.

He'd only made it halfway down the corridor when he heard the door go behind him, followed by hurried footsteps.

"I don't like it, Jack." Carmichael jogged at Jack's side as the pair made it down the first flight of stairs. "I don't like it one bit."

"I hear you, Rob. But what do you want to do about it? Go higher?" Jack pushed open his own incident room door, gesturing for Carmichael to follow. The place was empty. "There's already an experienced SIO on the team, and the Gold Command Group should know what they're doing. You could be stepping on some very angry toes if you take it any further." Jack knew they could go to Dougie King anytime they wanted — but he wasn't so sure they should rope the Chief Superintendent into something like this. Jack didn't have so many brownie points left that he could start squandering them.

Carmichael bit his lip. "I want to stay here. If she's staying, then so am I."

"You smell something?"

"Well, there's certainly something about this whole setup that I don't like. It's all this cloak and dagger shit — makes you think you're not being told the whole story."

'*I don't trust her.*' Jack heard Spearing's voice echo inside in his head. He glanced at the whiteboards gracing the incident room walls. If the operation to apprehend Katarina's kidnappers was a success, then — if the cases were really connected like they now suspected — it might just solve the *Operation Scarecrow* investigation too. "What do you want me to do?"

"Can you go to the ransom drop-off?" Carmichael paused, his jaw muscles tensing. "We might not care too much about Spearing but his wife isn't at fault here."

"After we've been expressly told not to set foot anywhere near the place?" Jack's mouth twitched into a smile. "Of course, mate. Nothing I'd like better."

"Just see where they take him — look to see if there really *is* back-up where she says there will be back-up. At the moment all we've got is her word for it — and right now I'm not sure that's enough." Carmichael paused. "And then we still have the necklace . . ."

"Boss?" DC Daniels and DS Cassidy blundered in through the incident room door. "We might have something on that thread."

* * *

Time: 3.45 p.m.
Date: Saturday 30 August 2014
Location: Cornhill and Sons, Weighbridge Lane

Bobby Neale stabbed at the phone's speed dial. It wasn't like Jimmy not to pick up. He'd called his brother three times already that afternoon, and each one had gone straight to voicemail.

As did this one.

It wasn't as if Jimmy was busy, either. All he had to do was sit in that flat. He'd been a bit vague about where exactly he was doing this babysitting job, and what he was doing it for — all on a 'need to know' basis, apparently. Well, Bobby *did* need to know and it didn't quell his disquiet that his brother had got himself mixed up in something he shouldn't. Jimmy was his younger brother and he felt responsible for him in the way that only older siblings could. And although Jimmy was handy enough to look after himself in a scrap if he had to, it wasn't really his brother that Bobby was worried about.

It was the Carsons.

Bobby didn't trust that pair one bit and rued the day when Jimmy got involved with them.

Stabbing the screen one more time, he willed his brother to pick up. Once again, it went unanswered.

Bobby sighed and slipped the phone back in his pocket. As troublesome as the continued silence from his brother was, Bobby had bigger things on his mind right now. "Boss says we need to be ready to move." He eyed the other three members of Ritchie Greenwood's new inner circle. All had been with the organisation for some time, and not all of them relished the new leadership.

"Again?" voiced one, his tone loaded with scorn. "We've only just dealt with the last move."

Bobby made a face. "Just telling you what he says. We're to get the place cleaned as best we can, then wait for his call."

Wait for his call.

Bobby didn't like the idea either — relegating them to nothing but puppets dancing to Ritchie Greenwood's tune. But what choice did they have? Now wasn't the time to question the man's authority, as much as some would like to.

"You three go on ahead. I'll follow in a bit. Start bagging stuff up and burning it."

Amid various grunts and expletives, the others did as they were told and left through the front door of the shoemakers. Bobby remained inside, pulling out his phone again.

Still a blank screen.

Still nothing from Jimmy.

* * *

Time: 4.15 p.m.
Date: Saturday 30 August 2014
Location: St Benedict's Street, London

"Just up here." DS Cooper pointed through the windscreen from the passenger seat of Carmichael's car. "Pull up behind that van over there."

Carmichael brought the car to a halt.

"Me and Jenny are in the ground floor flat, number eight. The old woman lives next door at number seven."

Cooper and Carmichael exited the car just as Jack's Mondeo pulled up behind. The three of them made their way to the small step that led to number seven. Carmichael noted the sturdy looking front door. Not fancying his chances in forcing it open, he rang the buzzer to the ground floor flat. DI Yates had been nowhere to be seen after the briefing — which suited Carmichael just fine. He wouldn't have to explain his sudden departure — but it wouldn't take long for her to figure out where they'd all disappeared to.

"Have you told DI Yates where we are?" It was as though Jack could read Carmichael's mind.

Carmichael grinned. "Must have slipped my mind, mate."

"You think she's up to her neck in this, don't you?"

Carmichael leaned on the door buzzer again. "Whatever I might think about her, my priority right now is Katarina. She might be in here."

"So might the kidnappers." Cooper raised an eyebrow. "Just saying."

Carmichael took his finger off the doorbell. "Any of these flats have a back entrance?"

Cooper shook his head. "Not that I'm aware of. We don't have one anyway."

Carmichael knew in all probability he should really call for back-up, not go charging into a situation that could be catastrophic — not just for them, but for Katarina too. He was about to defer to Jack's seniority when he saw movement through the frosted panel in the centre of the door.

Cooper edged forward as the door was pulled open. "Mrs Thompson? Betty? It's Chris — from next door."

It seemed to take a while for the name to register, but then the old woman's face broke out into a beaming smile. She released the safety chain and pulled the door open wide. "Hello, my dear. How lovely to see you." A frown formed on her powdered brow as she took in Jack and Carmichael hovering on the step behind. "Is there a problem?"

"Not at all, ma'am." Carmichael inched forward. "I'm Detective Sergeant Carmichael with the Metropolitan Police — we just have a few questions about who might be using the flat above you." Carmichael's eyes strayed over the old woman's shoulder towards the stairs behind. He kept his voice low. "Do you know much about who's living up there?"

"I'm afraid I don't really have too much to do with them. Barely see them really."

"When was the last time you saw or heard anyone go up to the flat?"

Betty frowned. "I'm not really sure, my dear. I can't keep track of the time so much these days. And I can't hear a thing without my hearing aids in. I looked all over for them today and eventually found them sitting in my knitting basket!" She gave a chuckle. "But there was someone here earlier, now that I think about it — I think it was a delivery."

Carmichael's eyes were still fixed on the stairs. "A delivery? Do you know what it was they were having delivered?"

"I really can't say, my dear. There was a van outside, I do remember that. I just let them get on with it and went back to my baking."

"And how many people did you see?"

"Oh, just the one. Nice gentleman. Very smartly dressed, he was. Nice eyes."

Carmichael gestured towards the internal door that led to the old woman's ground floor flat. "Why don't you just step back inside for a bit? We'll come and chat to you later if we need to."

With Mrs Thompson successfully ushered back inside her flat, Carmichael turned towards Jack. "We going up?" He nodded towards the stairs.

Jack took a step across the threshold. "In for a penny."

The stairs were narrow, leading up to a small landing. The door facing them was closed fast. Carmichael placed an ear to the door panel, indicating soon after that all seemed to be quiet from within.

The handle turned easily enough, opening out into a spacious yet unfurnished room. Curtains were pulled across the only window, a slim chink of daylight slanting in where they failed to meet in the middle.

"Jimmy Neale." Jack made his way towards an upturned wooden chair in the middle of the room and crouched down by its side. He was careful not to kneel in the pool of crimson blood that had accumulated beneath where Jimmy's throat had been ripped open.

"Why do I know that name?" frowned Carmichael. "Neale? Any relation to the guy you mentioned earlier who was meeting with Spearing?"

"Brothers. Bobby's the eldest. This here is Jimmy." Jack's knees creaked as he straightened up. "Bobby's been part of Geraghty's gang for years but the pair of them have been on our radar for a while. There's clearly not much we can do for this one now, but I think that crate over there needs our attention."

Without speaking, they approached the wooden crate. Jack noted the crudely attached bolts on the outside keeping the lid firmly shut and what looked like air holes punched into the sides. Carmichael pulled on a pair of protective gloves, throwing another pair at Jack. Suitably gloved, they slid the bolts free and lifted the lid.

A mixture of stale sweat, urine and worse hit them in the face, making them both recoil.

But the crate itself was empty.

CHAPTER THIRTY-TWO

Time: 4.20 p.m.
Date: Saturday 30 August 2014
Location: Canterbury Lane Industrial Estate, London

Lance Carson tightened the strappings on the wooden chair, feeling Dion Fuller's body tense. The man had been literally begging for mercy during the entire journey over after Lance had pulled him from the street. Again, he began to whimper.

"Button it, Dion. I'm not in the mood."

Lance checked his watch. He'd had to reschedule the rest of the afternoon's cash pickups in order to deal with Dion — and it hadn't placed him in the happiest of moods. But cash flow was cash flow, and Dion Fuller was becoming a liability he could ill afford. He'd considered finishing him off — wrapping his scrawny body up in tarpaulin and chucking it into the Thames, letting nature do the rest, but the man still owed him serious money. And Lance Carson wasn't about to throw that kind of cash out with the tide.

Dion began to rock back and forth on the chair, seemingly trying to gain enough momentum to knock himself to the floor. Lance had no idea what that would achieve, and quickly swung an arm around the man's neck, holding him in a deadlock.

"Cut it out! Unless you want me to rip your head from your shoulders."

Dion's eyes widened, the whites showing. He shook his head, vigorously. Lance had stuck a thick strip of masking tape over Dion's mouth this time, not having the patience to listen to the weasel's excuses any more. Whatever it was that Dion was trying to say, it remained lodged in his throat.

"Wayne? You ready?"

Wayne Carson appeared from the back of the warehouse, pliers in hand.

Just then, Lance Carson's phone burst into life. He recognised the number straightaway. "Problem?" A brief look of concern flashed across his features as he listened to the reply, the muscles in his jaw tensing. Then he relaxed. A small chuckle followed. "Calm down. Everything will go to plan if you do as you're instructed. Don't get sidetracked with rumours. Just make sure you show up on time."

Carson killed the call then turned back towards Dion Fuller.

"So, Dion, my friend. Which finger shall I pull out first?"

* * *

Time: 4.30 p.m.
Date: Saturday 30 August 2014
Location: Metropolitan Police HQ, London

DC Daniels gunned the engine of the unmarked Ford and pressed heavily on the accelerator, pulling out of the station car park before DS Cassidy had had a chance to strap on her seatbelt.

"The guv says be careful. Don't take any risks. If we see anything that needs following up, to call it in."

Daniels nodded. They were driving into the unknown, chasing a very loose lead which would most probably turn out to be nothing but a waste of time and petrol. But the boss had agreed with them — it was worth taking a closer look at the old shoemaker's shop. To rule it out if nothing else.

With three bodies turning up in as many days, who knew when there would be another.

Daniels shivered as he pulled the car out into the main road. Fleetingly, he saw images of himself flying through the smashed window of Lily McArthur's student bedsit last September. He'd jumped in feet first that time — almost literally — and nearly paid a very hefty price for doing so. Subconsciously, he placed a hand on his side where his spleen used to be.

But this was different. This time he had Amanda by his side.

The journey to Weighbridge Lane didn't take long in the light Saturday afternoon traffic, and they soon arrived at the small side street that led down to the old *Cornhill and Sons* shoemaker's shop.

"I vote we take a closer look." Daniels steered the unmarked car further into the lane at a steady fifteen miles per hour.

The one-way street was narrow — just a small uneven strip of pavement on one side. From Street View they knew the former shoemaker's shop was approximately forty metres ahead on the left.

"I'll take a slow drive-by." Daniels gripped the wheel as the car crept forward. "Then I'll see if there's somewhere suitable to pull over."

Cornhill and Sons soon came into view. It looked just as it had on the screen — run down and abandoned. The front door was dusty, with peeling and flaking paintwork. The window frames around the graffiti-strewn boards equally rotting.

"Doesn't look like anyone's been inside for a while," remarked Cassidy as they passed by. She sounded a little deflated. "It's certainly not used as a shop anymore."

Daniels spied a turning point ahead, in front of a double garage set back slightly from the road. "Looks can be deceiving, Amanda. I should know that." He gave her a quick wink before turning the car in a circle and pulling up in front of the garage doors, facing the disused shoemaker's.

Off to their right was another narrow street, this one lined with several parked cars. "Let's wait it out for a while and see what occurs."

In the end they didn't have to wait long.

A figure stepped out of the dusty front door of *Cornhill and Sons*, and turned towards them. Although he had his head down, staring at the pavement as he walked — oblivious to the unmarked police car and its occupants sitting only a matter of metres away — there was no question it was the man they'd seen on the bus CCTV.

Cassidy and Daniels watched as the man turned the corner into the narrow side street opposite, stopping at the side of the first parked car. Pulling a set of keys from his pocket, he unlocked the car and slipped into the driver's seat. Soon afterwards, he pulled away from the kerb and away from the detectives' watchful gaze.

Without a word needing to be said, Daniels started the Ford's engine and followed at a discreet distance. Cassidy made a note of the registration number and pulled out her phone.

"I'll call it in," she said, already stabbing at the handset as both cars re-joined the main road, heading west. "Where do you think he's going?"

Daniels shrugged, his eyes firmly fixed on the vehicle ahead. "No idea — but let's find out."

CHAPTER THIRTY-THREE

Time: 4.30 p.m.
Date: Saturday 30 August 2014
Location: St Benedict's Street, London

"Would you be able to describe him for us?" DS Carmichael eased himself down on to one of the packing crates that still littered the front room of number eight. "The man you saw earlier today."

"Sorry we don't have more chairs yet." Jenny led Betty to the only chair in the room. "It's next on the list."

"No problem." Carmichael kept his attention on Betty Thompson. "Anything you can remember about him would be useful."

Betty frowned as she lowered herself into the chair. "I'm really not too sure. He was quite tall; I do remember that. And smartly dressed — a suit, I think. Grey."

"Anything more about his appearance? Hair colour? Eyes?" Carmichael drew his notebook from his pocket. "Did he have an accent at all?"

Betty shook her head. "No accent that I recognised, no. But he was very well spoken. And well groomed, too — I remember smelling something nice. An aftershave. Made me think of my Harold." A wistful look entered the old woman's eyes. "And he had nice hair. Sort of swept back from his face. Then his eyes . . ." Betty broke off, accepting the teacup Jenny handed her. "He had the most unusual eyes."

Carmichael's eyebrows hitched a notch. "In what sense were they unusual?"

Betty took a sip from the cup. "Well, they were different colours, I'm sure of it. I didn't know you could have different coloured eyes. But one was a lighter colour — a grey or a blue. The other was darker — a brown."

"Heterochromia," said Jenny, settling down on the floor at Betty's side. "It's when one eye is a different colour to the other. Quite rare. I've only ever seen it the once."

So have I, thought Jack. *And recently.*

Carmichael made a quick note in his notebook. "And was this the same man that gave you the necklace before?"

Betty's hand went to her neck. "Oh no," she replied, twirling the necklace in her fingers. "That was another chap. He was much shorter, stockier. And he had a beard, too. He didn't stop to talk much — just gave me the necklace to apologise for any noise."

Jack's eyes gravitated towards next door where upstairs Jimmy Neale's body still lay in a pool of congealing blood. *Bearded* Jimmy Neale.

Carmichael closed his notebook. "And you didn't hear any voices from upstairs? Not a woman by any chance? Any shouts or screams?"

Betty shook her head. "No, but like I said — I don't always hear things very well these days." A worried look crossed her face. "Has someone been hurt?"

Carmichael got to his feet. "Nothing for you to worry about, Mrs Thompson. Thank you for your time. We'll be in touch if we need anything else. But I'm afraid the forensic team will be next door for some time yet — it might be best if you arrange to stay somewhere else tonight. Do you have any family that live close by?"

"No, not since my Harold passed. I have a daughter and granddaughter but they live in Milton Keynes. I wouldn't want to trouble them unless I really have to."

"You can stay here — can't she, Chris?" Jenny turned to Cooper who was getting ready to follow Carmichael through the door. "We've got a spare room. There's nothing in it apart from a bed at the moment, and a lot of boxes. You'd be more than welcome, Betty."

Betty's bottom lip started to quiver. "Well, if you're absolutely sure? This is all rather unnerving . . ."

"Absolutely." Jenny beamed, getting to her feet and heading towards the kitchen. "I'll put the kettle on again and see if I can rustle up something to eat."

Once outside, Carmichael headed towards his car. "I'll head back to the station — keep tabs on the DI. The ransom drop-off's in about forty-five minutes."

Jack headed for the Mondeo. "Cooper and I will swing by — see what it's all about."

Carmichael called over his shoulder as he jogged across the street. "The minute you think you smell a rat, Jack — call it in."

Jack waved a hand in acknowledgement as Carmichael's car pulled away. They hadn't told Betty Thompson about the dead body lying upstairs above her flat — news like that could wait a while. The scene of crime investigators would be descending before too long, and the inevitable circus could then begin.

"You heard anything more from Amanda or Daniels?" Jack swung the Mondeo away from the kerb. "Last I heard they were going to check out that shoemaker's shop along Weighbridge Lane."

Cooper dragged his phone from his pocket. "Nope, nothing so far."

Jack frowned as he edged out into the traffic. "As much as I admire their tenacity, Cooper — they need to be careful. Bobby Neale is up to his neck in something, and if the person behind all this is who I think it is . . ." Jack turned the

Mondeo in the direction of Flanagan Street and the ransom drop-off. "He's not someone you want to mess with. Tell them again not to take any risks."

Cooper dutifully tapped out a message while Jack turned his attention to the traffic queue ahead. With one of Joseph Geraghty's gang rubbing shoulders with Jonathan Spearing, Jack didn't like the way things were heading.

* * *

Time: 4.50 p.m.
Date: Saturday 30 August 2014
Location: The South Bank

The man took a right turn, the road running parallel with the river.

"Where do you think he's going?" Cassidy kept one eye on her phone while watching the car ahead disappear around a bend. "There's nothing much around here. It's all abandoned."

"Perhaps that's why." Daniels tailed the car around a bend, entering a disused industrial estate. Row upon row of abandoned units passed by them on each side. "Do we just keep following, or what? This guy could be leading us anywhere."

Cassidy glanced at her phone and the message received from Chris some fifteen minutes ago.

'*The boss says be careful. Don't take any risks.*'

"Your call, Trev. But let's not do anything daft."

An involuntary spasm stabbed at Daniels' side, right where his spleen used to be. "As if I'd do anything daft," he mused. Winding down the side window to get a better look at where they were headed, he noted the heavy grey skies above discharging yet more bulbous raindrops, the freshening breeze slanting them sideways through the open window. Thunder began to rumble in the distance.

The car ahead slowed and then pulled to a stop in front of an abandoned unit. Daniels steered the Ford into a parking bay outside what was once a tyre repair centre, keeping out of sight. Poking his head out of the open window, he was just able to see the man jump from the car and head for a sturdy looking corrugated iron door, not so much as glancing over his shoulder.

Daniels thought back to Lily McArthur again and hurling himself through her bedsit window like some Bruce Willis impersonator. He'd been lucky that time. He wasn't sure he'd be so lucky again.

"Let's wait a while — then call the boss and see what he wants us to do."

CHAPTER THIRTY-FOUR

Time: 5.10 p.m.
Date: Saturday 30 August 2014
Location: Flanagan Street, London

Jack pulled the Mondeo to a stop at the corner of Flanagan Street. He could already see the reporter through his rear-view mirror, hopping from foot to foot.

"I don't like this, Cooper." Jack flicked his attention back to the windscreen in front, eyes sweeping the road ahead. "I don't like this one bit."

Big, fat spots of rain began to splatter the windows.

On the way to the rendezvous point, Jack had driven along the two side roads where the unmarked surveillance and covert back-up vehicles were meant to be stationed. He crawled along as slowly as he dared without causing eyebrows to be raised, but saw nothing that even remotely suggested any such vehicles were in position. Not a single one. It made him nervous.

Flicking his gaze back to Jonathan Spearing, Jack put in a call to Carmichael. It was answered on the second ring.

"I don't like it, Rob. I can't see any back-up anywhere — covert or otherwise. And Spearing's hopping around like a one-legged leprechaun." Jack heard a door closing and Carmichael's strained breathing. If Jack didn't know better, the man appeared to be running.

"I can't find her, Jack. She's sodding well disappeared!"

Jack was about to reply when his attention was taken by movement in the rear-view mirror.

"Boss? Taxi's arrived." Cooper was sitting, half-turned in his seat, watching through the back window. "Looks like Spearing's about to get in."

"I've got to go, Rob. Spearing's getting in the taxi. I'll follow on behind and see where they go." Jack hung up and readied himself to pull out into the late afternoon traffic.

It didn't take long for the black taxi cab to rumble past. Jack noted the tinted windows as he let it get a few car lengths ahead before joining the stream heading south. He kept one eye on the taxi in front and another on his rear-view mirror. He still couldn't see any surveillance teams, unless they were so discreet he couldn't spot them. It was possible, but unlikely.

Just what was DI Yates playing at?

The route the taxi took crossed the city, the Mondeo remaining several car lengths behind. Every so often Jack glanced up at the skies above, hoping for the sound of a helicopter.

There was nothing.

More fat raindrops began to fall, accompanied by the distant rumble of thunder intensifying.

Just where were they heading?

* * *

Time: 5.15 p.m.
Date: Saturday 30 August 2014
Location: Metropolitan Police HQ, London

Carmichael sprinted along the corridor towards DI Yates' office. The last time he'd seen her she was ensconced in the incident room — but then she'd just vanished into thin air.

The narrow corridor housed mostly vacant offices — several used as makeshift storage cupboards, another rammed full of abandoned desks and chairs. One was full of cleaning materials. If any other detective had arrived at a new station to be tucked away in a darkened corridor that had seen better days, most would have made a fuss.

But not Detective Inspector Rebecca Yates.

Maybe she wasn't bothered because she didn't intend to be hanging around that long.

Carmichael wrenched open the DI's office door, not even stopping to give a cursory knock. He already knew she wouldn't be there.

He was proved right with one quick glance around the interior.

Heading over to the desk, he noted the computer was still on, but password protected. A further quick glance told him there was little else of note on the desk, other than a half-drunk mug of long-cold coffee, a pile of case files and a notepad and pen.

Knowing he shouldn't, but feeling an inexplicable compulsion he had no control over, Carmichael pulled open the desk drawers. Most were empty, but the topmost drawer contained another selection of notepads, some pens and a reel of Sellotape. Beneath the spare notepads, Carmichael spied a number of envelopes.

Before he knew what he was doing, he'd grabbed the envelopes and pulled out their contents. They were all communications from the Bay Tree Nursing Home, and they were all invoices. Carmichael stared at the eye-watering amounts set out in bold under '*NOW DUE*' at the bottom of each.

Getting old was an expensive business.

Stuffing the envelopes back where he'd found them, Carmichael headed back outside into the corridor.

He had a detective inspector to find.

* * *

Time: 5.30 p.m.
Date: Saturday 30 August 2014
Location: Southwark Bridge, London

Jonathan Spearing eyed the holdall sitting on the seat next to him. The taxi had barely waited for him to close the door before it had pulled away. As before, the windows were tinted — nobody from outside able to see in. The partition between the rear of the taxi and the driver was also tinted, as it was before. Was it the same driver? Spearing had no way of knowing.

As the taxi swung around a sharp bend, Spearing grabbed the holdall and pulled it into his lap. He felt sick. Last time the taxi only travelled for a few minutes before pulling to a stop and letting him get out. This time, however, the journey seemed to be taking forever. He glanced out of the side window. He had no idea where he was headed, or how long the journey would last. Or even if Katarina would be at the end of it.

Where were they going?

An uneasiness joined the sickness pooling in his stomach. He felt bare. Exposed. What if it all went wrong?

MacIntosh had caught his eye at the final briefing, and Spearing could see the memory stick in the detective's hand. It told him that he'd been back to the house — which was a start. But maybe it was all too late? And what if he'd merely shown it to that DI Yates? There was something off about her — he'd detected it the moment they'd met. Call it a reporter's instinct. Maybe letting her know about Spearing's link to the people-trafficking case would do more harm than good — and Katarina would end up in even more danger.

Swallowing past the painful lump in his throat, he winced at the acidic taste as his stomach contents threatened to make a swift exit. Staring out of the tinted windows, he watched roads and buildings flash by as the taxi continued on its journey. A quick glance over his shoulder, Spearing hoped and prayed that there were people following him.

* * *

258

Time: 5.30 p.m.
Date: Saturday 30 August 2014
Location: Canterbury Lane Industrial Estate, London

Lance Carson had been true to his word. "Didn't I warn you, enough Dion?" Straightening up, Lance held the now-blood-ied pliers out towards his brother, who swiftly placed them into a pocket. "I don't make empty threats. You should know that by now."

Dion Fuller continued to whimper, his body folding in on itself. He was once more fastened to the wooden chair in the centre of the disused warehouse, strappings holding his ankles and thighs in place. They'd picked him up surpris-ingly easily — queuing up to place a bet at the bookies just around the corner from his poky flat. He was nothing if not a creature of habit.

"Despite what you might think, I don't take pleasure in doing things like this, Dion." Lance knew that particu-lar chestnut was untrue. He'd felt the all-too familiar rip-ple of pleasure as each remaining fingernail was ripped from Dion's stubby fingers. There was something quite satisfying in hearing the man's tortured screams with every pull. He'd taken extra delight in taking the fingertips too this time, but he'd made the man wait for his punishment, keeping him strapped to the chair for the best part of an hour. His eyes flickered towards Dion's fake Nike trainers. "At least you still have your toes, eh?" Lance felt a smile twitch at the corner of his mouth. "For now at least."

Dion whimpered some more, cradling his bloodied hand in his lap. He'd vomited with the pain, bile and rem-nants of his earlier Chinese takeaway now decorating the front of his T-shirt.

With one last glance at Dion's fingernails lying scat-tered on the concrete floor, Lance turned his back and started heading for the corrugated iron door.

"Get rid of that mess, Wayne," he commanded, whip-ping out his phone as he reached the door. "Before I decide to shove them down his throat. We could do without this headache today."

Wayne Carson gave a grunt, lowering his hulking frame to the floor.

Lance stabbed at Jimmy Neale's number once again. He'd called several times that afternoon and the man had failed to answer any of them. He knew Jimmy had been leaving the flat on occasion, expressly against orders — the telltale takeaway boxes and beer cans giving him away — so maybe that was it. Lance swore beneath his breath as yet another call went to voicemail.

"What about the girl?" Wayne Carson got to his feet, his hand full of Dion's bloodied fingertips.

"The girl doesn't matter," replied Lance. "She can stay where she is for all I care." A cruel smile crept on to his face. "If that reporter thinks he's getting his wife back anytime soon, he can think again. That family are worth more than a poxy hundred grand."

Just then, Lance heard the tell-tale beep from his phone. The message was clear — and went some way to alleviate the irritation Dion Fuller had managed to instil in him.

"Get rid of those fingernails, Wayne. We're on."

CHAPTER THIRTY-FIVE

Time: 5.35 p.m.
Date: Saturday 30 August 2014
Location: Canterbury Lane Industrial Estate, London

The taxi came to a stop on the abandoned forecourt, the engine still running. As each minute of the journey passed by, Jonathan Spearing felt his heart rate increasing, reaching such a crescendo it was sure to burst. He clutched the holdall tightly towards his chest, his hands slick with sweat.

A hundred thousand pounds.

Glancing out of the side window, he felt the nervousness inside him multiplying. Where was everyone? As far as he could tell, they were completely alone — just him and the taxi driver. Where was the surveillance? The undercover officers? He'd heard it with his own ears in the briefing — officers would be tailing his every move to bring this kidnap situation to a swift end.

Nothing would go wrong.

But where were they?

Spearing's eyes trawled the various disused buildings on either side of the taxi — but there was nothing to see. Nothing and no one. Sickness started to spread like wildfire, making him grip the holdall tighter and tighter. What if it all went wrong, despite what they'd told him? What if it had *already* gone wrong? For all he knew the location for the ransom drop-off could have changed again — leaving him alone and exposed; a sitting duck.

And a sitting duck with a bag full of money.

He ran a finger around the neck of his T-shirt, feeling the dampness. There was only one way this would end.

A sob caught in Spearing's throat as he thought of Katarina. If she wasn't already dead, she would be soon. Why had he gone to the police when they'd explicitly told him not to? He could have swallowed his pride and approached Katarina's parents himself — they would have stumped up the money if it meant saving their daughter's life. Then he wouldn't have needed to involve the police at all.

But instead he'd done exactly what they'd told him not to. Katarina would die, and so would he. Not that he cared too much about that. A life without Katarina was no life at all.

Suddenly, the door to the taxi sprang open.

"Out."

Spearing's heart leapt into his mouth. That one simple word was the only one the taxi driver had spoken during the entire twenty-minute journey.

"Out."

* * *

Spearing placed one shaky foot on to the rough tarmac. Before his legs collapsed, he gripped the frame of the taxi door and hauled himself upright. The rain was falling faster now, coming down in sheets. Within seconds his hair was plastered to his scalp and thick, fat raindrops trickled down the back of his neck. But he barely noticed.

With his T-shirt soaked through and clinging to his chest, Spearing hugged the holdall tighter as he took a juddering step forward. What was he meant to do now? He took a wary glance over his shoulder towards the taxi behind — but the rain splattered tinted windows gave nothing away.

Another shaky step forward.

More rain thudded down from the angry clouds overhead, deep puddles already pooling on the tarmac as rumbles of thunder filled the air. Tears began to stream from his eyes, instantly washed away by the torrent from above.

I'm so sorry, Katie. I messed up.

Clutching the bag of notes to his chest, he stumbled on.

The warehouse had a corrugated iron door which was partially open. Spearing's heart jumped further up into his mouth as a figure came into view. The man strode confidently in his direction, dressed in a well-tailored pale grey suit, his face as thunderous as the skies above.

"You're late."

Spearing's mouth opened and closed, but no words emerged.

The man came to a halt in front of him, the rain already turning his suit a darker shade of grey. "You have the money?"

Spearing felt himself nod, still clutching the bag to his chest. "Y . . . yes. You . . . you have my wife? I need to see her."

The man ignored Spearing, instead holding out his hand. "The money," he repeated.

Spearing felt his legs quiver as he handed over the holdall.

Thunder cracked overhead as a fresh torrent hammered down from the skies. Spearing felt the handles of the holdall being ripped from his fingers at the very same moment a distinctive thud-thud-thud echoed from the clouds above.

Before Spearing could catch his breath, a flurry of cars and vans screeched up behind the idling taxi, bodies spilling from the doors before they'd even come to a halt.

The next thing he saw were guns.

And lots of them.

* * *

Time: 5.40 p.m.
Date: Saturday 30 August 2014
Location: Canterbury Lane Industrial Estate, London

Jack and Cooper sprinted from the Mondeo, just in time to see Jonathan Spearing being led away to safety by two armed police officers, his face white with shock. The warehouse was surrounded both on the ground and from the air, officers appearing out of nowhere, swarming around like angry black ants.

Even through the torrential rain, Jack could see the look of confusion on Lance Carson's face. The man was kneeling on the rain sodden tarmac, hands on his head, guns trained on him from all directions.

Jack shielded the rainwater from his eyes as he approached. Armed officers were already streaming in through the open corrugated iron door, an array of shouts and commands coming from inside — but thankfully no gunfire. At least not yet.

Jack hovered where he was, a wall of armed officers barring his way. He glanced anxiously towards the industrial unit, knowing full well that Jonathan Spearing would be thinking exactly the same as he was right now.

Where was Katarina?

If she'd been kept in the crate above Betty Thompson's flat in Covent Garden, as they now suspected, then she clearly wasn't there anymore.

So where was she?

The answer came just a moment or two later.

Officers emerged from the warehouse, guns by their sides. The expressions on their faces told Jack all he needed to know.

Katarina wasn't there.

Jack then saw Wayne Carson led from the building, handcuffed and confused — then another figure stumbled on behind with what looked like a badly injured hand. Over his shoulder, Jack watched members of the Gold Command Group arriving in a series of unmarked cars, several of whom strode towards the abandoned taxi cab. As they approached, the driver's door sprang open and the taxi driver stepped out.

Jack felt his mouth fall open.

CHAPTER THIRTY-SIX

Time: 5.50 p.m.
Date: Saturday 30 August 2014
Location: Canterbury Lane Industrial Estate, London

"I'm on my way." Jack swung the Mondeo in a wide circle and stepped on the accelerator, hard. He slotted the phone into the hands-free holder on the dashboard as he steered one-handed back out on to the main road. He couldn't quite believe what he'd just seen — *who* he'd just seen — but his own team needed him now. "Keep talking to me — I want to know exactly what's happening. I'm about . . ." Jack glanced at the dashboard clock. "Fifteen minutes away."

DS Cassidy's voice crackled across the airwaves. "We're outside a row of abandoned units and lock-up garages. The guy we've been following from the old shoemaker's shop in Weighbridge Lane went inside about an hour ago. As far as we can tell, he's still in there. Nothing has moved in or out."

"Have you asked for back-up?" Jack briefly swerved the Mondeo on to the opposite carriageway earning himself several honked horns in the process.

"On their way as far as I know, but there's a delay due to the Spearing kidnapping incident."

Jack pulled back into the correct lane and came to a halt behind a queue of traffic at a red light. "I'll be there as quick as I can. Ring me back with any update in the meantime. But don't do anything stupid. I've left Cooper to accompany Spearing to the station." Jack ended the call as the lights turned green, then stabbed at the handset once again, his face darkening.

"Where is she?" he barked as soon as the call was answered.

"Good evening to you too, Inspector. How lovely to hear from you. How's your day going so far?"

Jack bit back an expletive. "I said, where is she?"

"You're supposing I have the faintest idea what it is you're referring to."

"Don't dick me about. Just tell me where she is. We've got the Carsons. It's only a matter of time before they tell us how you're involved too."

Ritchie Greenwood gave a throaty chuckle. "Oh, I doubt that very much, Inspector. But I guess you'll have fun trying."

Jack counted to one and a half. "I know you took her. Katarina. You were seen at the flat. There can't be that many people with heterochromia. And I know it was you that dispatched Jimmy Neale. So, what have you done with her?"

Silence followed from the other end of the line.

"It makes no sense for you to keep her now. The Carsons don't possess a loyal bone in their bodies — they'll soon tell us everything we need to know. It would be better for you to come clean now — because if you've harmed her . . ."

Irritation entered Ritchie's tone. "You disappoint me, Jack. I thought our friendship went deeper than this. The Carsons are beneath me, and if you had an ounce of sense you would realise that. I wouldn't piss on them if they were on fire, let alone do business with them. I had nothing to do with their crappy little kidnapping scheme — I just discovered her in what I might call a happy accident. All I did was set the poor woman free."

"If that's the case, where is she?" Jack's own irritation earned him more honking horns as he sped over a roundabout, accelerating around a learner driver doggedly abiding to the speed limit. The phone line went quiet and Jack wondered if Ritchie had decided to hang up. Then the man's familiar tone filled the car.

"Tell your newspaper friend to just go home. There's a surprise waiting for him."

* * *

Time: 6.10 p.m.
Date: Saturday 30 August 2014
Location: Manchester Way Industrial Estate, London

"Just remember, Daniels. We don't need you hurling yourself through any broken windows this time, right? No heroics."

The rain had now abated, but the downpour had still left the air sticky and humid, another storm clearly needed. Jack led Cassidy and Daniels along a narrow alleyway that skirted around the back of a row of lock-up garages. After arriving at the scene, they'd sat in Daniels' car for a minute or two, watching the entrance — still nothing moved. It didn't take long for disquiet to set in. With back-up delayed indefinitely due to the events at the Canterbury Lane Industrial Estate, Jack decided to take control. Whether that was a wise decision or not would soon be discovered.

The alleyway was overgrown and led, as expected, to the rear of the garages. The one they wanted was easy enough to spot — a battered, white van sat parked opposite an equally battered looking wooden gate. Jack wondered if the registration would show up on Cooper's list he'd been checking out earlier — he had a feeling it would.

"That'll be them," muttered Jack, gesturing for Cassidy and Daniels to keep flush with the brick wall that lined the alleyway. The front of the van was facing them, and it was easy enough to see that the front cab was empty — despite the windscreen being covered in dirt and pigeon droppings. His eyes flickered towards the gate which had seen better days.

Several of the horizontal slats were missing, others riddled with damp and disease. Jack approached from the side and peered through one of the gaps to see an overgrown courtyard full of discarded boxes and piles of rubbish. There was the smell of burning in the air, and piles of blackened ash sat strewn in among the carnage.

There was just the one door that led into the rear of the garage — and it stood wide open.

Daniels appeared at Jack's shoulder just as a figure emerged through the door.

"That's him — that's the guy we followed."

The man was dragging two refuse sacks out into the courtyard — and whatever was in them looked heavy — the black plastic straining and threatening to rip. Jack didn't want to hypothesise just what might be inside.

It didn't take long for Jack to recognise the man's face.

Bobby Neale.

The man swung both sacks up on to a pile which was already waist height, giving an audible grunt as he did so. He then stood facing the fence, his back towards the gate.

It took Jack a split second to realise what the man was doing, and even less time to react.

CHAPTER THIRTY-SEVEN

Time: 6.30 p.m.
Date: Saturday 30 August 2014
Location: Acacia Avenue, Wimbledon

Becky brought the car to a stop outside the Spearings' house. The wheels had barely stopped turning before the reporter jumped out and sprinted up the short garden path. Killing the engine, she turned towards the passenger seat.

"We'll need to bring her in properly. Question her. She could have vital information to help in the case against the Carsons. As could Spearing himself."

DS Carmichael nodded. "Let's just give them their five minutes together first, eh? I don't think I've ever witnessed someone going through what he has over the last few days — the man's wrecked."

"I guess you're right."

The two of them watched Spearing fumble with his keys, dropping them on the doorstep before finally unlocking the front door and stumbling inside. As Becky reached for the door handle, Carmichael turned towards her.

"Plus, we need to talk." A bemused expression filled his face. "I really thought you were in on this — in with the kidnappers. Up to your neck in it. I never once dreamed . . ."

Becky smiled, the relief on her own face evident. "I've never been so petrified in my life. The SIO heading up the Gold Command Group had been watching the Carsons for a long time — we just needed to catch them in the act of doing something big. We truly had no idea where Katarina was being held — so luring them out into the open was the only way. With me new to the station, it was the perfect cover — let them think they had a bent copper on their payroll. I think it made them lower their guard a little, they're not the brightest pair."

"So I've heard. But you must have been bricking it — I've done undercover stuff before and it's not easy. You acted with a really cool head."

Becky laughed. "I can assure you I was at no time feeling cool! Under the surface I was a mess. It's honestly been the most nerve-wracking thing I've ever done, and not something I fancy repeating too soon."

"I'm sorry I jumped to conclusions, though." Carmichael gave a sheepish smile. "I saw the invoices from the nursing home — and what with the whole cloak and dagger thing, I thought the worst."

"It's OK." Becky gave a small chuckle. "I'd probably have thought the same in your shoes. I won't lie, money is tight at the moment. I can see where you thought my motivation might come from." She sighed. "Dad's decided to sell his house now, to pay for the nursing home fees. He's moving in with me, so at least that's getting sorted."

"And you driving the taxi? I'd never in a million years have dreamed that one up."

"I told Carson I was laying a false trail — made him think our eyes were diverted elsewhere. Like I said, he's not the brightest."

"I guess we should see what's happening inside." Carmichael gestured through the window towards the house.

They made their way up the garden path and in through the front door. In the front room, Katarina was seated on the sofa, Spearing by her side. Both looked shocked beyond words. Becky went over to kneel down by her side, taking hold of the woman's shaking hands.

"Are you OK, Katarina?" She knew it was a pathetic question to ask. "Did they hurt you?"

Katarina hesitated, but eventually she shook her head. "No," she whispered, her voice so faint it was barely audible. "I'm fine. They didn't hurt me. They didn't even touch me. They just . . . they just . . ." Fresh tears spilled from her eyes as Spearing pulled her close.

"We'll need to get you checked out at the hospital anyway. Just to be sure." Becky's eyes drifted to the small nest of tables next to them, spying a glass of water and an open packet of biscuits. "Can I get you anything more to drink? Something to eat?"

Katarina gave a slow shake of the head. "No . . . the man, he . . . he gave me some water and said I wasn't . . ." The words caught in her throat. "I wasn't to move."

"What man was this?" Becky and Carmichael exchanged a look. "Can you describe him for us?" She knew this line of questioning might be too much too soon, the woman looked so fragile. But she also might have vital information. "Was he the man that abducted you on Tuesday morning?"

Katarina's watery eyes widened. "No . . . no it wasn't him. The ones on Tuesday were . . . different." She paused and swallowed. "They scared me. They were strong, and very rough. But he was . . . he was nice. Kind, even. He had nice eyes."

Carmichael was hovering in the doorway. "Nice eyes? They weren't different colours by any chance?" The comment earned a frown from Becky. "One blue, one brown?"

Katarina nodded. "Yes, they were. But he was . . ." Again she broke off, her shoulders shuddering. "He got me out of that crate — that filthy stinking crate — and brought me back home. He was gentle. He didn't hurt me. He let me have a shower and a change of clothes. Then told me I had to wait here . . . not to move. Not to phone anyone or go after him."

Becky straightened up just as Carmichael's phone chirped.

"It's Jack," he said, glancing at the screen. "Looks like he's seen a bit of action himself tonight."

* * *

Time: 10.45 p.m.
Date: Saturday 30 August 2014
Location: The Hanged Man Public House

This time it was just the two of them.

Jack eyed the tumbler of whisky but shook his head. "This isn't a social call."

Ritchie Greenwood poured himself a large measure and sunk it in one. "Suit yourself, Jack. But I thought we might be celebrating."

"I don't quite understand why you moved her — Katarina. Why have anything to do with her if, as you are so keen to point out, the Carsons' attempt at extorting money had nothing to do with you? Which I have yet to be convinced of, I might add."

Ritchie grinned behind his crystal tumbler. "Joseph was right about you — you're tenacious." He poured himself another generous measure. "I saw what they were up to — amateurs, the pair of them. I just thought I'd step in — do my good deed for the day. For all I knew, whoever slit Jimmy Neale's throat might come back and do the same to her."

"Cut the crap — we all know it was you that ended Jimmy Neale."

"Do we?" Ritchie smirked. "Have you found any trace of me in that flat? Any forensic detail to put me there at all? If you had, I'm pretty sure you'd have come for me by now. As far as I can see, all you have is a little old lady whose memory isn't all that great. Who knows what she actually saw?" The smile widened. "I think we both know if she's your only witness then that's not quite enough."

Jack sighed and gave in, reaching for the whisky. "I still don't get it."

"I'm not all bad, Jack, despite what you might have heard. Sometimes I feel like doing my Good Samaritan bit — helping you out." Ritchie's eyes twinkled above the rim of his glass. "Let's just chalk it up to another reason why you owe me."

Jack bristled, swallowing a mouthful of the fiery liquid. "As I've said before — I don't owe anyone anything. And definitely not you." He placed the tumbler down and got to his feet. He wasn't quite sure why he'd come. "You know we have Bobby Neale in custody. It won't take him long to start talking."

"Oh, I think you underestimate our Mr Neale, Jack. If I know anything about the man — which of course I'm not admitting to — he'll keep his silence. He's old school. The fact you haven't charged him with anything yet and I don't have a wall of police officers outside baying for my blood, leads me to suspect he's not saying much."

Jack knew he was right. Bobby Neale wasn't saying much by all accounts, although it was still early days. They hadn't conducted a proper interview with him yet, that would come in the morning. And forensics had only really got started with their investigations at both the industrial estate sites. So, for the moment, they had nothing on Ritchie Greenwood — which the man clearly knew. And relished.

"Where are your little friends today?" Jack glanced around the empty bar. "Gone for a sleepover?"

Ritchie grinned. "I like you, Jack. You're my kind of person. I really do think we could become good friends. Look — I'll offer you a deal. You can arrest me here and now — and I'll come quietly. No fuss." He made a show of holding up his hands, ready for the handcuffs. "I'll be a model prisoner."

Jack held the man in his gaze before turning towards the door. He didn't have any claim on Ritchie Greenwood, and the man knew it. "When I do arrest you, I'll take great pleasure in wiping that smile off your face."

* * *

273

Time: 11.00 p.m.
Date: Saturday 30 August 2014
Location: The Hanged Man Public House

Jack slammed the door of the Mondeo behind him. What the hell was he doing giving someone like Ritchie Greenwood the time of day? All it would do was encourage the man.

Restraint was rarely Jack's strong point, and it seemed to be getting worse the older and crankier he got. He shoved the keys into the ignition and tried to focus his thoughts on what had happened so far that night.

Bobby Neale would remain in custody overnight. He'd had a brief trip to A&E to fix the wound on his head, but they wouldn't get round to interviewing him until the morning. Jack had no doubt his detention would be extended beyond the initial twenty-four hours — but it would only be of use if the man started to talk. Which so far he wasn't.

Jack had already decided to leave the interviewing to Cassidy and Daniels — the experience would be good for them — and he'd given Cooper a few days' leave to help with the unpacking back at his new flat. So, for now, Jack to take a back seat.

Both Spearing and his wife would be formally inter-viewed too — although possibly with less hostility. Jack had managed to speak to the reporter himself earlier, something unknown drawing him towards the man who had made his life such a misery in print. Although Jack wouldn't swear to it, something akin to a truce passed unspoken between them. Maybe it was a turning point — time would tell.

During their brief conversation, Spearing did elaborate on why he'd been so secretive about where he'd hidden the memory stick — why he didn't just come out and tell Jack where to find it.

'I thought you liked a puzzle, Inspector. You seem the type.'

But Jack saw the hollowness in Spearing's eyes as he spoke, and it wasn't long before the truth spilled from the reporter's mouth.

'I thought the interview room might be bugged — maybe even I *was being bugged. I was paranoid about being watched — that those who'd snatched Katie were watching my every move, listening in. I didn't know who to turn to or who to trust. Police included.'* He'd then held Jack in a rock steady gaze. *'Except for you.'*

Jack pulled out of the pub car park, wanting to put as much distance as he could between himself and Ritchie Greenwood. He had received a call from the Governor of Belmarsh prison an hour or so ago, thanking him for his intervention in the attempted assault on James Quinn. As he pulled the Mondeo out on to the main road, he couldn't help a small smile flicker. *Saving James Quinn — who would have thought?* Ritchie hadn't brought up the subject of the botched attempt, and Jack wasn't going to enlighten the man.

On Friday evening, at the Argyle Foundation talk, Jason Alcock had told Jack about the prison rumours concerning Quinn. And it had put Jack in an awkward position. Part of him would have been glad to see the man dealt with — whether that be strung up, stabbed, garrotted, whatever — but there was another part of him that wanted Quinn to suffer more. So, he'd done the right thing — he'd alerted the prison to the rumour. By the looks of it, they'd dealt with the threat in textbook fashion. Quinn was alive, and on his way to a different prison as a reward.

And as for Jason?

Jack would be in support of the man receiving some kind of commendation, or at least recognition for what he'd done. But he knew Jason would want this involvement kept under wraps. A prison grass wasn't a label that you necessarily wanted hanging round your neck for long. So, Jack suspected the whole matter would be hushed up, swept under the prison carpet, but hoped at least something would remain on Jason's file for future reference. Who knew, maybe it could earn him some Brownie points with probation if and when his name came up for parole.

Jack soon found himself on Horseferry Road. Passing Isabel's Café, he made a mental note to check in with his brother. Stu hadn't rung him in a while and Jack felt a faint flicker of concern. Stu had taken the news about Quinn's involvement in their mother's death on the chin — or at least he'd given that impression. But Jack wasn't fooled that easily. Stu had a sensitive side that went far beyond the bravado he often portrayed. He'd ring him tomorrow, maybe suggest a trip down to Surrey if he could spare the time away.

Turning the Mondeo in the direction of home, Jack yawned and prayed for a good night's sleep — one in which the nightmares kept their distance for once.

CHAPTER THIRTY-EIGHT

Time: 11.15 a.m.
Date: Sunday 31 August 2014
Location: Church Street, Albury, Surrey

He'd found the perfect spot. He could watch the house to his heart's content from up here, and no one would ever know. Not unless they looked closely that was — and why would they?

Ritchie Greenwood stretched his neck to the side to relieve the cramp that was setting in. He'd need to move on soon, he knew that. But watching her was so addictive.

He'd managed to glimpse Isabel a few times already that morning, as she stepped out into the rambling garden at the front of The Glebe armed with a pair of secateurs. He watched her cut back a few of the dead plants that lined the path, then swept it clean. If he wasn't much mistaken, it looked like she could be humming to herself. Of course, he was too far away to truly hear her, but she just had such a look of contentment on her face that he imagined she was humming.

He'd also spied Jack's brother that morning. He didn't venture out quite so often as his beautiful new bride, but the likeness was unmistakable. He walked with a faint limp, not unlike that waste of space James Quinn. Ritchie had read all about Stuart MacIntosh's brush with death in the fire last year. Lucky to come out alive had been the overriding feeling.

Lucky indeed.

Look at him now.

Ritchie stretched his neck once again and heard it click. Just a little while longer. Now he was here he couldn't bring himself to leave. Joseph had lived here once — not for very long, granted, but long enough to maybe have left some essence of himself here. And he'd died here, too. Which gave it a place of prominence in Ritchie's world.

When Ritchie thought about Joseph, which was often, he hoped the man was happy with how things were starting to turn out — and not turning in his grave. Ritchie wasn't exactly ecstatic that one of their own had led the police to their latest hideout, only just able to move out in time, but Bobby Neale was expendable and wouldn't be missed. Ritchie was never quite sure how much of the inner workings of the enterprise the man had blabbed to his brother — and therefore the Carsons.

Although he felt Lance and Wayne Carson were so far beneath him they didn't warrant the time of day, Ritchie wasn't so complacent as to be stupid. Loose tongues could cost him money. And Ritchie Greenwood didn't like losing money. Lives maybe, but not money.

At least Jimmy Neale wouldn't be squealing back to the Carsons any more — Ritchie had seen to that, permanently. The gaping hole in the man's neck was testament to that.

And if Bobby Neale went down for the trafficking ring on his own, then so be it. Ritchie wouldn't be sorry to see the man go — he was dead wood. Just like Mickey Hatton.

Ritchie hadn't been pleased when he'd heard about the botched job on Quinn — but it mattered not to him really in the grand scheme of things. Mickey had agreed to take the rap for the Roger Bancroft murder, which was good enough for Ritchie. James Quinn had just been a little bonus, the icing on the cake to reel Detective Inspector Jack MacIntosh in closer.

Jack MacIntosh.

The man made Ritchie smile. He was right where Ritchie wanted him to be — he just didn't quite know it yet. He was proving to be a bit of a prickly character, unpredictable and somewhat volatile when pushed. But he was certainly loyal — to a degree. Ritchie admitted these traits, but he'd bet his last fiver that Jack MacIntosh would overstep the mark on occasion. You only had to look at what he'd managed to cook up with Joseph in this very house to know there was a definite chink in the detective's armour.

And that was all it took — one chink.

Deciding he'd seen enough for now, Ritchie left the relative obscurity of his hideout in the churchyard and made his way back to the car.

* * *

She couldn't really put her finger on what it was, but several times that morning Isabel had the feeling she was being watched. It was subtle, easily overlooked, but it was there all the same.

Mac had scoffed at the idea when she'd mentioned it to him earlier, telling her that the sun must have got to her head.

Which might be true. The sun was still hot overhead, the dry summer weather carrying on without any signs of abating any time soon. They'd dodged the recent thunderstorms that had swept through over the last day or so, the ground still parched.

But she still couldn't shake it.

Bending down to snip the last dead heads from the flowering tubs that flanked the front door, Isabel pushed the thought from her mind. They only had a few more days left here — maybe a week — until they really ought to be getting back to the café. Sacha, Dom and Gina were doing a fantastic job of running the place in her absence, but she couldn't hide away down here forever.

As much as she might want to.

There it was again. Isabel flinched as she straightened up, checking over her shoulder towards the singletrack road behind. The house was very well masked from the roadside — the leylandii trees keeping most prying eyes away. There wasn't really anywhere along the road that gave a clear view of the house — but even so, Isabel felt a familiar prickle at the back of her neck.

Her eyes gravitated towards the churchyard on the other side of the road, which climbed up and all the way back to the chocolate-box church sitting in the distance on the brow of the hill. That would be the only place someone might be able to see down into the garden of The Glebe.

Squinting through the mid-morning sunshine, Isabel scanned the headstones. It was too far away to see anything really, but nothing appeared to be moving. Nothing out of place. Certainly, nobody watching her.

She chastised herself for being silly. Mac was right. It was all in her imagination.

* * *

Time: 1.30 p.m.
Date: Sunday 31 August 2014
Location: Kettle's Yard Mews, London

"You seem to have a thing about cracking people over the head, mate." Carmichael passed Jack another bottle of Budweiser. "And you've got a pretty good swing on you, by all accounts. Maybe you should take up golf."

Bobby Neale had been taking a piss in the back yard of the lock-up garages when Jack had swung a wooden fence post across the back of his skull.

Jack buried his laugh in a mouthful of beer. "First thing that came to hand, mate. It was either that or rugby tackle him — and I didn't much fancy landing on him with his trousers round his knees."

Carmichael made a face and pulled the takeaway cartons out of their paper bag. "Fair point."

Despite having no regrets at flooring Bobby Neale, Jack knew there would be repercussions. Another summons to see Dougie King would no doubt be heading in his direction before too long. He'd only just put to bed an internal inquiry into Jack cracking the Bishop over the head with a concrete block last September — Jack could just see the expression on the Chief Superintendent's face when he learned of Jack's latest exploits. *'Another one, Jack? Really?'*

"I can't quite get my head around the whole DI Yates thing, though. I was so sure she was up to her neck in it." Carmichael spooned rice out on to two plates. "I really read her wrong."

"Not your fault, mate. Like you said, all this cloak and dagger stuff makes you feel like you're not being told the whole story — which you weren't."

"Maybe. I asked her why the rest of the team were kept in the dark — about her special operation, being so closely involved with the Carsons. It would have made life a lot easier if we'd all known what was going on." Carmichael ripped the lid off a portion of lamb bhuna. "She said something about there being too many bent coppers in too many bent pockets. They couldn't take the risk of the Carsons being tipped off."

Jack leaned forward to tip a helping of chicken tikka on to his plate.

Bent coppers in bent pockets.

Thoughts of Ritchie Greenwood started to circulate. He took another mouthful of beer to push them aside.

Carmichael carried on. "The story behind it all is just starting to come out, though. Spearing's coming clean now that the shock has worn off. He rang in sick to the *Daily Courier* because he wanted to focus on his people-trafficking story. He'd been delving into the dark web, poking about in things he probably shouldn't — lord knows what hornets' nest he prodded. He's told us that Bobby Neale reached out to him some weeks ago — and the pair cooked up this way of getting the story on to the front pages, to expose the trafficking ring. Bobby told him he wanted out so he gave that Stefan fella — your third victim — a phone and arranged for Spearing to interview him. That's what you found on that memory stick."

Carmichael shovelled a forkful of rice into his mouth. "And when Katarina was being abducted, Spearing was meeting Bobby Neale to try and arrange getting another phone into the ring. But Neale was hesitant after what had happened to Stefan. What neither of them bargained for was the Carsons getting in on the act."

"How did the Carsons find out about the trafficking ring? I'm assuming they must have known about it — given that they then abducted Spearing's wife?" Jack speared a piece of chicken tikka. "Spearing was sure the motivation behind the kidnap was his story, and not the money."

"By all accounts, Bobby Neale isn't saying much. Neither are the Carsons. Spearing is singing like a canary, however." Carmichael reached for his beer bottle. "But it wouldn't take much for Bobby and his brother Jimmy to swap information — our working theory is that Bobby tells Jimmy about Spearing doing a story on people trafficking, and about how he wants out of the trafficking ring. If Spearing and Bobby Neale confided in each other, Spearing could well have mentioned his wife. Katarina's family are well-known in Croatia, and the business they run. All Bobby would need to do is let slip that Spearing's wife comes from money . . . It wouldn't stretch the imagination that far."

"So you think Jimmy tells his bosses, the Carsons, that there might be a nice little pay day there for them?"

Carmichael shrugged as he sunk the rest of his beer. "It's a theory. Kind of makes sense. Maybe this Bobby will talk eventually."

"He's one of Geraghty's old timers — I'm not so sure you'll get him talking. But if he was thinking of quitting the organisation, maybe that's a way in. He might have a thread of decency in him somewhere."

"Katarina's been talking, though. She's surprisingly nice, for someone being married to Spearing." Carmichael grinned. "Maybe you were wrong about him?"

"Maybe." Jack's tone told Rob he doubted that very much. "What's she been saying?"

"She's explained a few bits that were stumping us. Remember I said that we'd found some emails to a family law solicitor, asking about grounds for a divorce? She's told us it was on behalf of a friend — someone whose husband was tracking their phone and emails, so couldn't make the enquiries herself. Sounds genuine."

Jack scraped the rest of his chicken tikka on to his plate. "I guess that clears that one up."

"But, back to you clocking Bobby Neale around the head — what else did you find at the lockups? I'm guessing everyone had it away on their toes before you got there? Except for Bobby?"

Jack nodded. "Pretty much. We found thirteen trafficked people inside — men and women. One child. So I guess it was a success on that score. But just the tip of the iceberg I'm guessing. We got a name for the first body at any rate. Young woman named Elina. Bobby was in the process of clearing the place out ready to move on again when we got to him."

"And he's happy to take the rap for it all? He's not giving up any information as to who's behind the whole operation? It can't just be him, surely?"

Jack gave a rueful laugh. "I think we all know who's behind it, Rob — but whether we'll ever get to them is another matter. The place was gutted when we went inside. If Bobby doesn't start talking then I guess, yes, he'll be the one to take the rap."

"You know much about this Dion Fuller guy? Bloke found with the Carsons at the industrial estate?"

Jack shook his head. "Low-life pimp by all accounts. My guess is it was just a case of wrong time wrong place with him, I wouldn't think he was involved in anything like a kidnapping. I'd wager he owed the Carsons money — judging by the lack of fingertips he has left."

"Be good to get the Carsons off the grid for a while though." Carmichael pushed his plate away and settled back with the remains of his beer. "They might be small fry compared to Geraghty's lot, but they're still an irritant we could do without."

"They are indeed, Rob."

But not as much as Ritchie Greenwood.

It was as if Rob could read his thoughts.

"You heard anything more about that Mickey Hatton's confession? I heard there was a bit of an incident with him at Belmarsh yesterday — some botched attempt on James Quinn? Saw a few details coming in on the system but didn't really pay much attention to it." Carmichael drained his bottle. "And something else that been bugging me — how exactly did you come to know Katarina had been returned home?"

It was then that Jack knew he'd reached the end of the line. He couldn't lie to Rob any longer. The man had had his back more times than Jack could remember — and he deserved honesty if nothing else.

And honestly meant telling him everything he knew about Ritchie Greenwood.

Jack sighed, sinking the last of his beer. "Rob — you might want to open that bottle of birthday whisky. This could take a while."

THE END

MESSAGE FROM THE AUTHOR

There are many people I need to thank for helping get *Three Broken Bodies* on to the bookshelves.

First, I must thank Detective Inspector Steve Duncan once again — this time for giving me the heads-up on kidnapping and extortion. Your help is very much appreciated. If there are any remaining procedural inaccuracies, then I can assure you that they are mine and mine alone and they are there for entertainment purposes only!

I must also thank Dr Ryan Butel, Consultant Histopathologist, at West Suffolk Hospital in Bury St Edmunds for the help given regarding post- mortem bloods and malnutrition.

I also received fantastic support from Mandy Inniss, Keeley Saul and Helena Lancaster for the background information as to life inside prison (not that I'm suggesting any of you have served time inside of course!) — I thank each of you for taking the time to answer my questions.

My good friend Sarah Bezant once again deserves a very special mention — your brilliant attention to detail when reading my early drafts is invaluable. I honestly couldn't do any of this without you.

And, of course, I must thank everyone involved at my publishers, Joffe Books — and especially Kate Lyall Grant for continuing to believe in me and making my writing the best it can possibly be.

And, finally, it is you — the readers! Without you, none of these books would ever see the light of day. I thank each and every one of you.

To keep up to date, there are various ways to get in touch:

www.michellekiddauthor.com — join my author newsletter for information on future releases and special offers. I also give away free downloads, content not available anywhere else!

www.facebook.com/michellekiddauthor

Twitter @AuthorKidd

Instagram @michellekiddauthor

THE JOFFE BOOKS STORY

We began in 2014 when Jasper agreed to publish his mum's much-rejected romance novel and it became a bestseller.

Since then we've grown into the largest independent publisher in the UK. We're extremely proud to publish some of the very best writers in the world, including Joy Ellis, Faith Martin, Caro Ramsay, Helen Forrester, Simon Brett and Robert Goddard. Everyone at Joffe Books loves reading and we never forget that it all begins with the magic of an author telling a story.

We are proud to publish talented first-time authors, as well as established writers whose books we love introducing to a new generation of readers.

We won Trade Publisher of the Year at the Independent Publishing Awards in 2023. We have been shortlisted for Independent Publisher of the Year at the British Book Awards for the last four years, and were shortlisted for the Diversity and Inclusivity Award at the 2022 Independent Publishing Awards. In 2023 we were shortlisted for Publisher of the Year at the RNA Industry Awards.

We built this company with your help, and we love to hear from you, so please email us about absolutely anything bookish at feedback@joffebooks.com

If you want to receive free books every Friday and hear about all our new releases, join our mailing list: www.joffebooks.com/contact

And when you tell your friends about us, just remember: it's pronounced Joffe as in coffee or toffee!

Milton Keynes UK
Ingram Content Group UK Ltd.
UKHW030737071024
449371UK00005B/399